Taming the Wind:
A Novel

Joe R. Eagleman

CONTENTS

Joe R. Eagleman

1

THE LAB AND THE VORTEX

There was a quiet energy in the lab at the University of Kansas, the smell of ozone and fresh coffee in the air. Weather charts were pegged on the walls in the corner, a tangled mess of colored lines that indicated the ever-changing patterns of the atmosphere. Glass beakers and instruments were in neat rows on shelves and the soft light coming through the windows cast faint, mechanical shadows all around the room. There was a hum of fans, a continual low murmur, and it seemed that the room itself was a living being, breathing with the excitement of discovery.

Jack Engle was in the middle of it, and his hands were firm in spite of the tempest in his soul. He was a man of moderate accuracy mid-sixties, with reddish colored hair, and eyes behind wire-frame glasses that were both wise and tired with the years of following the whims of storms. His battered lab coat flapped around him and the sleeves were rolled up like they were waiting, like they were anticipating the work that had been his life. A half-emptied mug stood on the edge of his desk whose chipped surface could hardly be seen among the mess of paperwork, equations, and weather instruments.

Today was different, though. Today, something new was about to happen.

The fans were set. The steam was beginning to rise in the hot water tank beneath, and curl lazily in the ordered confusion of the laboratory. Three industrial-grade fans, which were installed on the ceiling through a circular hole, were placed at an angle, which would allow them to form an ideal vortex. Jack had designed them carefully, so that he could regulate the strength of the wind by the tilt of the fan. It had been years to come up with the correct equations, to adjust each machine to the correct calibration and now after months of testing and adjustment, it was all ready.

Jack was excited, his heart was beating like crazy, but his hands never trembled. He flicked the last dial on the control panel and his fingers moved like they were controlled by years of muscle memory. The switches clicked home with a small mechanical sound and the room resonated with building tension. He retreated, with an eye to the center of his room, where, in a few moments, he would produce something which had only be seen in the chaos of nature.

"Here we go," Jack whispered to himself.

He flipped the last switch, and the fans roared to life.

For a moment, nothing occurred. Then the air changed. There was a low frequency buzz followed by a strong whoosh as the fans started to blow air up to the middle of the lab. Jack remained rooted to the spot and watched the level of temperature and humidity increase on the monitor panel. The tank was steaming, and the steam rose in fine, curling wisps, which wreathed like a phantom in the room.

The air felt thick, alive with energy. The room seemed to hold its breath.

Then, it happened.

The steam came into sharpness, whirling around in a close, furious spiral. It was originally nothing but a twisting column of air, not any more than a dinner plate in diameter, but in a few seconds, it started to shape up. In the middle of the lab there appeared the miniature tornado, an impeccable, living copy of the destructive forces that Jack had spent his life studying. Its foundation started to move over the floor, a swirling vortex of power which shook the walls and tossed papers in the air. Beakers shook upon the counter, and rattled like the room was alive.

Jack's eyes widened, and a grin spread across his face.

"Unbelievable," he muttered under his breath, his voice a mix of awe and satisfaction. He stepped forward, his hands outstretched toward the swirling mass of wind and steam, as though he could touch the very heart of the storm.

It was a triumph moment. An invention that came as a result of years of research, failures and sleepless nights of calculating the inexplicable. It was that perfect storm bottled up in a laboratory, contained within the exact power of his device. The tornado ceased to be the element of nature fury; it became an example of human creativity.

But when Jack observed the vortex rotating and fluctuating in the controlled environment of his lab he went off daydreaming. It was the years of his life in academia, the study of the patterns of the storms that had brought him to this point. He remembered the time he spent reading and reading meteorological reports, the nights when he went out to the open air, facing the weather conditions in order to witness the force of nature at its best. But all this time he never had dreamed he would be here, making a storm out of nothing, manipulating nature to his will.

He was taken back in his mind to the field, to the time when he was a boy and had chanced to see a tornado. It was as clear as though it had just happened: how he had stood in the midst of a Kansas wheat field, how his feet were pressed deep into the loose soil, how the wind had lashed his hair, how his heart had bounded as the sky had swirled above his head. His eyes had been riveted on that funnel cloud, as it came down out of the heavens as a finger of God. He had stood like a statue, powerless to turn away, though his elder brother dragged him to safety.

Look at it move... Jack had whispered to himself back then.

That same sense of awe filled him now as he stood before the miniature storm. It was different, of course controlled, man-made but the power was the same. The sense of wonder, of discovery, was unbroken. As Jack stood before the miniature storm, a flicker of memory tugged at him — a memory from when he was a boy. He remembered standing in that Kansas wheat field, mesmerized by the swirling chaos above him, his heart racing as the winds pulled at him. He'd stood still, transfixed, until his brother Vern's grip tightened around his arm, dragging him away from the danger.

"What're you, stupid? Get your scrawny ass to the cellar!" his brother had yelled, voice sharp with concern. But Jack, even then, had only whispered, "Look at it move…"

That same pull—the same yearning for the storm, the need to understand its beauty—had never left him.

On a shelf above the workbench, a small transistor radio crackled through static. Jack had left it running for background noise, but now the announcer's voice cut through, flat and clinical:

"…in Topeka, the death toll has risen to twelve. Authorities report dozens injured after last night's tornado leveled several neighborhoods. The storm struck without warning. Critics are calling for improved forecasting systems."

Jack froze. His grin faltered as the miniature funnel danced across the floor of his lab. He could picture it. Splintered homes, cars tossed like toys, families clawing through wreckage. The number—twelve—lodged in his chest.

He adjusted the airflow, watching his tiny vortex steady itself again. A pale, fragile imitation of the real thing, but maybe… maybe this was the start of an answer. Maybe these experiments could one day give people a few minutes' warning. Time enough to save twelve lives, or twenty.

Jack's pencil scratched across the margin of his chart, the figures suddenly urgent, weighted. He thought briefly back to the nights he had spent in the university, his heart heavy with self-doubt as he faced pages of complicated equations that seemed impossible to solve. Back then, the storms seemed just out of reach. But now, standing here in his lab, his work had finally taken form.

"I've come a long way," he muttered to himself as the vortex swirled before him.

His pencil scratched across the margin of his chart, the figures suddenly urgent, weighted.

He leaned closer, whispering as much to himself as to the storm:

"We can do better than this."

The announcer's voice faded back into static, and Jack turned his focus once more to the ghostly funnel, a flicker of resolve cutting through the awe.

"Jack?" a voice called from the doorway.

He turned, shaking out of his daydream, and saw Darlie in the doorway. She was sipping a chipped mug that had the words, World Best Meteorologist, on it and the steam was coming out of it as a ghost. She was now in her fifties with gray streaks in her once dark hair but her presence had not changed. She was the steadying influence in his life-the one who had been with him when he had dreamed of becoming a tornado researcher and the one who was with him now as he crossed the line of what he ever thought he could have done.

"What do you think?" Jack asked, his voice still filled with wonder.

Darlie raised an eyebrow, her lips curving into a small, amused smile. She stepped into the lab, her eyes scanning the swirling vortex in the center of the room.

"Not bad for a bunch of fans and some steam," she said dryly. Her gaze shifted to the control panel. "How long until it blows the whole place apart?"

Jack chuckled, a low, self-deprecating sound. "We'll see."

Darlie's smile widened, but there was a flicker of concern in her eyes. She set the mug down on the counter beside him, the soft clink of ceramic punctuating the silence.

"You sure about this?" Darlie asked, her voice softer now. "All this working with Universal, the lawsuit…"

Jack looked at her, his expressions lost a little. He understood what she was saying. It had been only a few days earlier when the lawyer at Universal Studios had called him with an offer. But the bigger picture was his whole journey—university days when he nearly gave up, years of studying and failing.

"I'm not sure about much these days," Jack said quietly, his eyes drifting back to the vortex. "But I know this. I spent thirty years studying storms. Never thought I'd put one in a courtroom."

Darlie's raised eyebrow was met with Jack's usual self-deprecating chuckle.

He understood what she was saying. It had been only a few days earlier, when the lawyer at Universal Studios had called him, and given him an opportunity he had never thought he would have to take, to claim ownership of the tornado models and the science behind it. To name his price.

"I'm not sure about much these days," Jack said quietly, his eyes drifting back to the vortex. "But I know this. I spent thirty years studying storms. Never thought I'd put one in a courtroom."

Darlie did not answer at once. She took a slow sip of her mug instead, observationally examining him. The lab was steamy and full of electricity, but now, there was a burden between them that nobody could break, a certain comprehension of the situation that Jack found himself standing at.

"I'm with you, you know," Darlie said, her voice steady, but there was a hint of something more in her eyes, a quiet resolve. "Whatever you decide."

Jack nodded, and he liked her more than he could say. But it was not that only, it was something that troubled him, a feeling that he could not get rid of. He was no longer just a scientist. He was the contestant of a game much bigger than his laboratory, of lawyers, of companies, and the very core of the art he had devoted his life to mastering.

But now, being in the middle of his laboratory, with the vortex spinning in front of him, he gave himself a moment of rest. The storm was here; it was here, somehow, as it never had been before, and in a moment, it seemed all the intricacies of the outer world were swept away.

"Let's see where it goes from here," he muttered, more to himself than to Darlie.

The tornado was spinning, alive and beautiful with howling winds swirling in the lab. And Jack was, for the first time in a long time, allowed to believe that the world was indeed chaotic, unpredictable and wild but that perhaps it was now in his reach.

2

A BOY AND HIS STORM

It was midday in Kansas, and the sun was low in the heavens, and the sunbeams were golden on the broad, wide fields. The country appeared to reach away in every direction, and the horizon was lost in the warm cloud of the afternoon. Wheat fields danced lightly to the wind as their tall stalks swayed in time to an unseen song. The smell of the earth was heavy, of the freshly mown grass, and of the dry earth under Jack's feet.

It was a hot summer, the hot summer that comes down on you like a weight, physical as well as suffocating. It was one of those days when the air is too thick to breathe and hangs on the skin in a sticky damp hug. The air was very still, almost unnaturally so, the sort of stillness that had always seemed to me to predict a storm. It was a quiet world, except the faint rattle of cicadas and the intermittent rustle of leaves in the wind. The sort of stillness which hinted that something is going to happen something big, something that will burst the silence with the sound of something that cannot be ignored.

Eight-year-old Jack stood at the edge of the wide, golden wheat field, his sneakers crunching over the dry stubble left after the combine had passed a few days before. The air smelled sharp, like straw and sunshine baked together. His older brother, Vern, was already halfway across the field, his long legs carrying him in easy strides. Vern was fifteen and liked to pretend he was too grown-up for games, but Jack knew better.

"Wait up!" Jack shouted, waving both arms.

Vern turned, grinning. "You'd better hurry, slowpoke, or you'll miss it!"

Jack squinted toward the far end of the field. At first all he saw was a shimmer of heat, the kind that made fence posts look like they were melting. Then he noticed it—a swirling column of straw, dust, and chaff rising into the sky. The dust devil twisted and danced across the cut wheat, skinny at the bottom and wide at the top, like some crooked funnel.

Jack's heart thumped. He had seen little whirlwinds before, but never one this big.

"Come on," Vern said, shading his eyes with his hand. "We're gonna run right through it!"

Jack hesitated. "Is it safe?"

Vern smirked. "It's not a tornado. It's just wind. You're not scared, are you?"

Jack straightened his shoulders. "No way."

They set off together, the ground scratching under their shoes. The dust devil was moving toward them, slow and playful, as if it had chosen the boys for a game. The closer they came, the louder it grew—a low hiss, like a thousand whispers. Pieces of straw shot upward, whirling around like golden sparks.

"Look at it go!" Vern laughed, his eyes shining.

Jack felt the hot wind tug at his shirt, then suddenly he was inside the spinning wall. The world blurred. Straw stung his cheeks. Dust filled his nose. He threw his arms out, half-dizzy, half-thrilled.

"It's carrying me!" Jack shouted.

Vern whooped beside him, his voice muffled in the roar. He bent down, grabbed a handful of loose straw, and tossed it into the whirlwind. The pieces vanished instantly, sucked upward in a flashing spiral. Jack copied him, hurling handfuls of stubble and watching it rocket toward the sky. It was like feeding some wild, invisible beast.

For a moment Jack felt as if he was flying. His hair whipped across his forehead. His shirt ballooned out. The sun above was broken into shards by the spinning cloud, everything turning gold and silver.

"This is awesome!" Jack cried.

The whirlwind began to drift across the field, and the boys ran with it, leaping and dodging, chasing it like two puppies after a butterfly. Sometimes the dust devil outran them, skittering sideways as if it had its own mischievous mind, and sometimes it slowed, letting them catch up and dive back inside.

At one point Vern shouted, "Bet you can't stay in it longer than me!"

"You're on!" Jack yelled.

They both plunged into the center and tried to stand still, squinting against the grit. The force pushed them back and forth. Jack squeezed his eyes shut and laughed so hard his sides hurt. Vern lasted longer, of course—he always did—but when the dust devil finally thinned and unraveled, both brothers collapsed onto the stubbly ground, coughing, laughing, and covered in straw.

Jack lay on his back, staring at the endless blue sky. The spinning in his head slowly faded, but the thrill lingered.

"Did you see me?" he asked breathlessly.

Vern propped himself up on one elbow. His face was dusty and his hair stood in all directions. "You were flapping around like a scarecrow," he teased. Then, softer, he added, "But yeah… you did pretty good."

Jack grinned, proud of the rare compliment.

For a while they just lay there, listening to the soft whisper of the breeze moving over the empty field. Somewhere a meadowlark sang. The dust devil had vanished as quickly as it came, leaving only a faint trail of scattered straw.

Vern sat up, brushing dirt off his jeans. "You know," he said thoughtfully, "it's kinda like we were inside a tornado. A baby tornado."

Jack's eyes went wide. "Do you think real storm chasers ever do that?"

Vern shrugged. "Maybe not. But we did."

Jack hugged his knees, thinking about it. He liked the idea that today was something special, something only he and Vern would remember. Maybe years from now, when they were both grown, they'd still talk about the time they ran through a whirlwind together.

"Let's do it again if another one comes," Jack said.

"Yeah," Vern agreed. "But next time, I'm staying in longer."

They both laughed, their voices carrying across the wide summer field, while the wind drifted and the sun kept shining, waiting for the next dust devil to spin out of nowhere.

The next day, Jack Engle, with all the energy of youth, ran across the fields and his bare feet stirred up dust as he ran. The earth under his feet was warm and sun-drenched which felt like home. His legs pumped hard and he could feel the ground moving under him because he was running faster than he had ever run in his life. He was tall for his age, and somewhat gangling, with a mop of unruly reddish-brown hair which always had a tendency to fall in his face, but he was amazingly fast, considering the boy so young.

The sky above was a clear blue; a deep blue with no cloud expanse, but it was moving. It was the shifting of the air, a weird, faint pull at the atmosphere, which Jack felt. His heart beat faster. There was something wrong with the day, and it was not the heat. It was more than that, a kind of undertone of anticipation which appeared to vibrate in the very air.

Behind him, Jack heard his older brother, Vern, calling out in his teasing, yet somewhat exasperated voice, "Catch me if you can, Jack! You're too slow!"

But Vern's voice, although playful, always held an edge of concern. Jack could almost hear the warning in his brother's tone. "Be careful, Jack," he would've said. But Jack had always run faster when his brother told him to stop. Vern always had the practical answers, always focused on survival. But Jack wasn't like that. He couldn't ignore the storm calling to him, just as he couldn't ignore the pull of the wind as it whispered through the fields.

Vern was Jack's constant companion--when it pleased him. Vern was stout, and never motionless, and his movements were more flowing and restrained than the young sprawl of Jack. He had the kind of easy confidence that made him the center of attention and he liked it. Vern never appeared lost or unsure of what to do, where to go. Jack idolized his elder.

The legs of Jack burned as he made the effort to keep up, but he no longer had Vern in mind. He was now looking up into the sky. The wind was beginning to blow, and blowing in weird whirls and gusts around him, and he felt it swirling round him in wild fits. The air was tense, a weight seemed to be in the air, the world was standing on the brink of something. Jack started to feel his heart racing, not because of the sprint. It was not that, it was a feeling that pricked the skin at the back of his neck.

Behind him Vern's voice broke through Jack's thoughts. "Jack! Quit daydreaming and get over here!"

To Jack, the outdoors was his playground where he could get lost in the beauty of nature. He was naturally curious, and in the middle of a game he would always take off to pursue an insect or observe a blade of grass or a bunch of clods as though he had never seen those things before. His thoughts always wandered and he was full of questions that had no answer yet. His mind dwelt, more than once, upon the sky, upon the storms which swept down in summer, or the weird, exciting anticipation which invariably preceded a storm.

It was then, just as Vern ran past him, laughing and shouting a teasing challenge, that Jack noticed it. The sky had begun to change.

At first, it had been barely noticeable just a slight shift in the light. The sun, still high in the sky, started to lose its brilliance, fading to a dull amber. Jack paused mid-step, his legs stilling in the wheat as he looked up. The air had become heavier, thick with moisture, as if the earth was holding its breath. The usual chatter of cicadas faded, and a deep, unsettling stillness settled over the field.

Jack's breath caught in his chest as he felt the first drop in temperature. It was suddenly cooler, almost too cool for a hot summer afternoon. Jack raised his head to the heavens and his senses keen, and then he caught sight of it. High above in the sky, so far off you could hardly see it, a cloud was beginning to curl--gently at first, as if it were a sort of slow-dance of smoke. Then it started to come into shape. The slight turning of the clouds grew tighter and the shape of a tornado became obvious.

Jack's heart raced. The world around him got smaller and the adrenaline rushed in his veins. He could sense it, the attraction of the storm as though it were calling to him just like the dust devil. His legs started going before his mind had reached what was going on. The world moved and so did he.

He was not able to look away. The tornado was magnificent, so distant, and so very powerful. The manner in which the clouds were twisting and turning, with such a purpose, was something that looked like another power, something that was out of this world. It was lovely, it was awful, at the same time. Jack stood motionless a moment, fascinated by the simple strength of what he was seeing. He was not a boy playing in the fields any more, but a boy who saw the greatest show that nature ever put on.

His breath quickened, his heart thundering in his chest as he stood in awe of the storm. The air around him was electric, crackling with the promise of something immense. The wind picked up, tugging at his hair, as if urging him closer, encouraging him to get nearer to this force of nature that he had only ever read about in books or seen in pictures.

Jack felt something deep in his chest, a longing, an overwhelming desire to understand what was unfolding in the sky. It wasn't fear that surged within him; it was something much stronger: curiosity. He wanted to see it a little closer. He needed to see it, to experience it in a way no one else could. This wasn't just a storm; this was something alive, something that demanded respect. And Jack was filled with a desperate yearning to understand it, to be part of it, to feel its power.

Without a second thought, Jack began to run. His legs, filled with youthful energy, propelled him forward, and he surged ahead, his feet pounding the earth as he moved toward the tornado. His heart pounded in rhythm with his steps, and the world around him blurred. Vern's voice faded into the background, his friends' calls becoming distant sounds in Jack's ears. The only thing that mattered now was the tornado — the incredible, magnificent storm that was unfolding before him.

The pull was irresistible. He was too far away to feel its full force, but even from this distance, the sheer magnitude of it was intoxicating. It was more than just a windstorm — it was something beautiful, chaotic, and powerful. Jack couldn't think of anything else. His legs carried him through the field, the wheat brushing against his arms as he pushed forward.

Behind him, Vern had stopped running, and for the first time, Jack heard the urgency in his brother's voice.

"Jack! What are you doing? Get back here, NOW! That is not a dust devil. It's a tornado!" Vern's voice was sharp, filled with a growing panic. Jack didn't turn around, didn't stop. His brother was behind him, but Vern's concern was a distant thing. The tornado was all that mattered.

Jack's feet thudded against the ground as he ran, faster now, the wind in his face urging him onward. His gaze was fixed on the swirling mass above, the tornado now more distinct, more dangerous. But Jack couldn't stop. The storm was calling to him, pulling him closer, and every step felt like a step toward something he couldn't yet comprehend. He felt the electricity in the air. A crackling energy that was both frightening and awe-inspiring.

"Jack! You're gonna get yourself killed, idiot!" Vern's voice broke through the noise of the wind, but Jack couldn't hear the fear in his words, not like he could hear the storm in his own chest, growing louder, more powerful with every step he took.

Vern was closer now, his hand reaching out to grab Jack's arm. But Jack was too fast, too caught up in the storm's pull. His brother's words were drowned out by the roar of the wind. He was almost there so close to the edge of the field where the tornado was beginning to touch the earth. He could feel the storm's power now, a pressure building in the air, pressing against him like an invisible wall.

"Jack!" Vern's voice was frantic now, and Jack could feel his brother's grip tightening around his arm. "Come on! Get away from there! What are you, crazy?"

Jack didn't resist. He couldn't. The grip was strong, and he was pulled away from the edge of the field. The storm, the pull of it, began to fade as Vern tugged him toward shelter, toward safety. But as Jack was dragged away, the storm still called to him. Its roar, its fury, its power.

Jack stumbled, his legs dragging behind him as Vern pulled him back toward the house. There was a deep frustration burning inside him, a sense of loss. He didn't want to leave. He didn't understand why they had to run. The tornado, the storm, it was beautiful, wasn't it? Why was everyone so afraid? Why couldn't they see what he saw?

"Are you crazy, Jack?" Vern growled, still holding him firmly by the arm. "That's not something you mess with. You could get killed, you idiot."

Jack's chest tightened, and for a moment, he wanted to shout back. He wanted to tell Vern that it wasn't about fear. It was about understanding. The tornado wasn't just something to hide from; it was a mystery to be unraveled, a force to be experienced. But the words didn't come. His brother's voice had a finality to it, a certainty that left no room for debate.

As they reached the barn, Jack stopped for a moment, looking back toward the horizon. The tornado was still there, twisting in the distance. It was fading now, but Jack's mind raced. He didn't understand why everyone else was so afraid.

"Let me go," Jack whispered, barely audible over the rush of wind.

But Vern didn't let go. Instead, he gripped Jack's arm tighter, guiding him toward shelter, away from the storm.

Jack didn't resist this time. The doubt in his mind settled heavily. He couldn't explain why he felt this way, but deep inside, the fascination had only deepened. The storm was no longer just a force of nature; it was an obsession.

Jack's heart thudded in his chest as Vern dragged him away from the barn. The wind had picked up again, pushing against them as they moved into the small, cramped cellar in the back yard. The door slammed behind them with a hollow, heavy thud. Vern, though relieved to be out of the storm's path, was still frantically pacing, muttering under his breath. He kept his eyes on Jack, giving him quick, worried glances, but Jack couldn't focus on his brother. His mind was still far away, up in the sky, following the tornado that had just come so close.

From the small, dusty window of the cellar, Jack caught his first glimpse of the storm as it rolled toward the horizon. It was moving quickly, but the tornado's powerful spin was unmistakable as it twisted toward the edge of the field. Despite the danger, Jack could not look away. The fascination he felt for it was as sharp as ever, and it tugged at him, urging him to understand it, to get closer.

Jack crouched down by the window, pressing his palms against the cool, damp stone as he peered through the grimy glass. The storm in the distance was gradually dissipating, its funnel weakening as it stretched upwards into the sky, its once formidable shape now curling into the clouds, leaving nothing behind but a faint memory of its power. Jack's breath caught in his throat.

It was moving away, almost gone, but not before leaving its mark on him.

Vern was behind him, the sound of his footsteps heavier as he drew closer, his voice sharp and firm. "Jack, get away from the window. You're gonna make yourself sick staring at that thing. You're safe here, okay? Stop looking."

Jack didn't move. He didn't want to listen. His fingers tingled, a strange electric charge running through him as he stayed rooted in place, unable to break free of the grip the storm still had on him. The wind outside howled, and the sound of the house groaning under the weight of the storm's remnants filled the air. It wasn't the roar of the tornado anymore, but it was the deep, lingering echo of something wild and untamed.

"Jack," Vern urged again, softer this time, "The storm's done. It's over."

But Jack couldn't take his eyes off the storm's fading imprint. The tornado had passed, but it wasn't gone in his mind. There was an ache in his chest, a kind of longing that he couldn't explain. He could feel the sadness gushing inside him, a deep, heavy disappointment that he had been pulled away before it was truly over. He didn't want to be here, hidden away in the cellar. He wanted to be out there, feeling the air crackle with power, watching the storm move, witnessing its grandeur.

The tornado was gone from sight now, lost to the horizon, but Jack couldn't forget the way it had looked, a swirling column of chaos and beauty, an unstoppable force. The image of it would stick with him long after the storm had passed. In the quiet after the storm, in the thick, damp air of the cellar, Jack sat still, his gaze never leaving the darkening sky. The world felt still, almost eerily so, as if it too were holding its breath.

Sitting in the silence of the cellar, Jack let the storm's memory wash over him. He tried to explain it to himself, the way his heart had raced, the electricity in the air, the sheer magnificence of the storm. What had driven him to run toward it, to feel it, to experience it up close? His brother had pulled him away, but it wasn't just Vern's warnings that held him back now. It was something else, something much deeper, something Jack had never truly been able to put into words.

Jack was not like Vern. He was not like other members of his family. Where they experienced storms as something to be feared, he experienced storms as something to be understood. His brother did not know what was so appealing about the tornado; Vern did not find the beauty in it, or the uninhibited, chaotic energy that made it so appealing. The storm to Vern was simply something that can destroy everything in its path. To Jack it was something different as if it was alive.

The tornado was not only a threat. It was not a destructive force alone. It was mystic, beautiful, powerful, and all this was bound up in one chaotic, whirling mass. It was something that made Jack feel small and insignificant but at the same time, it made him feel that he was part of something bigger than himself.

Jack started thinking about his family, his parents, his brother, and understood how he was different than them. His family labored in the farm with scratchy hands all the time and their minds were on the matter. His father was pragmatic and never went after something that would not give him a concrete outcome. His mother was caring and hard working but with the same practical mindset. Their issues were to do with ensuring that the farm ran smoothly, that there were all the necessary things to run the farm the following day. The storms were not an exception; they were part of the scenery they knew how to take care of, to live.

But to Jack, the storm wasn't something to survive. It was something to study, something to be embraced.

He sat back against the cold stone of the cellar, his legs crossed beneath him, his gaze still fixed on the sky through the tiny window. His mind raced with the memory of the tornado. He thought about how it had moved, how the clouds had spun and twisted, how the air had hummed with power. It was chaotic, unpredictable, and dangerous, yes — but there was something about it that called to him. Something in the way it seemed to have a purpose, a life of its own.

Jack's mind buzzed with questions. How did it form? Why did it move the way it did? What made it grow so strong, so fast, and what caused it to eventually dissipate? He wasn't afraid of the tornado. He was fascinated by it. The more he thought about it, the more he realized how deeply drawn he was to it.

The tornado represented everything Jack longed to understand, power that was beyond his control, yet beautiful in its chaotic form. It was everything in life that could not be tamed or explained, yet it was something that, to Jack, could be studied and understood if only he had the tools and the knowledge.

It was this fascination, this deep yearning to uncover the mysteries of nature, that would shape his life. As he sat in the dim cellar, Jack felt a quiet fire ignite inside him. He didn't want to just live with the storms. He wanted to understand them. He wanted to study them, to learn how they worked, to unlock the secrets of the sky.

The tornado was chaos and it was beautiful.

As the sounds of the storm slowly faded into the distance, the world outside returned to its usual stillness. The roar of the wind that had once seemed so deafening now felt like a distant memory. Jack could hear Vern's voice from behind him, still speaking in that half-frustrated, half-relieved tone. "You really are crazy, you know that?" Vern muttered under his breath. But there was no anger in his words only an undertone of concern. Vern's protective nature always showed itself, especially when it came to Jack. He was the oldest, after all, and had taken on the responsibility of looking out for his younger brother for years.

Jack didn't respond to Vern right away. Instead, he sat on the stone floor of the cellar, leaning against the cool, rough wall, his gaze lost in thought. The warmth of the storm had faded, leaving the air damp and heavy. Outside, the last remnants of the tornado slowly swirled away, dissipating into the sky, leaving behind only the ripples of its power. Jack watched the faint twisting clouds above, their once-prominent rotation now nothing more than a distant, almost imperceptible wisp of vapor.

"Next time, Jack," Vern said, his voice more solemn now, "just listen to me, okay? You can't go running out into the field like that. Tornadoes aren't something to mess around with."

Jack heard his brother's words but couldn't shake the feeling of yearning that still filled him. He had always admired Vern, but in this moment, he felt a deep disconnect. It wasn't fear that had drawn him to the storm—it was something far more powerful, something Vern couldn't see.

Jack pushed himself up from the cold cellar floor, brushing off the dirt and dust that clung to his clothes. Vern's concern was clear, but so was the sense of resignation in his voice. Jack knew Vern didn't understand not like he did. He didn't share Jack's fascination with the storm. His brother had always been practical, grounded in the realities of life, always thinking in terms of safety and consequence. Tornadoes, to Vern, were just a dangerous force to be avoided. But Jack... Jack wasn't like that.

"I'll be careful next time," Jack muttered, more to appease his brother than because he truly agreed. He nodded, even though inside, he could feel the rebellion stirring within him. His brother's warnings, though well-intentioned, couldn't quell the burning curiosity that raged inside Jack. And no matter how much Vern or anyone else told him to stay away, Jack knew in his heart that he couldn't just ignore it.

The two of them walked back toward the house in silence, but Jack's mind was elsewhere, still chasing the storm that had faded into the distance. He couldn't stop thinking about it — the way it had moved, the beauty in its raw, untamed power. There had been something so majestic about it, and Jack found himself yearning for another chance to see it, to experience it up close.

***

Back inside the house, Jack sat at the wooden kitchen table, absently picking at the crumbs of his sandwich, but his thoughts were miles away. The kitchen smelled of baking bread and simmering stew, but Jack barely noticed. His mother moved around the room, preparing dinner, while his father sat at the table, quietly reading the newspaper. The rhythmic sound of the table scraping under his father's hand was the only sound that broke the silence between them.

Jack's mind wandered back to the tornado, the way the wind had howled, the way the air had vibrated with power. It was beautiful. Chaotic. And it had called to him like nothing else ever had. He felt a restlessness growing inside him, an almost insatiable curiosity about the storm. He needed to understand it. The tornado had been alive, in a way, a living, breathing thing that was both terrifying and magnificent. It wasn't just about the danger; it was about the mystery of it.

His brother, Vern, didn't understand. He never would. To Vern, everything had a place, a purpose, a time. The world was neat and tidy, and storms were to be feared, not admired. Jack tried to reconcile the difference between himself and his brother, but it felt like there was a growing gap between them. Vern's protective instincts were rooted in practicality. He wanted Jack to be safe. But safety, to Jack, felt like a cage. He couldn't ignore the storms. They drew him in.

For as long as he could remember, he'd been intrigued by the forces of nature. The wind, the dust devil, the rain, the power of a storm had always fascinated him, but the tornado—this tornado—had changed everything. It wasn't just about surviving nature. It was about understanding it, unlocking the secrets it held. What made it spin? What made it so powerful? Jack couldn't explain it, but his heart raced whenever he thought about it.

He glanced over at his brother, who was talking to their father, discussing something about the crops, but Jack barely heard them. His mind was filled with the image of the swirling clouds, the air thick with electricity. That's what he wanted to understand. That's what he had to learn. Storms weren't something to hide from. They were something to be unlocked.

As Jack sat there, listening to the dull hum of conversation around him, he could still feel the storm tugging at him. The feeling was still there, a faint longing, a curiosity he couldn't shake.

The storm had passed, and the day was settling into twilight. The sun was low, casting long shadows across the field. Jack stood from the table, moving toward the window. The sky outside was clear now, the storm gone, but his mind still churned with questions.

He pushed open the window, the cool evening air brushing against his face, and for a moment, he stood there in silence, gazing out at the vast expanse of land. The world around him was quiet, calm again, but Jack's mind was still racing.

He didn't know when he would see another tornado, but he knew one thing for certain: he would be ready. He would watch, study, and learn. And he wouldn't stop until he understood the storms that fascinated him so.

Jack's curiosity had only deepened. The tornado had become something more than just a storm to him. It had become an obsession one that would drive him for years to come.

For now, he was looking out of the window, at the great Kansas sky, his heart full of a kind of quiet excitement. This storm had taken its toll on him and it was apparent that nothing would be the same anymore.

***

Years later, that memory never truly left him. In lecture halls, in the lab, even decades later when storms were recreated for paying crowds, he could still hear Vern's voice as clearly as the rush of wind through the wheat: 'You're the last person who should be out in a field when a storm comes.'

The warning echoed like scripture, yet it was always paired with another vision. The sight of that first funnel cloud, beautiful and merciless, descending from the heavens as though the sky itself had split open. That moment stitched itself into the fabric of who he was.

Jack Engle would spend his life carrying both truths inside him: his brother's caution, and the irresistible pull of the storm. He never stopped chasing that feeling. Not really.

The most unpredictable and raw force of nature, tornadoes, had become a part of Jack's life. And he intended to have the knowledge of all about the

3

THE STORM WITHIN

The sound of the kerosene lamp hissing in the dark kitchen filled Jack's memory as though it were happening again. It was a ritual, every evening on the Engle farm. The warm glow of the lamp cast long shadows over the rough wooden table where Jack's mother Elsie laid out the meal: biscuits fresh from the oven, a pot of beans that had simmered all afternoon, and a simple stew with potatoes and carrots. The air was thick with the familiar scent of home, but it was always charged with a silent tension.

Edger Engle, Jack's father seated at the head of the table, held his fork like a gavel, his silence demanding obedience. The children knew to speak only when spoken to.

Elsie, ever the peacemaker, would sprinkle in soft questions, "Did the hens lay well today, Wanda?" or "Jack, you washed your hands, didn't you?" She tried her best to keep the conversation flowing, but her words often seemed swallowed by the weight of Edger's presence.

Wanda, sharp-eyed and quick-tongued, couldn't resist poking at her brother. She nudged Jack with her elbow, smirking.

"Got hay sticking out of your hair again. Maybe it's growing there."

The younger siblings erupted in laughter, bits of biscuit tumbling from their mouths. Jack flushed, keeping his eyes on his plate. Edger's fork clicked sharply against the tin dish, silencing the table.

"Let's eat with less chatter," Edger commanded.

The moment passed, but Jack's thoughts drifted, as they often did. Each meal was a pleasant gathering with little conversation but plenty of food. He often wondered if life on the farm was meant to be a constant balancing act between silence and noise, with more work than rest.

***

The mornings came early, often before the first rooster crowed. Jack carried buckets from the well, the wooden handles biting into his palms, the water splashing against his legs. He milked cows in the dim light of dawn, the rhythm of the streams hitting the pail interrupted by the occasional swat of a cow's tail. In the hen house, chickens scattered at his feet when he reached for eggs, their feathers swirling in the morning air.

Wanda followed him into the yard, already muttering complaints. "You're slow as molasses, Jack. I'll be old before you finish."

Jack scowled, his patience wearing thin. "At least I don't leave half the eggs cracked."

Their bickering caught Edger's attention. He inspected the pails and baskets with the critical eye of a foreman. "Sloppy work," he remarked, his voice biting. "If you're gonna do a job, do it right."

Jack knew that he was right this time. He bit his tongue, knowing better than to argue.

While Wanda hurried through her chores, eager to escape scolding, Jack lingered. He crouched down to watch a line of ants marching near the chicken coop, each carrying crumbs twice its size. Dew glistened on the grass like tiny jewels, and Jack traced patterns on the barn wall, as though the morning held secrets that only he could see.

When the chores were done, Jack's mind was free to roam. Behind the barn, he shaped mud into miniature towns, streets, huts, and walls, using beetles as his "citizens." He watched them wander, recording their choices with a stub of pencil in his pocket notebook.

"They turn left more than right," Jack whispered to himself, fascinated by their predictable patterns.

Sometimes his curiosity became daring. Watching hawks wheel overhead, Jack decided that man should fly. He found two thin boards and strapped the makeshift wings to his arms. From the barn loft, he leapt into a mountain of hay, flapping his arms furiously.

The result was always the same—a crash, a grunt, and straw sticking to his clothes. Wanda doubled over laughing.

"One day, you'll break your fool neck!" she teased.

But Jack grinned, brushing hay from his face. "One day," he muttered to himself, "I'll fly." The bruises from his attempts were badges of honor, proof that he dared to try.

While the others laughed or rolled their eyes, Vern's calm gaze lingered with curiosity. When Jack showed him his beetle charts, Vern studied them with genuine interest.

"Keep looking, Jack," he said softly. "The world tells its secrets to those who pay attention." But at the same time, Vern wanted his little brother safe from any kind of storm.

Vern's quiet support meant more to Jack than any scolding from Edger or teasing from Wanda. Vern shielded him from their father's stern discipline, offering a steady hand on his shoulder, unspoken encouragement that made the hard days bearable.

***

At night, after the last chores were done, Jack sometimes sat with Vern on the porch. The field stretched endlessly before them, fireflies blinking in the tall grass. Thunder rumbled far off, a storm crawling across the horizon. Wanda played with her doll. Edger and Elsie fell asleep in their rocking chairs after a full day of labor. But Vern leaned back in his chair, watching the sky.

"Storms come and go," Vern murmured. "What matters is how you stand through them."

Jack tucked those words away in his mind. The farm was not just a place of hard work and hardship, it was a crucible, shaping him with every meal, every chore, and every experiment. In the flicker of the kerosene lamp and the quiet of Vern's voice, Jack began to understand: resilience and imagination were his true inheritance.

***

Later, in school, Jack felt the weight of his family's expectations and the sharp sting of failure. Mr. Smith, the stern teacher, demanded conformity above all else, and Jack's daydreaming was often met with harsh reprimands.

"Engle!" Mr. Smith's voice cracked like thunder, pulling Jack back to reality.

Jack jerked his head, heart racing. The teacher's cold gaze pinned him to his desk.

"Repeat the rule for diagramming compound subjects," Mr. Smith demanded.

Jack's mind went blank. The clouds, always calling him, wiped away every trace of grammar from his thoughts.

"I—I don't remember, sir," Jack stammered.

Mr. Smith's mouth tightened. The ruler slammed against his palm. "Daydreaming, again. There is no place for idle thoughts here. The world is hard enough without fools who waste their minds staring out windows."

Jack lowered his eyes, his cheeks burning. He wasn't trying to be foolish. The sky always called louder than the chalkboard.

***

Later that day, as Jack walked home, the boys who had seen his failure in the classroom found him again.

"There he is," one sneered. "The daydreamer. Can't add two numbers, but knows every cloud in the sky."

They blocked his path, jeering at him, kicking his books out of his hands. The humiliation burned. But instead of walking away, Jack's fists clenched.

For a moment, the older boys hesitated. Jack, though smaller, had a wild look in his eyes — something untamed, like the storms he loved.

***

This wasn't just about Jack being punished or mocked. It was about the **gospel** — the beliefs and rules that held power in his world. His father's stern authority, Mr. Smith's unwavering discipline, and the societal expectations that demanded conformity, they were all part of the **gospel** Jack was expected to live by. Yet, Jack's nature, his curiosity, his imagination, and his refusal to fit neatly into these rules was beginning to challenge it.

Just as Vern had encouraged him to keep looking, to watch for the patterns that others missed, Jack's confrontation with the older boys was his first act of rebellion against the gospel. The rigid expectations of his father, the harsh critiques at school, and the silent pressure to conform were all pieces of the gospel he now saw as flawed. What mattered was not following the gospel, but finding his own path.

Jack didn't fight because he was angry. He fought because he was learning that **resilience** was not just a survival mechanism, it was the key to questioning the rules that limited him. And the gospel, Jack now realized, wasn't an unquestionable truth. It was a set of patterns that could be challenged, just like the storms he loved. The world, and his place in it, wasn't as fixed as the gospel had led him to believe.

***

The sound of the wind howling outside the lab's walls reminded Jack of a memory, one that had been tucked away for years. He stood at his workstation, his hand gripping the small joystick that controlled the wind turbines he'd set up, manipulating the air pressure to simulate the early conditions of a tornado. The machines hummed to life, and Jack's mind wandered back to his childhood, the countless days spent trying to understand the world around him.

He could almost hear the voice of Vern in his mind, telling him to "keep looking." Vern had always seen Jack's potential, even when Jack himself couldn't. It was Vern's quiet belief in him that had propelled him through every hardship on the farm and every challenge in his youth. And now, it was that very belief that allowed him to build this—something tangible and real. A miniature tornado, the very thing that had eluded him as a boy, could now be studied, understood, and even manipulated.

As the winds inside the chamber swirled, Jack felt a quiet pride. The world wasn't chaotic, as he had once thought. There were patterns just like the storms of his past, just like his childhood, and just like the gospel that had shaped his life.

He'd challenged that gospel long ago, and now, he was creating something that could save lives.

Jack smiled softly to himself. Vern would have been proud.

With a deep breath, Jack pressed the final button, watching the storm he had created whip around the room. This was no longer just a child's dream. This was science. This was Jack's life's work. And the storms, both inside and outside, had led him here.

4

THE CALL TO HOLLYWOOD

The hum of the lab was what Jack Engle had heard for hours. Today, the room was quieter than usual, with the fans turning lazily to and fro overhead, and the low mechanical hum of instruments transferring data out of the air. There were a couple of loose pages which flapped on the fringe of the desk, stirred by the low puffs of the ventilation system. Outside, the air was a silver haze, and the light fell through the windows that were set high, and made the shadows long and slanting on the polished concrete floor.

Jack was sitting hunched over his workbench squinting at a complicated scatterplot of atmospheric pressure readings. The monitor light caught the lines cut into his eyes, years of staring up at skies and screens having their effect. His hand traced, with the ease of a machine, wind shear anomalies in green, which circled outliers in red. He had a pencil hanging behind his ear which he had forgotten. It had three coffee mugs on the desk, one of them empty, one half-full and one long since cold.

He didn't mind the silence. He preferred it, most days.

This was the only place where things worked out for him. Equations did not break laws. Weather, at its chaos, had patterns, so long as you knew where to find them. In this steel-and-paper shrine he could reproduce what nature threw forth in spasms of wrath and beauty. Tornadoes did not debate. They rotated and annihilated, yet they did not challenge his ways. People did.

Jack took his old brass-bound sketchbook, where he kept all his tornado models, airflow concepts, vortex variations, and opened it to a half-done page. Margins were filled with spiral diagrams. Numbers, formulas, small drawings of fans, and a question that was barely readable in the middle of the page: *What is the price of curiosity?*

He sank in his chair, and rubbed his temples. Since early morning he had not spoken to anyone. Darlie had called a few minutes ago, to say that dinner was ready, and to remind him that it was time he was getting home, before it grew dark which he had forgotten. Again.

He felt a tightening in his chest which he had not before observed; it was not pain, however. Something else. An ache. A hunger. As though his mind was stretching to get something beyond the picture. His work was worthy. Groundbreaking, even. The predictive system, the vortex model, the little tornado -years of his life in a whirling air. But recently, a doubt had begun to creep into his mind:

Was anyone watching?

His colleagues were polite. The papers were cited. His students were respectful. But beyond the walls of academia, beyond the halls of government policy where he'd once pitched tornado shelter standards who really knew what he had done? What he had built?

The first sign of recognition came through an unexpected email. Jack scanned the subject line with surprise: *"Invitation to Contribute: Groundbreaking Work in Tornado Simulation."* He opened it quickly. The National Meteorology Conference wanted him to submit his latest research on tornado models for an upcoming conference. He hadn't expected this. Not yet. His mind raced. He had barely finished his last round of revisions, but here they were, inviting him to present. His breakthrough was starting to gain attention. This was recognition. A foot in the door. But was it the kind of attention he wanted?

Jack looked over the lab, where the remains of his last controlled vortex still filled the room. It had spun for only a few minutes, but it had moved like something alive. The real storm lived in there, just for a moment.

The rest of the world? They only saw destruction. They only saw *Twister* on a movie screen, wind machines in a theme park, a ride, a thrill. They didn't see what he saw. What he felt.

Jack's phone buzzed. He glanced at the screen. An email from Science Weekly. The subject: "Feature Story Opportunity: A New Era in Tornado Simulation." He paused before opening it. His work was beginning to spread beyond academic circles, being noticed by the media. They wanted to feature him and his work. The recognition felt like a shadow he wasn't sure he wanted to welcome.

He bent over, took the old dial caliper, and set the dial on a copper coil nearby. His hands were steady enough, but his mind was wandering again. It was becoming more frequent in the recent past. Flashbacks of the past, remnants of storms and skies and many questions unanswered. This solitude was joyful, yes, but there was also a dull side of dissatisfaction growing upon it.

A sudden beep startled him.

The landline. Rare enough to hear these days.

Jack turned his head, the sound dragging him back to the present. The phone sat on the far end of the table, half-buried under reports and a wrinkled old newsletter from the National Weather Service. He stared at it for a moment, letting it ring again, then reached out and answered.

"Dr. Engle," he said automatically, voice still coated in the fog of calculations.

There was a pause — half a second too long.

Then came a smooth, polished voice on the other end.

"Good afternoon, Dr. Engle. My name is Asher Quinn. I represent Universal Studios, and I think we may have something rather exciting to discuss."

Jack straightened slightly in his chair, brow furrowing. The voice on the line was polished. A practiced calm, with the faint accent of someone used to making offers people didn't know they were waiting for.

"This is Dr. Jack Engle," he replied slowly, suspicion slipping into his tone. "You said... Universal Studios?"

"Yes, sir," the voice continued. "Asher Quinn. I'm a legal and talent representative with Universal. I'm reaching out in regard to some rather exciting developments on our end—specifically, the science behind our tornado simulation for a major attraction at our theme park in Orlando."

Jack blinked. He wasn't sure what response he had expected. A grant offer, maybe. A university collaboration. But not this.

"I'm sorry," he said, leaning forward, bracing his elbows on the desk. "Did you say tornado simulation?"

"That's correct," Quinn said, as though he were confirming an appointment. "We've been developing a live, interactive storm experience for our Twister attraction. Your name came up during internal technical reviews as one of the foundational figures in tornado model research—particularly small-scale vortex dynamics. Some of your work appears, let's say… inspired the engineering behind our systems."

Jack went quiet. The hum of the lab, the tick of a weather gauge, the faint whoosh of air. It all seemed to pause.

"Inspired," he repeated slowly.

"Yes," Quinn said, not missing a beat. "Your vortex model more specifically, the controlled vertical airflow method you published in the

Journal of Atmospheric Phenomena, and in your book, *Severe and Unusual Weather.* We also saw the demonstration you gave at the National Conference years back. Our engineers referenced that work during early development. Quite groundbreaking. We believe you may have a claim or at least an interest — in what's being built."

Jack's mouth felt dry. His book had been published several years earlier. That paper had been buried under a decade of more recent work.

"I... I don't follow," he said. "Are you saying you are building an attraction using my design?"

"Well," Quinn said smoothly, "let's just say it draws heavily on your intellectual groundwork. Now, before this becomes a formal legal matter, my team and I would like to discuss a more amicable arrangement. A partnership, of sorts. We're very interested in working with originators like yourself to ensure the spirit of the science is preserved and appropriately credited, of course."

Jack's hand tightened around the receiver. "Credited. And what exactly are you offering?"

There was a pause — then a chuckle. "Dr. Engle, we're asking you to name your price."

Jack stared at the opposite wall, blankly. The phrase hung there in the air, heavier than anything else Quinn had said. *Name your price.*

He should have felt triumphant. Validated. But instead, he felt… uncertain. The offer was unexpected, unnerving. Was this what recognition looked like? Corporate lawyers with silky voices and checks behind curtains?

"I'll have to think about this," he said finally, his voice low.

"Of course," Quinn said easily. "Take your time. My number's on your caller ID. We'd love to fly you out to Orlando next month to see the prototype. Just give me a call. And Dr. Engle — congratulations. Your work is changing the way people experience nature."

The line went dead.

Jack sat there for a long time, holding the receiver, not moving.

Across the lab, the steam chamber released a faint hiss. A curl of vapor lifted upward in the still air, turning once like a dancer before dissolving into nothing.

Jack stood by the window now, staring out at the flat Kansas skyline. The phone still sat on the table behind him like an unanswered question. He ran a hand through his hair and exhaled sharply. It wasn't every day that a global entertainment giant came calling. And it definitely wasn't every day they offered to throw money at you, no questions asked.

He was still turning it over in his mind when the phone rang again.

This time, he answered it before the second ring.

"Dr. Engle," the voice said again. Same smooth, poised cadence. "Asher Quinn, Universal Studios. Hope I caught you at a better time."

Jack glanced at the clock. It hadn't even been fifteen minutes.

"I'm listening," Jack said, cautious.

"Excellent. I'll keep it brief," Quinn replied. "Universal Studios is currently developing a high-profile attraction—a full-scale immersive tornado experience for our Orlando theme park. Think cutting-edge simulation, high-speed airflow chambers, sound design, even artificial debris. Think *Twister*, but tangible. The idea is to drop guests in the center of a storm."

Jack raised an eyebrow. "So, you're building chaos for fun."

"We're building awe," Quinn said with a light chuckle. "And as we began digging into the science of how to make that awe feel real, your name kept surfacing. Your tornado simulations, vortex stability research, even that rotating fan model with layered wind shear? We found the tech specs fascinating."

"And now you want to… buy them," Jack said slowly, testing the words.

"Exactly," Quinn confirmed. "Universal is prepared to purchase the rights to your tornado models and associated simulations. Full licensing, full credit. No strings. You'd retain name recognition, of course. We'd include a plaque, maybe even an interview segment in our promotional rollout."

Jack's gut tightened. "And the data?"

"All yours," Quinn said. "We're not asking for exclusivity, just the rights to use your models for the park attraction. We respect that this is your life's work. We just want to bring it to the public in a form they can touch, feel, remember."

Jack was quiet again. The part of him that had spent decades buried in books, equations, and skeptical peer reviews bristled at the thought. A theme park. Screaming kids. Flashy lights. But another part — the one that had stood in the wheat field as a boy and looked up at the sky in awe, wondered what it would feel like to share that sense of wonder with the world.

"What's the catch?" Jack asked finally.

"No catch," Quinn said. "No fine print. Just a check, some contracts, and your blessing. Honestly, Dr. Engle—name your price."

That phrase again. So easy. Too easy.

Jack ran a hand along the edge of the table. The surface was chipped, scarred from years of hot mugs and soldered circuits and storm notes. *Name your price.* What was the price of wonder? Of years spent decoding the violence of the skies?

"I'll think about it," he said, more firmly this time.

Quinn didn't push. "Of course. We'll send over a draft agreement. Feel free to have your legal team review. If you're ever in Orlando, we'd be honored to give you a tour. The prototype's nearly complete. I think you'll be impressed."

Jack hung up without saying goodbye.

He stood still for a moment longer, the quiet of the lab wrapping around him again, but it didn't feel the same. There was something foreign now in the air — opportunity, temptation, the faint electric buzz of his legacy being pulled into a world he didn't quite trust.

Behind him, the steam chamber exhaled once more. The air twisted into a soft spiral - small, elegant, and utterly real.

Jack sat alone at his desk; the room dim now as the light outside had begun to change. Evening shadows stretched across the concrete floor, long and quiet, as if the lab itself had slipped into contemplation with him.

The call had ended, but the words lingered, clinging to the corners of the room like static. *Name your price.* That phrase haunted him, replaying over and over, not just in his ears but in his bones. How many times had he wanted to hear something like that? Acknowledgment. Respect. Someone outside the cloistered walls of academia recognizing the depth of his work, not because it passed peer review but because it moved people.

He reached absently for the cooling mug beside him, sipping out of habit. The coffee was bitter now, but he barely tasted it. His mind spun faster than the models on his monitor.

What if this was his chance?

For decades, Jack had tried to bring tornado science out of the lecture hall and into the light, into public awareness where it could matter, could save lives. He thought about the towns that hadn't gotten the warning in time. The families who'd never known what hit them. What if his work, twisted into something theatrical and immersive, actually *reached* people? What if a boy somewhere, years from now, walked into that attraction, stood in front of that swirling vortex, and felt the same wonder Jack had felt in the Kansas fields?

Would that be such a terrible thing?

He stared at the vortex sketch tacked to the wall above his desk. A spiral in pen, neatly labeled airflow equations beside it. He remembered staying up all night to finish that drawing before his first conference presentation. Back then, he didn't care who saw it, he only cared that it worked. That it was *true*.

But now…

Now they wanted to put it behind velvet ropes and strobe lights. They wanted to sell it in a gift shop.

Jack pushed back from the desk, the wheels of his chair squeaking against the concrete. He stood and began to pace slowly across the lab, his hands behind his back, brow furrowed. He tried to shake the feeling, but it clung to him like storm humidity.

He imagined the crowd standing beneath a simulated storm, children gasping, parents filming with their phones. He imagined the awe on their faces. He imagined a plaque with his name on it: *Based on the tornado models developed by Dr. Jack Engle.* Was that so wrong?

But then another image came: his work reduced to a marketing tagline. Science watered down into spectacle. Years of trial, error, and rigor recast as entertainment. The nuance, the precision - lost beneath the noise.

He remembered how Asher Quinn had said it. *We just want to bring it to the public.*

He hadn't asked about the equations. He hadn't asked about the simulations, or the airflow dynamics, or the controlled humidity ratios. Just a check, a contract, a smooth line about "awe."

Did they really care about the science? Or just the spectacle?

Jack stopped pacing and stood in front of the vortex chamber. He saw himself — older, thinner, and worn by time. He had spent a lifetime trying to understand something untamable. Now, someone wanted to turn that understanding into a ride.

He pressed a hand lightly into the swirling vortex. It reacted quickly and curled around his fingers.

The world might finally notice his work.

But at what cost?

The following afternoon, Jack was back in the lab, but his concentration was fractured.

He had tried — genuinely tried — to lose himself in his data, running simulations on wind velocity over uneven terrain, recalibrating a fan array, even cleaning a few shelves that had been dusty since 1998. But every time he reached for a notebook or turned a dial, he would hear the words again: *Name your price.*

So, when the phone rang, again, he already knew who it was.

He hesitated for a second before picking up. "Dr. Engle."

"Good to hear your voice, Doctor," Asher Quinn said, all polished edges and charm. "I hope I'm not interrupting."

"You are," Jack said flatly, "but go ahead."

Quinn chuckled, unbothered. "I just wanted to follow up. My team has reviewed your publications in greater depth, and we're more certain than ever that your work forms the conceptual backbone of our simulation. It's elegant. Precise. More than what we expected, frankly."

Jack said nothing. He was already tired of the compliments.

"And Universal is prepared," Quinn continued, "to offer a figure that reflects our appreciation of that foundation."

Jack exhaled slowly. "Let's skip the setup. How much?"

There was a pause, just long enough to signal gravity.

"Two hundred and fifty thousand dollars for licensing rights. An additional retainer if you agree to consult during final attraction development. Plus expenses covered for travel to Orlando and lodging. You'd retain name credit. And, if we move forward with future weather-based attractions, your name would be at the top of our advisory list."

Jack leaned back in his chair. He let the number settle in the room.

It wasn't just generous — it was life-altering.

He could rebuild the lab. Fund real fieldwork. Set up scholarships. Or, for once, just... breathe. Two-hundred-and-fifty thousand dollars could stretch a long way in Kansas.

But something inside him didn't stretch so easily.

"I appreciate the offer," Jack said carefully, "but this work... it wasn't designed for entertainment."

Quinn didn't hesitate. "But it *can* be. And isn't that the point of good science? To reach people?"

Jack didn't answer right away. The silence between them crackled like static.

"The science I do saves lives," he said finally. "It predicts patterns, improves shelters, protects communities. What you're proposing is a thrill ride."

"A thrill ride based on *truth*," Quinn said smoothly. "Built on your truth. What better way to bring the public into that reality? Into that awe?"

Jack rubbed his forehead. He wanted to argue but part of him couldn't deny it. He remembered the face of that little girl at the science fair last spring, how her eyes lit up when she saw the tabletop vortex he'd built for a demo. She'd looked at it like it was a miracle. Was that so different?

Still, this felt… rushed. Unclean.

"I'm not saying no," Jack said slowly. "But I'm not ready to say yes. This isn't the kind of decision I make on a Tuesday afternoon over the phone."

"Completely understood," Quinn said. "We want you to feel confident. But I should be honest with you, Dr. Engle this offer won't sit on the table indefinitely. We're entering final build-out, and we need all licensing and technical partnerships in place soon. I'd suggest we reconvene within the next few days. End of the week, ideally."

Jack narrowed his eyes at the phone. The voice on the other end was still friendly, still measured. But underneath, there it was, the deadline. The unspoken *or else*.

"I'll think about it," he said again.

"I hope you do," Quinn replied, tone upbeat but conclusive. "And I hope you realize how rare this kind of recognition is. Most scientists never see their work come to life in a way people can touch. You have that chance. We'd be proud to help make it happen."

The line clicked off.

Jack set the phone down gently and stared at it for a long time, as though waiting for it to ring again. Outside, the wind rustled against the glass. He could almost hear thunder, though the sky was clear.

A storm was coming but not the kind he could model.

The lab was silent again.

Jack sat in his chair, motionless, one hand resting on the desk and the other still loosely curled as if it clung to the ghost of the receiver. The call had ended, but the conversation continued to echo in his mind.

Two hundred and fifty thousand dollars.

His name, in lights. His model, spinning in the middle of a billion-dollar theme park, surrounded by speakers and fog machines and gasping tourists.

He leaned back slowly in his chair, the old leather creaking beneath him. Outside, the Kansas sky was bruised with the coming dusk. Wide, endless, unchanging. It made the lab feel smaller than it had a moment ago.

He stared out the window, and for the first time in a long while, Jack Engle didn't know what to feel.

He should be thrilled. Someone wanted his work. Not just to footnote it or cite it at the bottom of a paper — but to *use* it. To build something with it. Something big. For years, he had labored in obscurity, pushing against institutional indifference and grant committees that didn't return his calls. Every breakthrough, every calibration, had felt like shouting into a void.

Now, that void had answered.

But at what cost?

He turned back toward his desk, scanning the chaos of papers and prototype notes. A piece of chalk had snapped on the table earlier. He picked it up, absently rolling it between his fingers. There were equations scribbled on the wall behind him in fading white lines, an unfinished sequence about rotational velocity he'd meant to double-check days ago.

Is this what it takes? he wondered. *Not a paper. Not a peer review. But a roller coaster and a legal department?*

Jack sighed and rubbed his forehead.

This wasn't how he'd imagined his work would gain traction. He'd hoped for recognition in journals, on panels, maybe a speaking spot at a national climate symposium. He hadn't dared to dream of *popularity*. That wasn't the path of a scientist. Scientists didn't get famous. They didn't get theme park deals.

But maybe… maybe that's exactly why this mattered.

He thought about that moment in the vortex chamber just a few days ago — when the steam had caught the light just right, forming that perfect spiral. He'd watched it spin with the same awe he'd felt as a child watching the sky turn dark, watching the clouds twist like they were alive.

What if someone else could feel that, too?

What if millions of people, people who never picked up a textbook, never sat through a lecture, could walk into that attraction and feel the wonder he'd spent a lifetime chasing?

Was it so wrong to want that?

And yet, beneath the thrill, the unease remained. What if they got it wrong? What if they turned it into a cartoon? What if they stripped away the science and left only spectacle? Would his life's work become just another backdrop for popcorn and plastic souvenirs?

He closed his eyes, trying to imagine it. His name on a plaque. The crowd walking past. A parent reading it out loud to a kid who wasn't listening.

"Dr. Jack Engle... developed the tornado model used here."

Would that be enough?

He wasn't sure.

But he was sure of one thing: this offer was *something bigger* than he'd ever been part of. Bigger than any grant, any academic accolade. Bigger than Kansas.

And that realization scared him more than any storm he'd ever chased.

For the first time in years, he felt like he was standing on the edge of something, something new. Not a front of weather, but of consequence.

His hand finally let go of the chalk. It rolled off the table and hit the floor with a soft tap.

Jack didn't move to pick it up.

Instead, he sat in the silence of the lab, staring out at the last amber light of the evening, and felt a quiet, undeniable truth settle inside him.

This could change everything.

The lab had grown dim, but Jack hadn't turned on the lights.

The last light of the day slid down the walls like molasses, painting long amber shadows across the desk, the floor, the chalk-stained whiteboard covered in equations that had once felt like gospel. Now, they just looked… distant.

Jack sat in his chair, still, as if movement might break the fragile moment that had settled around him. Before him lay his notes, his diagrams, his miniaturized models of the tornado chamber. Years of trial and error. Pages written by hand, curled at the edges, coffee-stained and underlined a hundred times over. Equations that had taken him decades to balance. Simulations that had nearly cost him his funding. Models built with more belief than budget.

And now, they were something else. Not just science.

They were currency.

He leaned forward and gently picked up a plastic scale model of his airflow generator. It was worn from handling; edges dulled from years of demonstration. He ran his thumb along the base, remembering how it once sat in a conference room while he tried to explain to a panel of funders why controlled vortex systems mattered.

Back then, no one had listened.

Now, a studio did.

He felt the tug of something deep — something equal parts hunger and hesitation. Was this it? The moment he'd been waiting for? Or was it something more dangerous: the slow undoing of everything he'd built for the sake of visibility and a dollar amount?

What's the price of being understood? What's the cost of being seen?

Jack stood and walked slowly to the wide window overlooking the edge of the campus. Beyond the rows of redbrick buildings, the Kansas horizon stretched — flat, infinite, humming with possibility. The sky had begun to bruise with evening. Heavy clouds hovered, not quite storm-ready, but close enough to whisper to someone who knew how to listen.

He crossed his arms, staring out into the deepening twilight.

Fame had never been the goal. Understanding had. But understanding didn't pay for lab equipment. It didn't build outreach centers. It didn't land like a check in your mailbox.

He could almost hear Quinn's voice again: *You have that chance. We'd be proud to help make it happen.*

Jack closed his eyes.

He could see it: tourists walking through the ride, wind swirling around them, artificial lightning splitting the ceiling. Somewhere in the corner, his name, etched into a plaque. A boy, wide-eyed, watching the tornado take shape — just like he had, once. Would it be enough?

He didn't know.

But he knew this. The offer had changed something in him. It had cracked open a door that couldn't be closed again.

Maybe this was the next frontier. Not just the science of storms, but the science of *how people experience them*. Maybe he could shape both.

Or maybe he was making excuses.

Behind him, the lab exhaled - quiet, steady, full of the ghosts of ideas.

He looked back once at the vortex chamber.

Then turned again to the sky.

The clouds were heavy now. Low. Heavy with something unidentified.

Change was coming.

And Jack didn't know whether to chase it or run from it.

5

THE KITCHEN DEBATE

The clock ticked too loudly. In the living room, Jack stalked up and down the length of the room, his socks swishing across the well-worn hardwood in silent, rhythmical movements. There was a cup of coffee standing on the window which had not been touched. The house, which was always a quiet place, seemed restless tonight as even walls were preparing for something they could not define.

The conversation with Asher Quinn played on a loop in his head.

Name your price.

The phrase had followed him home, settled in the corners of the room, woven itself into the cushions of the couch and the shadows cast by the lamp. It wasn't just a line anymore. It had become a challenge, a temptation, a ticking clock.

A few hours ago, Jack had received yet another email, this time from a media outlet. They were offering him a feature story, praising the very research that had once felt like a never-ending cycle of failures.

He stopped at the bookshelf and rested a hand on the spine of an old meteorology textbook— *Atmospheric Turbulence and Stability*. He'd taught out of it for years. Now, it felt absurdly heavy. He let his hand fall away.

***

He tried to sort the storm inside him, but it did not break into neat categories the way his models did. It spun wide and fast, sucking in memories, regrets, and hopes alike.

Recognition. That was the word Asher had used. And hadn't Jack wanted that? Not out of ego—at least not entirely—but out of longing. To be understood. To be valued. To be seen not just as the man in the lab coat, but as the mind that had dared to replicate one of nature's most dangerous wonders.

And wasn't that what all of this had been about from the start? Helping people understand storms. Giving them tools. Warnings. Wonder.

But now they wanted to turn that wonder into an amusement park ride.

He rubbed his temples. A part of him--the weary part, the part which had been rejected by grant boards, ignored by academic conferences--wanted to say yes. Take the money. May the storm carry his work out into the world and may he at last sleep well.

But the other part—the stubborn part, the idealist that still lived somewhere in his gut was not ready to sell what he hadn't built for sale.

What if they got it wrong? What if they turned the science into spectacle? What if his life's work became a flash of wind and noise, followed by cotton candy and a souvenir shop?

***

He moved to the window and looked out over the lawn. The wind had picked up slightly—just enough to rustle the leaves. He used to find comfort in wind. Now it felt like a reminder.

This wasn't just a choice between money and integrity. It was a choice between *what kind of scientist* he wanted to be. The kind who holds the line or the kind who steps out of the lab and into the world, no matter how messy that world might be.

For a long moment, he stood there, watching the breeze tug gently at the branches.

Then, softly, aloud, as if confessing it to the night:

"I don't know which is worse... being ignored, or being misunderstood."

***

Jack wandered into the kitchen, the scent of onions and garlic soft in the air. Darlie stood at the stove, stirring a pot of soup, her sleeves rolled up and her hair tucked behind one ear.

"You're quiet," she said without turning. "Everything okay?"

Jack hesitated. He picked up a slice of bread from the counter and tore off a piece. "Yeah... just thinking."

Darlie glanced at him. "That 'thinking' looks like pacing from room to room. Want to tell me what's going on?"

He took a breath and leaned against the kitchen counter. "I got a call yesterday. From a guy named Asher Quinn. Works for Universal Studios."

She blinked. "The movie people?"

Jack nodded. "Yeah. Theme Park division. They're building a tornado attraction down in Orlando. Something immersive, with a large artificial tornado, sound effects... the works."

Darlie stopped stirring. "And?"

"They want to use my vortex models," he said. "The ones from my laboratory."

She turned toward him, eyebrows raised. "Seriously?"

"They said my simulations were the best they'd seen. Said it would help the experience feel real. They're offering... a lot. A quarter of a million dollars for licensing rights. Maybe more if I consult."

Darlie leaned against the table, absorbing that.

Jack rubbed the back of his neck. "I haven't told anyone else yet. Just needed time to process."

Darlie gave a short laugh, half surprise, half disbelief. "Well... that's something. Did you ever think this kind of offer would come?"

He shook his head. "No. Not in a million years."

She paused. "So… what's the catch?"

Jack shrugged. "They get to use my work in a theme park. Flashing lights. Special effects. Tourists with cameras. That kind of thing."

"And you're okay with that?"

He hesitated. "I don't know. That's the problem."

Darlie walked over and placed a hand on his arm. "Jack, it's incredible. Recognition, money, your name on something millions of people might see. But… do *you* feel good about it?"

"I want people to understand tornadoes," he said. "To feel the awe, the danger, the beauty. I just don't know if a ride at Universal is the way."

Darlie studied his face. "Do you think they'll treat it with respect? Or just turn it into a thrill ride?"

Jack didn't answer right away.

"I don't want to sell out," he said finally. "But I don't want to disappear either."

Darlie gave a soft smile. "You won't. Not to me. Not to anyone who knows what you've built."

She returned to the stove and gave the soup another stir. The kitchen was quiet for a few moments.

"Sleep on it," she said gently. "Not every storm needs an answer right away."

Jack looked at her, grateful.

"Thanks," he said.

***

Later that night, Jack sat alone in the study.

The lamp beside him gave off a warm, soft light, but his mind was anything but calm. A notepad lay open in front of him, though he had not written a single word. He just sat there, staring at the blank page, his thoughts swirling like the storms he studied.

What am I doing?

He leaned back in his chair and rubbed his hands together slowly. His fingers felt cold. Maybe it was the air, or maybe it was something deeper uncertainty settling into his bones.

The offer from Universal had stirred something in him. Excitement, sure. But also doubt. And now that Darlie knew, the reality of it felt heavier.

Is this what I've worked for? he wondered. *To see my research used in a theme park?*

He had spent years perfecting those vortex models, tweaking airflow, studying humidity levels, testing storm behavior under controlled conditions. They weren't just machines. They were the result of late nights, failed experiments, stubborn belief.

And now… they wanted to turn all of that into a thrill.

Jack frowned.

Would people walk away from the ride thinking, *wow, that's how tornadoes really work*? Or would they just laugh and take selfies, never realizing the science behind the wind?

Was this about education or entertainment?

He got up and walked to the window, folding his arms across his chest. Outside, the yard was still. A few leaves danced across the driveway. A quiet night.

He thought about the children he'd spoken to during school visits, the curiosity in their eyes when he explained how air could spin into something so powerful. Maybe this ride could spark that same curiosity on a larger scale.

But will it be accurate? Will it respect the science?

He didn't know. And that's what scared him.

***

He thought of the other scientists he admired. People who had never bent their research for profit, who stayed true to the academic world. Would they see this as selling out?

Would *he*?

But then, another part of him, again the tired part, the part that had watched his grant proposals go unanswered year after year spoke up.

This is a chance to reach people. A real chance. Maybe it won't be perfect. But it'll be something. People will finally see my work.

The money would help. Sure. But it wasn't just about that.

It was about being heard.

***

Jack returned to the desk and sat down slowly. He looked at the notepad again and finally picked up his pen.

He wrote one word.

"Why?"

And under it, he wrote:

Why did I start this work?

He tapped the pen against the page, thinking.

Because tornadoes mattered. Because science could save lives. Because if people understood the storms, they could survive them. That had always been the goal.

So maybe… just maybe… if the ride was done right—if he stayed involved, it could still serve that goal.

But that meant fighting to protect the science. Not handing it over blindly.

He closed the notebook, leaned back, and sighed.

No answers yet. Just questions.

But at least now, he was asking the right ones.

***

The next morning, the kitchen was quiet.

Darlie stood by the sink, pouring coffee into two mugs. Jack sat at the table, shoulders hunched, still wearing the same T-shirt from the night before. He looked tired not from lack of sleep, but from the weight of too much thinking.

She set his mug in front of him gently. "You've been up since before dawn," she said.

Jack gave a small nod. "Couldn't sleep. My head's too full."

Darlie sat across from him, both hands wrapped around her own cup. She watched him carefully. "Still thinking about the Universal offer?"

He looked up, eyes cloudy. "I just don't want to make the wrong choice."

Darlie was quiet for a moment. Then she said softly, "Can I say something you might not like?"

Jack managed a faint smile. "Since when has that ever stopped you?"

She smiled back then grew serious.

"I think you're excited," she began, "and I don't blame you. This offer… it's huge. It could change everything for us. The money, the recognition, finally having people see your work the way it deserves."

Jack nodded, but didn't speak.

"But Jack," she continued gently, "is this really *you*? Is this what you've always wanted?"

He opened his mouth, then hesitated. "I've always wanted people to understand tornadoes. To feel the urgency. To respect what these storms can do. And this… this could be the way."

"Could be," she repeated softly. "But it could also be something else."

Jack looked at her, waiting.

"It could be loud music, fake thunder, flashing lights. It could be tourists eating popcorn while your life's work spins in front of them like a toy." She paused. "And I worry… if they turn it into a show, and you don't have control over it… will you still be proud of it?"

Jack looked away. That part had haunted him too.

Darlie reached across the table, resting her hand on his.

"I've watched you spend years chasing storms, running models, failing and trying again. You didn't do it for money. You didn't do it to be famous. You did it because it mattered to you. Because the truth mattered."

Jack gave a slow nod. "But what if this is how I *get* people to care?"

Darlie squeezed his hand gently. "Then be sure that what they're caring about is the *right* thing. The truth—not a version of it made for thrills."

They sat in silence for a moment.

Then she added, more quietly, "Just promise me something."

He looked up.

"Whatever you decide, do it for the *right reason*. Not just because the number is big. Not just because they're offering a shiny stage. Do it because it helps the work. Do it because it feels like *you*."

Jack swallowed hard.

"I don't want to lose you to this," she said. "Not the man who stayed up until midnight tweaking airflow just because a decimal didn't look right. That's the man I believe in."

He smiled, barely.

"Still here," he said quietly.

"I know," Darlie whispered. "I just needed to make sure."

***

Later that evening, Jack stood on the back porch, watching the wind push gently through the wheat fields beyond the fence. The sky was streaked with the last gold light of day, quiet and wide.

Darlie came out, drying her hands on a dish towel.

"You've been out here a while," she said.

Jack didn't look at her just yet. He took a deep breath, then said, "I've made my decision."

She nodded slowly, waiting.

"I'm going to say yes," he said. "To Universal."

Darlie walked over and leaned beside him on the railing. "You sure?"

"No," he said, with a small laugh. "Not completely. But I think it's the right thing to do."

He looked at her now, eyes serious.

"I know it's not perfect. I know it's commercial. But what if this is the only way people ever *see* it? Really see it. I have spent decades trying to explain tornadoes in classrooms, papers, models and it barely leaves the lab."

Darlie stayed quiet, listening.

"But in a theme park?" Jack went on. "Millions of people. Families. Kids. Maybe one of them sees it... and *gets it*. Feels what I felt the first time I saw a storm twist above the Kansas fields."

He looked down at his hands.

"I'm not doing it for the paycheck though it'll help," he added with a wry smile. "I'm doing it because I think this might be my shot. To make people care. To make them respect nature. To show them how powerful and beautiful these storms really are."

Darlie gently touched his arm. "And the science?"

"I'll be part of it," he said firmly. "I'll consult. I'll make sure it's done right. If they want my name on this, they get *all* of me not just the show version."

He looked at her again. "I won't let it become a circus."

Darlie gave a soft, understanding nod.

"I believe you."

Jack exhaled, and with it, some of the weight he'd been carrying seemed to lift.

"I'm scared," he admitted.

"That means you still care," she said.

They stood together in the quiet for a moment longer. The sky above them slowly deepened into blue, and in the far distance, a lone gust of wind stirred the trees.

Jack squeezed her hand gently.

"I'm doing this, Darlie. But I'm doing it on *my* terms."

She smiled. "Then I'm with you."

***

The next morning, the kitchen was filled with a low hum—the kettle on the stove, birds outside the window, the soft clink of a spoon in a mug.

Jack stood by the phone, hand hovering just above it. His heart beat faster than he liked to admit.

Darlie sat at the table, sipping her tea. She'd been watching him since he walked into the room.

He finally turned to her. "They're expecting a call today."

She nodded, her face unreadable.

"I'll say yes," he said. "I'll do it."

A long pause followed. Darlie looked down at her cup, then back up at him.

"I figured you would."

Jack waited for more approval, disappointment, anything—but her voice was steady.

"I still have my doubts," she said honestly. "I'm not sure if it's the right path."

Jack gave a small nod. "I'm not sure either. But I feel like I have to try."

Darlie stood, walked to him, and placed her hand lightly on his chest. "Just promise me one thing."

He met her eyes.

"Promise me you won't lose yourself in this," she said softly. "Promise me you'll still fight for the truth behind your work—no matter where it takes you. Even in the middle of lights and noise and spinning wind machines... don't forget why you started this."

Jack swallowed. Her words settled into him like roots.

"I promise," he said.

Darlie gave him a small, tired smile. "Then go ahead."

He picked up the phone, took a breath, and dialed.

As it rang, Darlie turned back to her tea, but not before glancing over her shoulder one last time—her eyes full of love, and something else he couldn't quite name.

Maybe it was hope.

Maybe it was fear.

Maybe both.

***

Jack pressed the phone to his ear as it rang. Once. Twice.

A quiet click. "Asher Quinn," came the voice on the other end.

Jack cleared his throat. "It's Jack Engle."

"Ah, Professor Engle," Asher replied, his tone bright. "I was hoping to hear from you."

Jack hesitated just a second longer, then said clearly, "I'm in. I'll do it."

There was a pause, then the sound of a satisfied exhale.

"Excellent. I'll get the paperwork in motion. This is going to be the start of something very big."

Jack forced a smile that Asher couldn't see. "Let's hope so."

They exchanged a few final words, details about next steps, scheduling, legal documents — and then the line went dead.

Jack lowered the phone slowly.

He stood there for a moment, alone in the quiet, his thumb still resting on the edge of the receiver. A part of him felt lighter like something long denied had finally opened. He was stepping into the spotlight. People would finally see the work. The storm would no longer stay in the lab.

But underneath that small victory, a thread of worry tugged at him.

Will they treat it right? Will I still be proud of it a year from now? Five?

He turned toward the window. Outside, the Kansas sky stretched wide and pale, the early morning light beginning to warm the edges of the clouds.

The wind stirred faintly across the field.

He watched it, searching for answers in the air, like he always had.

This is it, he thought. *The door has opened.*

But as the clouds shifted slowly above the prairie, Jack couldn't help but wonder.

Am I walking into something great... or walking away from everything that ever mattered?

6

THE STORM CHASER'S DREAM

The desk lamp buzzed softly in the corner, its yellow light pooling across a clutter of notes, weather maps, and open textbooks. Jack sat in his study, elbows on the table, head resting in one hand, staring at a swirling diagram of airflow patterns he'd drawn years ago. Outside, the wind nudged the branches against the windowpane, as if trying to remind him of something.

The house was quiet. Darlie had gone to bed an hour ago but Jack remained where he was, too restless to sleep.

Pride and uncertainty wrestled silently inside him. He had made the call. The deal was real. Contracts were coming. Universal Studios was going to build their tornado attraction in Orlando and his models would be at the heart of it.

It was everything he had once wanted: visibility, validation, a stage big enough for the whole world to see what he had built.

And yet, as he sat among the very things that had shaped his life – weather journals, storm footage, old lab notes. He felt something unfamiliar pressing in around him. Not regret, exactly.

Something quieter.

A disconnection.

His eyes landed on a framed photo on the shelf above his desk. He and his mentor, Dr. Wayne Decker, standing beside an early tornado probe they'd tested during grad school. Jack smiled faintly. They'd been soaked to the bone that day, caught in an unexpected downpour out on the plains, laughing like kids as their equipment sputtered in the mud.

Back then, there had been no talk of money or theme parks or branding. Just the work. The science. The raw, thrilling chase to understand what no one else had.

Now, he wondered. *Had he drifted too far from that boy in the field?*

He looked again at the swirling airflow model on the page, then reached for a pen. Without thinking, he began retracing the lines, adjusting the curve of a vortex, tightening the central pressure line, reflexes of a man who had done this a thousand times.

But as he worked, the same question returned, stubborn and quiet: *Will any of this mean the same, once it has its own building with flashing lights?*

He leaned back and closed his eyes for a moment, letting the hum of the lamp and the rustle of wind fill the space. For all the celebration, all the congratulations that were surely coming he couldn't shake the feeling that something precious was slipping away. Not just his models. Not just the data.

But the purity of it.

The purpose.

He opened his eyes again, suddenly needing to remember how it all started, not the research, not the models, but the moment this obsession with storms had first taken hold of him.

The answer was simple.

He had seen a tornado.

He had stood in the middle of Kansas as a boy, watching the sky split open and spin itself into something alive.

And that moment had changed everything.

***

The memory came rushing back like a sudden change in wind direction, uninvited but welcome. One moment Jack was staring at the dim light of his study lamp, the next he was nineteen again, walking into a college lecture hall with a worn spiral notebook and more questions than answers.

It was the fall of 1967. The University of Kansas was buzzing with the kind of nervous excitement only incoming students know. Jack had chosen meteorology as a major, mostly because he couldn't imagine doing anything else. Ever since that childhood moment standing in a field, watching the sky twist into a living monster, he'd been chasing that same feeling, equal parts fear and awe.

That first class changed everything.

The room wasn't much to look at, chalk-streaked blackboards, a stack of textbooks on a metal cart, ceiling fans creaking above but the man at the front of the room had presence.

Dr. Wayne Decker.

Gray hair, heavy brows, and a voice that cut through the classroom like a cold front. He didn't teach so much as challenge.

"Most people think tornadoes are just chaos," Decker said, scribbling a tight spiral on the board. "They're wrong. Every storm has structure. Every vortex probably follows rules even if we don't understand them yet. The tornado is just waiting for someone to unlock its secrets."

Jack was hooked.

He sat up straighter, his pen flying across the page. That one sentence opened a door in his mind. The idea that there was **order inside the storm** that you could *know* it, maybe even *predict* it was like a spark in dry grass.

After class, Jack stayed behind.

"You really think we can predict them?" he'd asked.

Dr. Decker had studied him for a second, then said, "Not yet. But someone will."

Jack remembered the way that sentence had struck him. Not yet. But someone will.

That was the moment Jack stopped being just curious. That was the moment he decided: *Why not me?*

***

The flashback swelled with color, the smell of chalk dust and cold air, late nights in the lab surrounded by wind charts and Doppler radar printouts, hours spent outside in Kansas fields launching weather balloons and watching storm fronts roll in like ocean waves.

Jack wasn't the best student in every subject, but when it came to the atmosphere, he was obsessed. While other students crammed for finals, Jack was building rudimentary vortex simulations out of plexiglass and box fans. He spent hours in Decker's office, debating pressure gradients, moisture layers, and convective indexes.

And Dr. Decker, for all his sternness, noticed.

"You have fire," he told Jack once, during a thunderstorm field observation. "That's good. But fire needs focus. Otherwise, it just burns itself out."

Those words stuck.

So did the deeper lessons about integrity. Decker had once turned down a funding offer from a media network because they wanted sensational footage of storms, not accurate data.

"This field is not about putting on a show," he'd said firmly. "It's about understanding something bigger than us and helping people survive it."

That ethic carved itself into Jack 's bones.

***

Back in his study, Jack leaned forward again, fingers gently brushing the edge of a brittle lab notebook from those early years.

He smiled faintly.

That fire Decker spoke about… it was still there.

But now, as the world opened a door labeled *fame*, Jack wondered if he'd be strong enough to remember why he walked through the first one.

***

The flashback lingered, growing clearer, more personal.

Jack could still remember the warm smell of old paper and coffee in Dr. Decker's office. Books lined every wall, most of them so worn their spines were unreadable. In the corner sat a weather radio that never stopped humming. It was a quiet space, sacred almost, filled with curiosity, calm, and the quiet ticking of a desk clock that seemed to measure time in questions, not seconds.

It was in that office, one fall afternoon, that Decker leaned back in his chair and shared something Jack had never forgotten.

"You know what they wanted me to do once?" the old man said, folding his hands. "Some news station in Chicago offered me five grand to go on live TV and stand in front of a green screen, narrating tornado paths like a game show host."

Jack had blinked. "Did you do it?"

Decker chuckled, shaking his head. "No. I was younger than I am now, but I wasn't stupid. I told them if they wanted a circus, they should hire a ringmaster."

Jack laughed. But Decker's face grew more serious.

"This field's changing, Jack. People don't want slow truths anymore. They want spectacle. Noise. Flash. You'll get your chance someday to go big. Just make sure it's still *you* talking when the microphone turns on."

He leaned forward then, voice low but firm. "Science is not about fame, Jack. It's about *truth*.

Understanding the universe. Don't let the world turn you into a show. You're here to *discover,* not to *entertain.*"

Jack had nodded quietly, those words settling deep.

That moment wasn't just a lesson. It was a vow.

***

They shared more than equations and field data. There were long drives through storm-chasing routes, during which Decker would share stories of storms that almost took them out, of grants that never came through, of nights sleeping in station wagons just to stay close to a promising cloud formation.

"Sometimes," he once told Jack during a roadside meal, "I think we're just trying to get close to something too big to hold. That's what makes it worth it."

It wasn't just his knowledge that shaped Jack. It was the way Decker walked through the world with humility, with restraint, and with respect for the natural forces he studied.

In him, Jack saw the version of himself he *wanted* to become not the man on magazine covers, but the one in the trenches, eyes to the sky, chasing meaning in patterns of wind and light.

***

Jack 's rise in meteorology came quickly under Decker's mentorship.

He published early. Led data teams. Built a reputation for accuracy and innovation in tornado modeling. His work wasn't flashy but it *worked.* And it saved lives.

And through it all, Decker's voice stayed with him. Not just in memory, but in practice.

When Jack was offered an early corporate grant, he turned it down. When a cable network asked to film his research for a "tornado special," he said no unless the science stayed intact.

It was integrity, not just knowledge, that shaped his path.

***

Back in his present-day study, Jack opened a drawer and pulled out a faded photo: him and Decker, standing next to a storm-chasing van, arms crossed, wind tearing through the tallgrass behind them.

Decker was gone now. Past three years ago. But his presence lingered in the pages of Jack 's notes, the careful measurements, the questions still unanswered.

Jack stared at the photo for a long time.

"Am I still the man you taught me to be?" he whispered.

The room said nothing. Only the faint whistle of Kansas wind outside the window, like an old friend knocking gently on the glass.

***

The years after graduation came fast and full.

Jack threw himself into his work, long days in the lab, longer nights chasing storm data across the Kansas plains. He had a gift for finding patterns in the chaos, for seeing the logic buried inside the wind.

By his late twenties, he had developed a new algorithm –one that used air pressure, temperature shifts, and wind velocity to model tornado formation more accurately than anything else at the time. It wasn't perfect, but it was promising. His mentor, Dr. Decker, had praised the work, calling it *"a rare leap forward in an old science."*

Jack's first published paper made ripples in the meteorological community. For a while, it felt like everything was unfolding just as he'd imagined, respect from his peers, invitations to speak at conferences, even a mention in a regional science journal.

He still worked in modest labs, drove an aging truck, and bought his field gear secondhand but he was chasing the truth, and the truth was finally looking back at him.

Until it wasn't.

***

It started small, an unexpected failure in a field test. One of his storm-tracking prototypes malfunctioned just before a major supercell moved through Oklahoma. The data was lost. The funding agency was not impressed.

Then came the critiques.

"Too theoretical," one reviewer had written about his model.

"Needs more real-world application."

"A promising idea, but unproven in dynamic storm conditions."

Jack pushed back, presented his data, refined the models, ran more simulations—but the feedback didn't change. More than once, he sat through panel reviews where his work was praised for its ambition, then passed over for grants in favor of flashier, media-driven projects.

The work that once thrilled him began to feel like a fight.

***

The hardest part wasn't the rejection. Jack could handle rejection. It was watching *other* researchers, those who simplified their work to fit media soundbites or leaned heavily on commercial funding, get the attention he believed his research deserved.

At one conference, a company unveiled a new "twister simulator" for schools, a plastic cylinder filled with fog, spinning with a light show. It was enclosed in a container, but the crowd clapped anyway.

Jack had sat in the back of the room, arms folded, jaw tight.

"They're cheering for smoke and mirrors," he muttered to a colleague.

"People like spectacle," the man had shrugged. "Truth doesn't sell as well."

That comment stuck with Jack far longer than it should have.

***

He never stopped working. But the edge of doubt began to creep in.

Will any of this matter?

Will anyone ever care about the science if it doesn't come with lights and ticket sales?

The truth was, funding was scarce. Public interest came in waves, usually right after disasters. To survive in the field, Jack had to start making compromises: shortening papers, simplifying models, accepting smaller grants from sponsors who didn't fully grasp the work.

It hurt. But it kept the lab open.

***

Still, late at night, he clung to the core of it.

The wind. The data. The moment before the funnel touched ground when everything felt on the edge of being understood.

Those were the moments that reminded him why he started.

But even then, a quiet question began to settle in his gut:
What if I never get to finish what I started?

***

The flashback shifted again, memories stringing together like storm cells across a dry plain.

Jack was in his early thirties now, a few more papers under his belt, and finally, finally, people were starting to notice.

He was invited to speak at a regional meteorology summit in Denver, his first big conference presentation. The lecture hall wasn't packed, but the audience was serious: researchers, weather professionals, a few journalists.

Jack had stood behind the podium, nervously adjusting the collar of his button-down shirt. On the screen behind him, a time-lapse played — one of his early tornado model simulations, a slow spiral of calculated fury building over flat Kansas land.

"My work focuses on early identification of tornadic potential using upper-level wind shear and surface dew point interactions," he began.

"What you're seeing here is a predictive pattern based on five years of collected data…"

At first, they listened politely.

By the end, they were leaning forward.

***

That night, someone from the local paper pulled him aside for a quick interview.

"The guy with the digital twisters," they'd called him in the article.

Jack clipped that piece and stuck it in a file.

Then there was the science magazine that picked up his research summary. Then a radio show — just a quick call-in segment about tornado safety, but still. It was something.

He didn't seek the spotlight. Not exactly. But when it found him, it felt… good.

Like proof.

Proof that all the long nights, the failures, the doubts – they hadn't been wasted.

***

In the quiet that followed, Decker's words returned like distant thunder:

"Just make sure it's still you talking when the microphone turns on."

Jack hadn't forgotten. He never would.

But still, something stirred in him now that hadn't been there before.

A hunger — not just for truth, but for impact. For reach.

He started to wonder:

What if more people understood tornadoes the way I do?

What if the public didn't just fear storms — but respected them, knew how to prepare for them, knew how they worked?

Jack 's models could save lives. If he could just get them out there — *really* out there — not buried in academic journals, but into classrooms, newsrooms, maybe even onto TV screens.

It wasn't ego. Not completely.

It was the belief that truth — real, tested, scientific truth — shouldn't be kept behind university walls.

It should belong to everyone.

***

The sound of wind brushed gently against the lab windows.

Jack blinked and exhaled, the memory fading like vapor from a warm field. He was back in his lab, surrounded not by crowds or lecture halls, but by silence only the steady hum of old computers and the quiet tick of the analog clock above the whiteboard.

The screen in front of him still showed the rotating funnel—a simulation loop he'd been watching for nearly ten minutes without realizing.

He leaned back in his chair, suddenly aware of the heaviness in his chest.

When did the dream change?

He thought back to those long-ago lectures, the passion in Decker's voice, the joy of unlocking even a small part of a storm's secret structure. Back then, his work had been pure—a calling, not a commodity. But now?

Now it felt... different.

Not wrong. Just—entangled.

***

He had accepted the deal. That was done.

The contracts would come, and soon there would be emails and meetings and consultants talking about ride layouts and visual effects. His tornado would become an attraction—part of a thrill-seeker's day between roller coasters and overpriced churros.

And yet, even as he tried to reassure himself—*It'll educate people. It'll reach millions*—a small voice inside whispered:

Or it'll become noise. One more storm in a world already drowning in spectacle.

He rubbed his forehead and looked again at the simulation.

The tornado spun in perfect symmetry, a swirl of raw beauty and destructive promise.

It had always meant more to him than danger or chaos. To Jack, the tornado was truth, undeniable, wild, and elegant. It demanded respect. It was the great humbler of man. The final say in any argument with the sky.

And now he'd sold it. Or at least, handed it over.

Was that betrayal? Or evolution?

Jack couldn't tell anymore.

***

His eyes drifted to a dusty model on the corner shelf—the first tornado chamber he'd ever built. Just glass and air and a whirring fan. It hadn't looked like much, but when it worked, when the vortex rose and curled in the middle of the chamber, he'd felt like he was touching a secret of the universe.

He stood and walked to it, fingers grazing the rim of the old display. The storm inside it was gone now. Just still air and memories.

And maybe… a warning.

He closed his eyes.

Don't lose yourself, Darlie had said.

The tornado had been his obsession, his teacher, and now, maybe—his mirror. A beautiful, powerful force that began with pure purpose… and spun out of control the moment it touched the ground.

***

Jack stood by the window, the lab behind him fading into shadows as evening settled across the plains.

The sky was wide and soft with cloud. Those slow-drifting Kansas kinds, smeared pink and gold by the dying light. Somewhere far off, a hawk wheeled alone against the horizon.

He pressed a palm to the cool glass.

This was the sky I grew up under.

And somewhere within that sky — years ago — he had seen it.

The storm that had changed everything.

He had been just a boy then, barefoot in the fields, frozen as the funnel dropped like a divine exclamation point from the clouds. It had scared him, thrilled him, made him feel small in the way only nature could.

That tornado hadn't just torn through his town.

It had carved a purpose into his soul.

***

He closed his eyes and let the memory return. The smell of rain on dust. The stillness before the wind. The rush in his chest. That was the moment he'd started chasing storms — not for fame, not for grants, not for anything but the need to understand.

Can I still be that person, he wondered, *now that the world is watching?*

The Universal deal was happening. The wheels were turning. The stage was being set for something bigger than he'd ever imagined. And yet… he wasn't sure if he was stepping toward his destiny or turning his back on it.

He thought of the old dream: traveling backroads, measuring wind speeds, logging field notes under the open sky. There had been such freedom in that — such clarity.

Now, there were contracts. Cameras. Lawyers. Press.

A whole storm of a different kind.

***

Behind him, the lab was silent.

Before him, the sky waited.

What do you really want, Jack? he asked himself. *The storm, or the spotlight? The truth, or the applause?*

He didn't know yet.

But he knew one thing: whatever came next would define everything.

And the storm—always the storm—was still calling.

7

THE COURTROOM BECKONS

The house was unusually quiet that morning. The kettle on the stove whistled softly, the only sound in the still kitchen. Jack sat at the table, papers spread out before him like a battlefield map, legal documents, contracts, and a thick manila folder with "Universal Studios" scrawled in permanent marker across the front.

He hadn't touched his coffee. Darlie moved quietly around the room, the kind of quiet that only comes when both people are trying not to speak first. She poured hot water into two mugs, letting the steam rise between them.

Jack rubbed his temple with the side of his hand and exhaled slowly. "I never thought it would come to this," he muttered.

Darlie slid a mug toward him and sat across the table. "You mean lawyers and courtrooms? Or fighting for something that was always yours?"

He gave a dry smile. "Both."

***

The documents in front of him were sterile, full of clauses and countersuits, legal jargon that made his head hurt. Somewhere inside them, though, was his life's work.

This wasn't just about a tornado model anymore. It was about the principle behind it. The ownership. The recognition. The right to tell the story of what he'd built with his own two hands and what others now claimed was theirs to commercialize.

Jack shook his head, staring at a paragraph he had already read five times.

"They make it sound like I should be grateful they even looked at my research."

Darlie sipped her tea, watching him. "They don't know what it cost you. The years. The fieldwork. The nights you didn't come home because you were chasing storms across state lines."

Jack gave a small nod. "They see a theme park attraction. I see a decade of weather data, three broken laptops, and one near-death experience outside Topeka."

A pause.

Then: "You don't have to do this alone, Jack."

Her voice was soft, but steady.

"I know," he said.

And he did.

***

The morning light filtered through the curtains, turning the papers gold around the edges. The kitchen smelled like mint and paper and quiet resolve.

Jack leaned back in his chair and looked across at Darlie.

"I just… I keep asking myself — when did being a scientist turn into being a plaintiff?"

Darlie reached out and touched his hand. "Maybe when someone decided your work was worth stealing."

Jack looked down at their hands, hers strong, calm. A steadying force.

He nodded once.

"I'm going to fight."

"I know," she said, squeezing his fingers gently. "And I'll be there. Every step."

***

The legal papers sat in a neat stack on Jack's desk now, but nothing about them felt tidy.

Jack turned a page, eyes scanning dense paragraphs filled with phrases like *derivative rights* and *exclusive use agreements*. Somewhere between the lines was his storm—his vortex of passion and science—boiled down into a list of contested claims.

He leaned back, tossing the pen onto the table with a soft clatter. "How did it go from sharing a discovery... to defending ownership of it?"

Across the room, Darlie sat on the couch with her laptop open and a legal pad balanced on her knee. She was quiet for a moment, then spoke gently, "Because you said yes."

Jack looked up, brow furrowed.

Darlie met his eyes. "You accepted their offer. You opened the door. And when you do that with people who see opportunity first and science second, they walk through it carrying contracts."

***

She set her laptop aside and stood, crossing to the table. "Jack, I've been reading up on it. Intellectual property law is not built for guys like you. It's built for companies. For control."

He gave a tired smile. "I thought it was for protecting ideas."

"It is," she replied. "But only if you can afford to fight for them."

She sat down across from him. "In science, we publish, we share, we build on each other's work. But Universal isn't a journal or a peer-reviewed community. They want to take your tornado model, tweak it, and call it theirs. And once they do that legally… you may not be allowed to use it yourself."

Jack blinked. "You mean I could be locked out of my own research?"

"If the court sees it their way — yes."

The words hit like a sudden gust, tipping something in Jack 's gut. He stood, walking to the window, arms crossed.

Outside, a thin band of clouds stretched across the sky—harmless, for now. But he knew better than anyone how quickly things could turn.

"It wasn't supposed to be like this," he said. "It was just supposed to be a way to share the work. To help people understand the storms."

"And maybe it still can be," Darlie offered. "But only if you protect it first."

He turned back to her. "Since when did we need lawyers to do science?"

Darlie hesitated. "Since corporations realized there was money in it."

***

Jack fell silent, watching the light shift on the floor.

He thought of Decker, his old mentor, who had once said, *'Science is about truth, Jack. Keep it clean. Keep it honest.'*

Would Decker be proud of him now? Or disappointed?

Jack didn't know.

All he knew was that if he let this go, if he let Universal shape the narrative—his work could become a spectacle, stripped of meaning, sold for thrills.

He sat down again, quieter this time.

"We've got the lawyer," he said softly.

Darlie nodded. "Dr. Callahan. IP specialist. She's good."

"But are we?"

She didn't answer right away.

Then, gently: "We're ready enough."

Jack looked back at the papers.

The storm was coming. This time not on the horizon, but in court filings and cross-examinations.

And he would have to weather it.

***

The wind outside had picked up, rustling the sycamore leaves against the kitchen window. Inside, the air felt still, heavy with unspoken worry.

Darlie sat back down, setting her tea aside. Her hands folded over her lap, her voice low but firm.

"Jack … I need to ask you something."

He looked up from the papers. "Go ahead."

"Is this fight worth it?"

The question lingered.

She didn't say it with judgment. She said it with love, the kind that knows how to hold up a mirror without shattering someone's pride.

Jack rubbed the back of his neck, already feeling the weight of where the conversation was headed.

"I mean it," she continued. "You've worked your whole life to build something meaningful. And now you are about to enter a battle with people who don't see science the way you do. To them, this is just leverage. Business."

He gave a small nod. "I know."

"Do you?" she asked gently. "Because this… it could consume everything. Our time. Our savings. Your peace of mind. And even if you win, you might not come out whole."

Jack leaned forward, elbows on the table.

"I've thought about all that," he said, his voice steadier now. "Believe me, I have. I know they don't care about the science. To them, it's a feature for a ride. A selling point."

He paused, tapping a finger on one of the folders.

"But this is my life's work, Darlie. I can't walk away and let someone else slap their name on it. I chased storms for this. I spent nights driving across state lines, built models from scratch, fed them with real data, risked my life out in the field. It's not just research—it's part of who I am."

Darlie looked at him, eyes soft. "I know. That's what scares me."

Jack reached across the table and took her hand.

"I'm not doing this for ego. Or for the money. I'm doing it because if I don't stand up for this… then what message does that send? That corporations can rewrite science? That discovery belongs to whoever has the bigger lawyer?"

***

A moment passed.

Then Darlie gave a small, resigned smile.

"You sound like .your mentor."

Jack smiled faintly. "He'd probably tell me I'm being foolish."

"No," she said, squeezing his hand. "He'd say you're being brave."

The clock ticked quietly in the background, marking the calm before the real storm.

Jack knew Darlie was right to worry. He wasn't blind to the cost. But for the first time in days, his resolve felt solid.

They would fight.

And he would not let go of what was his.

***

The house had gone quiet again, save for the occasional ticking of the clock and the distant hum of wind brushing against the trees outside.

Jack gathered the files on the table into a neat stack, clipping them together with steady hands. Darlie stood beside him, flipping through a checklist of documents their lawyer would need in the coming days—emails, blueprints, drafts of his tornado models, early research notes.

"They'll want everything," she said. "Timelines. Evidence of development. Anything that proves this started with you."

"It did start with me," Jack replied, voice firm.

"I know," Darlie said, softly. "Now we just have to make them see that."

***

They worked in silence for a while, filing, sorting, assembling the armor they'd wear into court. It didn't look like armor—just folders and printouts, sticky notes and highlighted margins. But Jack knew the truth: every piece of paper was a story. A moment of insight. A night of doubt. A breakthrough, sometimes bought with tears or sleepless nights.

This was not just about a model of a storm.

It was about the years that led him to build it.

***

Later, as the sun dipped below the Kansas horizon, Jack stood by the window, his gaze lost in the vast stretch of amber sky. Clouds moved slowly overhead, casting long shadows over the fields. Somewhere out there, the wind was changing. He could feel it.

His thoughts drifted back—to his first field study, to Decker's warning, to the quiet awe of watching a tornado swirl into being in the distance, like nature drawing breath.

Back then, it had all felt so simple. So pure.

Now, it was something else.

But still — worth it.

***

"I just want to do what's right," he murmured.

Darlie joined him at the window, placing a hand on his shoulder.

"Then fight for it," she said.

He nodded slowly, letting the words settle in his chest.

The battle was about to begin.

And whatever storms lay ahead, inside the courtroom or out — Jack was ready to face them.

8

THE LAWSUIT BEGINS

The courtroom was quiet, but the tension inside was thick like the air before a storm. Jack sat at the long wooden table next to his lawyer, a stiff folder of documents resting in front of him. Darlie sat just behind him, her hands folded in her lap, watching everything with quiet concern. Her presence gave him comfort, even though his stomach was a knot of nerves.

This was not his world. Courtrooms, suits, cross-examinations—all of it felt far away from the lab where he had spent most of his life, lost in weather charts and swirling storm data. But today, he wasn't a scientist. He was a man defending his life's work.

Across the room, Universal Studios' legal team was easy to spot. They looked polished, calm, and far too confident. Their lead attorney was a sharp-looking man in a navy suit who barely glanced at Jack. He opened his briefcase with smooth, practiced hands, then began arranging his papers like someone setting the pieces of a chessboard.

Jack tried not to watch him.

He leaned forward, whispering to his lawyer, "Do you think they'll go hard right from the start?"

His lawyer, a middle-aged woman named Karen Barnes, gave a small nod. "They didn't fly in a lawyer like that to play nice."

Jack took a deep breath and nodded slowly, trying to steady his hands. The judge entered moments later, and everyone rose from their seats.

"All rise," the bailiff announced.

As the judge took her seat and called the room to order, Jack felt the weight of it all settle onto his shoulders. This wasn't an academic debate. This wasn't a university meeting. This was real, and it had already begun.

He looked down at the papers in front of him, his models, his calculations, the fruit of decades of work—and reminded himself why he was here.

They weren't just fighting over numbers.

They were fighting over the truth.

***

The Universal lawyer stood, buttoned his suit jacket, and stepped calmly toward the bench. Everything about him was smooth—his voice, his expression, even the way he held his notes.

"Your Honor," he began, addressing the judge with the confidence of someone who had done this a thousand times. "What we have here is a man claiming ownership over the weather itself."

A few people in the courtroom chuckled under their breath.

Jack stiffened.

The lawyer went on, "Let's be clear - tornadoes, storm behavior, atmospheric patterns—these are natural phenomena. No one can own the sky. No one can own a storm."

He glanced toward Jack but didn't hold the gaze for long.

"Mr. Engle's research is, without question, impressive. However, impressive does not mean original in the legal sense. His models are based on public data, shared knowledge, and long-standing meteorological principles. He did not invent tornadoes. He did not discover storms."

Jack could feel the words chipping away at his reputation. Like slow hail cracking glass.

The Universal lawyer paused dramatically before delivering the final blow.

"This is an attempt," he said, "to privatize knowledge that belongs to the public. To claim credit—and profit—for something that belongs to no one."

Karen, Jack's lawyer, stood next.

She didn't raise her voice. She didn't need to.

"Your Honor," she said firmly, "Mr. Engle is not claiming to own the weather. What he created after decades of work is a functional model of storm behavior that has already been applied in real-world safety protocols. It's innovative. It's specific. And it's his."

She held up a thick folder. "These designs are not pulled from textbooks. They are the result of original research, unique algorithms, and first-of-their-kind visual models. That is what Universal Studios used to build their attraction and that is what Dr. Engle deserves credit and compensation for."

The judge nodded thoughtfully, scribbling notes.

Jack leaned forward in his seat, listening carefully. His heart was beating fast, but he felt a small flicker of pride hearing his work defended so clearly.

The judge adjusted her glasses. "Very well. Let's proceed with testimony. Mr. Engle, please take the stand."

Jack's stomach tightened. He rose, walked stiffly to the witness box, and raised his right hand for the oath. The words felt heavy on his tongue; truth, the whole truth, nothing but the truth, but he spoke them steady.

Karen approached first, her voice calm and deliberate. "Dr. Engle, can you tell the court, in your own words, what exactly you created?"

Jack exhaled slowly. "I designed a working model of storm behavior. It isn't just equations on paper. It simulates the mechanics of tornado formation in a controlled environment, something no one else had done."

Karen nodded. "And what was the purpose of this work?"

"To help people understand storms. To help warn communities before disaster strikes," Jack said. His voice grew firmer as he continued. "This was never about profit. It was about safety."

Karen gave a small smile. "No further questions."

The Universal lawyer rose smoothly, buttoning his jacket as he approached. His eyes were sharp. "Mr. Engle, you speak of safety, but isn't it true that your models rely on publicly available weather data? Information anyone could use?"

Jack stiffened. "Yes, the data was public. But the model, the algorithms, the application—that was mine. My design."

The lawyer leaned in slightly. "So, you admit nothing here is truly original. You borrowed, repackaged, and now you're trying to call it your own."

Heat crawled up Jack's neck. He gripped the edges of the witness stand. "I built something new from that data. That's how science works. We build on what came before, but we innovate. That's what I did."

The lawyer's voice hardened. "Or is it what Universal did, once they took your notes and turned them into something people could actually use?"

The words stung. Jack's pulse hammered in his ears, but he forced himself to meet the lawyer's stare. "They took my work. They polished it, yes—

but without the foundation, without the model, there would be nothing to polish."

A murmur rippled through the courtroom. The Universal lawyer smirked faintly, then stepped back. "No further questions, Your Honor."

Jack swallowed hard, his palms damp. As he returned to his seat beside Karen, Darlie caught his eye from the gallery. She gave him the smallest of nods, her expression calm but full of strength.

Then, the Universal lawyer stood again.

"If Mr. Engle's real concern is education," he said smoothly, "then why demand ownership? Why not share this with the world? Could it be," he paused, looking directly at Jack now, "that what he really wants is a payout? That he's more interested in fame than science?"

Jack clenched his jaw. The lawyer had struck a nerve.

The courtroom fell quiet. All that remained was the tapping of keys from the stenographer, and the faint creak of chairs as people shifted uncomfortably.

The battle lines were clear now and they were drawn right through the heart of Jack's career.

***

The Universal lawyer adjusted his tie and took a few slow steps in front of the jury box.

"With all due respect," he began, his tone cool and measured, "we're talking about a collection of ideas. Equations. Theories. This isn't something that could ever stand on its own in a commercial setting."

He turned slightly toward Jack, gesturing loosely. "Mr. Engle's research is interesting, yes. But useful? Only in a lab. Only under the safety of fluorescent lights and chalkboards. His models were never designed for the real world certainly not for something as complex and high-profile as a theme park attraction."

Jack 's hands tightened around the edge of the table.

The lawyer continued. "What Universal Studios built was the result of collaboration. Engineering. Imagination. Our attraction is not a replica of Mr. Engle's storm—it's an experience. Something his academic theories alone could never produce."

There it was.

The air in the courtroom seemed to shift like the sudden stillness before a storm.

Jack could hardly believe what he was hearing. Only useful in a lab? Was that what they thought of his work? Of the years he had spent chasing storms, mapping out their secrets, staying up late poring over patterns until his eyes blurred?

He glanced at Darlie. Her face was calm, but her eyes spoke volumes she was just as insulted as he was.

Jack took a deep breath, steadying himself, but inside he was boiling.

They had no idea what it took. The danger. The data. The dedication. He wasn't just fighting for himself now. He was fighting for every scientist who had ever been brushed off as "just academic."

He leaned in toward his lawyer and whispered, "They think this is a game. Let's show them it's not."

Karen nodded.

Jack sat back, jaw clenched. The doubt he had been carrying was burning away, replaced by something stronger.

Conviction.

***

Darlie sat on the wooden bench at the back of the courtroom, her fingers laced tightly together in her lap. From where she sat, she had a clear view of Jack —his shoulders tense, his eyes fixed on the proceedings, his jaw clenched like he had not unclenched it in hours.

She knew that look.

Jack wasn't just thinking about today's testimony or the legal arguments. He was reliving years of work—formulas scrawled on napkins, storm chases in the middle of the night, days and weeks spent building models that no one else believed in.

She could see the weight of it all pressing down on him.

Later that night, back at home, Jack dropped his briefcase on the hallway table and sank into his chair at the kitchen table. He looked exhausted.

Darlie placed a warm mug of tea in front of him and sat beside him.

"You hardly touched your lunch," she said gently.

Jack gave a tired shrug. "Didn't feel like eating."

Darlie reached for his hand. "You're burning yourself out, Jack."

"I'm fine," he muttered, though his voice lacked conviction.

She studied his face. The lines that had deepened these past weeks, the dark circles under his eyes, the stiffness in his shoulders.

"This... this isn't just about the courtroom anymore," she said softly. "It's about you. I know how much this matters, but I need to ask—are you okay with what it's doing to you?"

Jack looked at her, really looked, and for a moment the wall of determination in his eyes softened.

"I didn't start this to win a fight, Darlie. I started it because I couldn't let them take credit for something I gave my life to. If I let it go, it won't just be me they walk over. It'll be every scientist who ever poured their soul into something just to have it snatched away."

She nodded, still holding his hand. "Just... promise me you'll know when to stop. If it becomes too much, promise me you'll let go."

Jack hesitated, then gave her a tired smile. "I'll finish what I started. But I won't lose myself in the process."

Darlie gave his hand a squeeze and stood up. "Then I'm with you. All the way."

***

"All rise," the bailiff called.

The judge stood, looking weary but firm. "We'll take a brief recess. Court will reconvene in thirty minutes."

With a soft bang of the gavel, the courtroom emptied into a low hum of footsteps and murmured conversations.

Jack didn't move at first. He sat still in the witness box, hands folded in his lap, eyes fixed on nothing. Darlie touched his shoulder gently.

"Come on," she said. "Let's get some air."

They stepped outside the courtroom into the quiet hallway, the hum of the fluorescent lights above the only sound. Their lawyer, a calm but serious woman, Karen, leaned against the wall, flipping through her notes. "They came out swinging," she said quietly. "But we're not out of moves."

Jack nodded but said nothing. His jaw was tight, his thoughts clouded.

In his mind, he kept hearing the Universal lawyer's words— *"Only useful in a lab."* It echoed like a bad tune stuck on repeat.

He leaned against the wall, staring at the tiled floor. Darlie stood beside him, silent, giving him space.

Jack's hands clenched at his sides. This courtroom wasn't like the lab. There were no data points to correct, no simulations to rerun. Here, facts twisted into arguments, and passion was mistaken for pride.

He looked up at the courtroom doors, still closed, still looming.

"This isn't just a trial," he said under his breath. "This is my name. My work. Everything I've spent my life building."

Darlie looked at him, eyes soft with worry. "Then fight for it. Just don't forget why you started."

Jack didn't answer. Instead, he turned back toward the doors, his spine a little straighter now.

He didn't know what the judge would say tomorrow. He didn't know if the courtroom would respect science the way a storm did.

But one thing was clear—he wasn't walking away.

Not yet.

9

JACK'S LEGACY

The soft buzz of fluorescent lights filled the weather lab, broken only by the occasional creak of old floorboards or the low hum of machines still running, even after all these years.

Jack sat at his desk, the same desk he had used for decades, surrounded by stacks of papers — some yellowed at the edges, others covered in fresh scribbles and graphs. Tornado models, pieced together from foam, wire, and plastic tubing, lined the shelves like trophies from another lifetime. Some were dust-covered. All were well-used.

Outside the windows, the Kansas sky rolled out flat and wide, streaked with the early color of dusk.

Jack leaned back in his chair, hands folded across his stomach, eyes fixed on a faded photo tacked to the corkboard him and his mentor, standing side by side in front of their first field station van, both of them younger, brighter-eyed, and full of big ideas.

A half-smile tugged at his lips.

He wasn't that young man anymore. His hair had grayed at the temples, his back ached when he bent too long over charts, and sleep didn't come as easily. But the fire that had burned in him all those years ago, it was still there. Just quieter now.

The lawsuit with Universal had left a mark. So had the fame, the headlines, the attention from people who didn't know a funnel cloud from a wind tunnel. And yet, through it all, the work had endured.

He turned slowly in his chair and looked at one of his earliest models — a clear plastic cylinder with a small motor on top, still faintly smelling of glue and solder. That little tornado had once made a room full of scientists lean forward in awe. Not because it looked cool but because it explained something no one else had made visible before.

Jack sighed and tapped the model with one finger. "You held up better than I thought," he murmured.

He wasn't sure what the future held anymore. Hollywood had changed things. So had the courtroom. His place in the university was stable, but he felt more like a relic than a rising mind these days. Still, the impact of his work echoed far beyond this room.

He knew students were still reading his papers. Storm chasers were still using his prediction models. And somewhere out there, a kid was probably building a mini-tornado in a bottle for a school science fair — just like he once had.

Jack sat quietly for a while longer, letting the hum of the lab fill the space around him. The storm outside his window hadn't formed yet, but the clouds were gathering.

Whatever happened next, he'd done something that mattered. And that mattered most of all.

***

The hum of the present faded, replaced by a buzzing glowing light and the quiet tap of fingers on a keyboard. Suddenly, it was the 1970s again.

Jack was younger — maybe thirty. His lab back then was nothing like the one he had now. The walls were yellowed, the equipment old, and the air carried the smell of solder, paper, and black coffee. There was no sleek software, no high-end sensors — just grit, books, and wires.

Jack sat hunched over a desk cluttered with graphs, notebooks, and weather maps. He scribbled notes with a pencil, paused, checked wind speeds on a dial, then typed a few lines of code into an early-model computer the size of a filing cabinet.

Lines formed on the green screen — lines that told stories. About pressure drops, shifting air masses, the birth of something fierce.

Outside the small window behind him, the Kansas sky stretched wide, full of motion and mystery. But Jack wasn't distracted. He was trying to trap a storm with numbers.

Back then, he wasn't famous. He wasn't even respected. Most of his colleagues dismissed him with polite nods and quiet chuckles. Tornado prediction? "Too unpredictable," they said. "Too niche."

He'd written papers no one read. Applied for grants he didn't get. His name rarely appeared in conference schedules. He often worked alone, late into the night, eating sandwiches at his desk and listening to the wind howl outside.

But Jack didn't give up.

Because every now and then, his models worked. They caught something—a pattern in pressure, a twist in the data. A whisper of warning before a storm touched down. And when that happened, when the numbers lined up just right, Jack would smile to himself. Not because someone else had noticed but because nature had spoken, and he'd understood it.

His tools were simple, his office plain, and the paycheck small. But his heart was full.

Even when no one else believed in him, he believed in the work.

He saw tornadoes not just as chaos, but as poetry. As puzzles to be solved. Beautiful, dangerous, spinning questions from the sky.

And back then, that was enough.

***

It happened one spring afternoon—quiet at first, like most big moments.

Jack was in his lab, sipping cold coffee, staring at lines of code that had begun to blur after hours of checking and rechecking. Charts were pinned to the wall, maps rolled out across the floor. Numbers were everywhere.

Then... something clicked.

His model — based on air pressure, temperature shifts, wind flow — predicted a sudden drop in pressure over northeast Kansas. It matched a pattern he'd only seen twice before, once in his student years and once in old records from the 1950s. The data told him a storm was coming. Not just a storm — a twisting one. A tornado.

He double-checked everything. Then again. The system was sound.

Jack called the local station in Topeka, his voice steady but urgent. "There's something forming. Fast. You'll see a spiral in Jefferson County by 5:30 PM. Maybe earlier."

They didn't laugh this time. They listened.

At 5:22 PM, a tornado touched down just outside Oskaloosa. Narrow, sharp, and fast-moving — just as Jack's model had predicted.

The next day, his phone didn't stop ringing.

Reporters, professors, emergency planners — they all wanted to talk to the man who'd "seen the storm before it came." His name started appearing in science journals. Invitations arrived for conferences and guest lectures.

For the first time, Jack's work wasn't just interesting—it was important.

He stood in front of a chalkboard one evening after the media buzz had settled, staring at the equations that got him there. His hands were ink-stained. His shirt untucked. But his heart felt full.

He had done it.

He had proven that storms could be understood—not just feared. That prediction was possible. That science mattered.

In that moment, he wasn't chasing a prize or a paycheck.

He was chasing understanding. And for a brief, shining moment, he felt like he'd caught it.

***

The years rolled on. Recognition came slowly but surely, and with it, a new chapter in Jack's career.

He found himself no longer just behind a desk or buried in storm maps, but standing before packed rooms at weather conferences, pointing to swirling lines on projection screens and explaining how upper-level wind shear, pressure and temperature could foretell chaos or calm.

At first, he had been the quiet one at these conferences, scribbling in notebooks and taking it all in. Now, colleagues waited to hear what *he* had to say. His models, once questioned, had become a new standard. And with that respect came invitations — to collaborate, to lead, to guide.

In one of those sessions, Jack met Dr. Lin, a sharp-minded atmospheric physicist from Colorado. Together, they refined a new tracking algorithm that could detect rotating storm systems earlier than before. In another joint project, Jack and a team from Texas worked on low-cost sensors for rural areas. The collaboration energized him — it reminded him that science was not a solo journey, but a team effort.

But what surprised Jack the most was how often younger scientists approached him — some nervous, others full of bold ideas. "Your paper on the 1987 model — it's what got me into weather science," one said. Another admitted, "I saved your lab tornado picture in the *Weekly Reader* from '82 and stuck it on my wall as a kid."

Jack never quite knew what to say to that.

Still, he took the responsibility seriously.

Back at the university, he began to teach more classes. Not just lectures, but real, open conversations — walking students through data, asking them what they *saw*, not just what the books told them.

He developed a new class at the university using his knowledge about storms that he had collected from real storm observations and from his work with weather data. This class, called Unusual Weather, grew until it filled the largest auditorium on campus and still had to turn students away.

He remembered his own mentor's words: *"Science is about truth. Not applause."*

Now, Jack passed that same wisdom on.

In time, he became more than just a researcher. He became a mentor. A guide. A quiet force behind the next generation of storm chasers and data analysts, who respected not only his models, but the principles that guided them.

His legacy, Jack began to realize, wouldn't live in one moment of fame — but in many small ones. In students who looked at clouds differently. In young minds who dared to ask, *what if we could predict the storm before it started?*

***

The room was quiet except for the soft hum of his old desktop computer and the scratch of Jack 's pencil across a notepad. Outside, a Kansas wind rattled the lab windows. Jack barely noticed. He was deep in thought, staring at a swirling map of storm data on his screen.

After years of research, late nights, and fieldwork in muddy plains and windblown farms, Jack was finally pulling everything together. His papers, his storm-chasing notes, thousands of weather readings—they were all feeding into something new.

A model.

Not just any model.

His tornado model.

Jack had always believed tornadoes followed hidden patterns, and now he was close to proving it. He began designing a system that could read the small signs—sudden wind shifts, changes in temperature, vertical rotation in the clouds and use them to predict tornado formation more accurately than anything before.

At first, it was just numbers on a screen. Then came simulations, color-coded maps, and eventually, real-time forecasts that tracked with eerie precision. Jack felt like a musician discovering the notes behind a thunderclap he was tuning into nature's code.

His excitement was contagious. Students gathered around him during testing. "We're getting a five-minute lead time increase," one exclaimed. Jack grinned, his eyes bright. "Let's make it ten."

He upgraded his software. Added satellite data. Pored over storm footage frame by frame.

Every version of the model became faster, smarter, more precise.

It became his life's work.

The meteorological community was cautious at first. Jack's ideas were bold, and not everyone welcomed change. But slowly, as his predictions proved reliable especially during a particularly dangerous spring season—experts began to take notice.

His model was used in a pilot program in Oklahoma. Emergency sirens went off ten minutes before the storm touched down. Ten minutes that saved lives.

By the end of the year, Jack 's model was being reviewed for national implementation.

He didn't want praise. He wanted impact.

And that's what he got.

Hospitals reported fewer injuries. Schools ran smoother drills. Families had time to reach shelter.

Jack stood in his lab late one evening, watching a simulated storm swirl on his screen. He didn't smile, exactly—but there was peace in his eyes. He whispered softly, "We're getting closer."

The tornado model would become the crown jewel of Jack's career—respected, taught, and refined for generations to come. A tool forged not for profit, but for people. A quiet legacy hidden in radar maps and storm alerts, spoken in sirens and saved lives.

***

The room was quiet again.

Jack sat in his lab, just as he had so many times before. Papers surrounded him, their corners curled from years of use. His old tornado models—battered but still precise—lined the shelves like trophies of quiet victories.

The flashbacks of his younger years drifted from his mind, leaving behind a soft ache. He wasn't that young man anymore. The one chasing grants, drawing patterns on chalkboards, or driving through rain just to get closer to a storm. But part of him still was. That fire never fully went out.

Jack leaned back in his chair, gazing at the ceiling for a long moment before turning toward the window. The Kansas sky stretched wide outside, soft with clouds. It looked calm now — but Jack knew better than most how quickly calm could change.

He had come a long way.

From a struggling student ignored by the scientific elite to a respected voice in meteorology... and now, a man locked in a legal battle over his own work. It was strange to think that the models he built to save lives were now at the center of lawsuits and corporate deals.

He ran a hand slowly over the edge of his desk, his fingers brushing against the blueprint of his first tornado model. A small smile tugged at the corner of his mouth. It hadn't been easy, but it had been worth it.

He didn't regret chasing storms.

He didn't regret the long nights, the failed prototypes, the skepticism from his peers.

Because he had made something real.

Something that mattered.

Jack stood and walked toward the window. The hum of the lab machines faded behind him. As he stared at the sky, he thought about the word "legacy." What would his be?

Would it be court transcripts and licensing agreements? Or would it be the moment a young student picked up his research and made it even better?

He hoped it would be that second one.

Because Jack had never been in it for the money. He had never cared much for awards or magazine covers. What he had always wanted since he was a boy staring at a spinning funnel in the distance — was to understand the storm.

And to help others understand it too.

The battle with Universal Studios was far from over. But in that moment, with the sky above and the hum of data behind him, Jack felt centered. His models, his work, his purpose — they all still mattered.

The next chapter of his life might be shaped by lawyers and headlines, but his legacy would be written in science.

And the storms would keep coming. But so would the people he'd inspired.

10

THE FIGHT FOR RECOGNITION

The courtroom was still and silent, like the eye of a storm just before it shifts. People sat upright in the benches, waiting. The air buzzed with quiet tension as the judge called, "Dr. Jack Engle to the stand."

Jack stood slowly. His hands trembled slightly, but his eyes were steady. Darlie gave him a soft nod from the gallery. Beside her sat Karen, his lawyer, calm as ever, flipping through her notes.

Jack took the stand. The bailiff swore him in, and he adjusted the microphone.

He looked across the room. It wasn't just a courtroom to him — it was the battleground where his life's work was now on trial.

The lawyer for Universal, sharp-eyed and smooth-talking, rose first. "Dr. Engle, would you please tell the court about your role in the creation of the tornado models being discussed today?"

Jack cleared his throat, feeling every eye in the room fixed on him. "I've spent over thirty years studying tornadoes—tracking, modeling, predicting their behavior. It began when I was a student, fascinated by the forces of nature. Over the years, I developed a detailed model—one that helped improve early warning systems and deepen scientific understanding of tornado dynamics."

He glanced at the jury, trying to connect. "My models aren't just diagrams and laboratory tornadoes. They save lives. They have helped meteorologists predict storm paths more accurately. The work is not entertainment—it's research built from real storms, real data, and real consequences."

The opposing lawyer didn't flinch. "So, you're saying your work was directly used in Universal's Twister attraction?"

Jack hesitated only for a breath. "Elements of it were. The simulations, the structure of the storm behavior, the actual ability to create an artificial tornado. Those things didn't come out of thin air. They were built from models I created."

Karen stood next. "Dr. Engle, can you explain how your models differ from public weather data?"

Jack nodded. "Public data is raw — temperature, wind speed, pressure. My models interpret that data, map it, and predict how it evolves into tornadic systems. It's the difference between ingredients and a recipe. What Universal used was the recipe that I created for producing an artificial tornado."

He could see some of the jurors nodding.

Karen continued, "And why is it important that this work be credited properly?"

Jack looked straight ahead, his voice steady. "Because science is about truth and responsibility. If companies can take research without permission and turn it into profit, we risk turning knowledge into something disposable. I'm not here because I want fame or fortune — I'm here because I want recognition for what I created. I want younger scientists to know their work matters, and that it should be protected."

The room was quiet again. Not from boredom but from attention.

The judge called for a short recess. Jack stepped down from the witness box, feeling both drained and proud. Darlie reached for his hand as he returned to their table.

"You did great," she whispered.

Jack gave her a tired smile. "Let's hope it was enough."

That evening, back home, Jack dropped his jacket over a chair and froze at the sound of his own name. On the television, a local newscaster stood in front of the courthouse steps, describing the case in clipped, urgent tones. Behind her, a still image showed Jack shielding his face from cameras as he left the building.

Darlie muted the sound, watching him carefully. Jack sank onto the couch, staring at his own likeness—drawn, tense, older than he imagined. "I look like I'm hiding," he muttered.

"You look like a man under fire," Darlie said gently.

Jack rubbed at his collar, unsettled. In the lab, he had always been the observer. Now, he was the one being observed—and judged.

And with that, they waited. The fight for recognition was far from over—but for the first time in a long while, Jack had spoken his truth out loud.

***

Jack took a slow sip of water before the next round of questioning began. Karen stood and approached the bench, her tone calm but direct.

"Dr. Engle, let's talk more specifically about the Twister attraction. Can you explain to the court how your scientific models are connected to what Universal Studios created?"

Jack nodded. "Yes. The fifty-foot tornado featured in the Twister building wasn't just a random visual effect. It was created from very specific movement patterns, rotational velocity, wind shear, vortex structure—all of which mirrored the exact behavior found in my research models and in my own laboratory tornado."

He leaned forward slightly, eyes scanning the jury.

"I spent years studying how tornadoes form, how they move, and what conditions lead to their development. Universal used those models to recreate a 'realistic' tornado experience. The timing, the way the funnel formed and spun, even the debris pattern—all of that was based on scientific data I compiled through field research, lab simulations, and weather analysis."

Karen continued, "Was the intention of your work ever to be used for entertainment?"

Jack gave a small, thoughtful smile. "Not originally. I created these models to help meteorologists predict storms and warn people. But I also believe in science communication—bringing knowledge to the public. That attraction could have been an incredible way to educate people if it had been done with the right credit, the right context."

He paused, letting that land.

"My work was not meant to be a spectacle. But I do understand its power to reach people. If even one child walked out of that Twister building more curious about how storms work, then maybe it did some good. But it was built on science. My science."

The courtroom was quiet again. Even Universal's lawyer seemed momentarily still, adjusting his tie but not rising for a rebuttal.

Darlie sat a little taller in her seat. For all the years she had seen Jack chase storms and build models late into the night, this was the first time the world was truly hearing what it meant to him.

And maybe—just maybe—they were starting to understand.

***

Jack shifted in the witness chair as another Universal Studios lawyer rose. The man moved slowly, confidently, like someone used to being in control. His name was Carlton Drake — a corporate attorney with a polished voice and a habit of smiling when he was about to strike.

"Dr. Engle," he began, walking toward Jack with a stack of papers, "you've spoken at length about your tornado model. Impressive work, I'm sure. But isn't it true that your research was never officially licensed for the Twister attraction?"

Jack sat up straighter. "They used my laboratory tornado model without permission. The structure, the simulation algorithms — "

Drake cut in smoothly. "But is there a patent? A formal trademark? Anything that says, 'This laboratory tornado belongs to Jack Engle'?"

Jack's jaw tightened. "Scientific models are not always patented. In academia, we share findings, publish work. It's about contribution, not commercialization."

The lawyer raised an eyebrow. "Then how can you prove that Universal didn't simply build their tornado based on common scientific knowledge?

Tornadoes are natural phenomena, Dr. Engle. You didn't invent them."

There was a low murmur in the courtroom. Jack's chest tightened.

"No," Jack said firmly. "But I studied them. I analyzed their behavior and I described how to make an artificial tornado. The way Universal portrayed the tornado—the speed, the formation, even the way the debris moved—was not generic. It mirrored my specific findings."

Drake flipped through a few papers, deliberately taking his time. "Yet you can't produce documentation proving Universal directly copied your work. Isn't it possible, Dr. Engle, that you're simply upset that someone else made money from something similar?"

Jack leaned forward, voice tense but clear. "I'm upset that years of research—real science—was taken and turned into a tornado attraction without respect, without credit. I don't want fame. I want acknowledgment. I want the truth to matter."

The judge called for order as murmurs rippled again through the room.

Jack felt heat rise in his chest. This wasn't just legal sparring—it was personal. His life's work was being dismissed as a side note in a corporate project. He glanced over at Darlie. She gave him a small nod—reassurance. He wasn't alone.

But the pressure was building. Drake was skilled, and the courtroom, with all its rules and rhythms, was not Jack's natural environment.

Still, he wasn't backing down.

Not now. Not ever.

***

Two days later, Jack tried to reclaim some normalcy. He and Darlie went to the grocery store with Darlie, a quiet errand to break the courtroom tension. But halfway down the cereal aisle, a young reporter with a cameraman appeared, microphone in hand.

"Dr. Engle! Channel 4 News—can we get your reaction to Universal's latest filing?"

Jack froze, a box of cornflakes in his hand. Shoppers turned, whispering. Darlie's hand went instinctively to his arm, but the reporter pressed forward with questions about money, fame, and motives. Darlie cut in sharply, "He's here for groceries. Leave him alone."

Jack managed only a clipped, "No comment," before steering the cart toward the registers. His hands trembled as he placed items on the belt. "I never wanted this," he muttered. Darlie met his eyes softly. "Maybe not. But it's here now."

Jack glanced at the sliding glass doors of the store — doors that suddenly felt less like an exit, and more like the beginning of another stage he never asked for.

11

TENSIONS RISE

The courtroom was heavy with silence, broken only by the soft shuffle of papers and the occasional creak of wooden benches. Jack sat in the witness box, his hands resting stiffly on his lap. The overhead lights buzzed faintly, casting pale shadows across the polished floor. He took a deep breath, trying to steady himself.

Carlton Drake, the lead attorney for Universal Studios, stood with the poise of someone used to being in control. Tall, composed, and impeccably dressed, he approached the witness stand with slow, deliberate steps. There was a faint, polite smile on his face but it didn't reach his eyes.

"Dr. Engle," he began, voice smooth as silk, "let's talk about your tornado model."

Jack nodded slightly.

Drake continued, "You've stated that your research formed the backbone of what eventually became the Twister attraction. Would that be correct?"

"In part, yes," Jack replied. "My models were used to simulate storm behavior and to create my laboratory tornado model. They were based on years of meteorological research."

Drake tilted his head. "Interesting. Because from what I understand, the Twister attraction was built by a team of designers, visual effects engineers, creative directors, ride mechanics, and sound technicians—all working together under Universal's vision. That doesn't exactly sound like a scientific experiment, does it?"

Jack didn't respond immediately. He could feel the shift in the room—the way Drake's tone subtly turned the crowd's focus. He wasn't attacking the science; he was questioning its *relevance*.

Drake stepped closer. "Isn't it fair to say that your research, however respectable—was simply one of many sources of inspiration for the attraction? A reference point, perhaps? Not the foundation?"

Jack's jaw tightened. "Without the data in those models, the simulations wouldn't have had the same realism. They weren't just references; they were blueprints for creating my laboratory model."

"But you never patented your artificial tornado, correct?" Drake pressed. "You didn't copyright any visual designs. There were no contracts that named you as a co-creator of the attraction."

Jack hesitated. "No, I didn't patent the artificial tornado. But that doesn't mean that it wasn't used without permission."

Drake turned to the jury, speaking as if explaining something obvious. "Ladies and gentlemen, tornadoes are natural phenomena. They're not inventions. They've been studied for over a century. The idea of simulating a tornado isn't new — it's public knowledge. What Universal created was a show. A themed artificial tornado attraction. Science may have informed it, but it didn't define it."

Jack's hands clenched slightly. He could feel the direction this was heading. Drake wasn't trying to disprove the science — he was trying to erase it from the conversation altogether.

"Would you agree," Drake added, "that what audiences experience in the Twister attraction is primarily the result of visual effects, animatronics, sound design, and storytelling — not academic meteorological models?"

Jack looked straight at him. "I would say that without understanding the science behind the storm, the attraction would be nothing more than flashing lights and loud noises. The attraction could not have been created if I had not shown how to form such an artificial tornado."

There was a brief silence.

Drake gave a slight smile, turned, and walked slowly back to his table.

The damage, however, was done.

***

Jack sat stiffly in the witness chair, but something in his posture had changed. The careful confidence he had carried at the start of his testimony was beginning to crack under the weight of the cross-examination. His hands were clasped tightly in his lap, the knuckles white. Every clipped word from Carlton Drake echoed in his mind like a gavel strike, each more dismissive than the last.

He had expected pushback — this was a courtroom, after all — but he had not expected to feel so belittled. The lawyer hadn't attacked his work directly; that would have been easier to defend. Instead, he had eroded it, subtly suggesting that Jack's research was irrelevant, outdated, or worse — insignificant.

Jack's jaw tensed as he stared down at the polished wood edge of the witness stand. His throat felt tight. He forced himself to breathe slowly, but his thoughts raced.

He thought back to the early years — the long nights alone in the lab, where the only sounds were the clicking of his keyboard and the hum of outdated equipment. He remembered the endless coffee, the stacks of weather data, the whiteboards covered in swirling equations. He had given everything to his work.

He had missed Darlie's anniversary dinner one year — she had waited with candles lit and a homemade pie, but he had been in the lab, tracking a fast-forming supercell in the Midwest. He'd skipped birthdays, turned down trips, and let friendships fall away. He'd sat for hours in vans on dirt roads, chasing storms across open plains, soaking in hail and wind just to collect data that might never be published.

And now, in this sterile courtroom, it was being reduced to a footnote.

Drake's words replayed in his mind. *"A reference point, perhaps? Not the foundation."*

His lips pressed into a thin line.

He wanted to speak out, to shout that this was more than a footnote. That his research had meaning. That science wasn't just numbers — it was sacrifice, sweat, and sleepless nights. It was lonely, thankless work in pursuit of truth.

But instead, he sat still. His eyes fixed forward, his breath shallow. His pulse pounded in his ears. To lash out now would only help Drake's case. He knew that. He couldn't let emotion make him reckless.

Still, the hurt ran deep. It wasn't just about ownership — it was about being seen. Being respected. Being *understood*. Jack had never done this for fame. But to see years of effort shrugged off like it was nothing — it cut deeper than he expected.

He adjusted his glasses and cleared his throat quietly. His voice, when he next spoke, was calm. But the tremor behind it was not lost on anyone.

For the first time in the trial, the room could see it — Jack Engle, a man built on quiet conviction, was struggling to keep the weight of disappointment from breaking through the surface.

***

The courtroom lights had begun to feel harsher as the day dragged on, casting long shadows across tired faces. Jack sat at the plaintiff's table, quietly watching the opposing counsel finish another volley of arguments. His notebook lay open in front of him, but he hadn't written anything in a while. His pen sat idle in his hand, forgotten.

The trial was shifting.

What had started as a straightforward intellectual property dispute was evolving into something larger, messier, and more important. Carlton Drake continued to hammer away at the same narrative: that Jack's research, while "respected," was not essential. It had merely served as background reading—one of many scientific sources consulted during the development of Universal's Twister attraction. "Inspirational," yes. But *foundational*? No. Not enough, Drake insisted, to warrant ownership or compensation.

Jack's attorney, Karen, rose from her seat, this time with a slightly different posture—less defensive, more resolute. She began to speak not just of contracts and citations, but of principle. Of what it means to devote a lifetime to discovery. Of how the line between science and commerce had become dangerously blurred.

"This isn't just about who owns what," Karen said clearly. "It's about whether the work of researchers — real scientists — can be taken, repackaged, and monetized by corporations without so much as a handshake."

Jack looked down at the table, his fingers tightening around the pen. He wasn't sure when it happened, but the case no longer felt like it was just about him. It wasn't just about his tornado model or the years he'd spent perfecting it. It wasn't even just about Universal Studios.

It was about *what it meant to create something out of curiosity, out of care,* and then to watch it be swallowed whole by a system that valued spectacle more than substance.

He glanced at Darlie, who gave him a steady nod. Her expression was calm, but her eyes were fierce. She understood. This wasn't just a fight over past work — it was about every scientist who'd ever had their contributions minimized, every researcher whose quiet labor had been exploited without credit or compensation.

The air in the courtroom had shifted. The legal teams were no longer just discussing Jack Engle's legacy — they were shaping a precedent. What happened here could decide how future creators were treated. Would innovation be respected? Or would it be something for corporations to mine, mold, and monetize at will?

Jack felt his spine straighten as Karen continued. She wasn't just defending one man's career now — she was standing up for every unsung scientist, every unheard voice.

The stakes had grown, and Jack knew it.

He looked toward the jury. They were listening closely now, pens still, faces thoughtful. For the first time, Jack sensed that they *saw* him—not just as a man in a suit behind a microphone, but as someone who had spent his life chasing storms so others could survive them.

The battle lines were drawn. And win or lose, this was no longer just his fight.

12

A FAMILY DIVIDED

The rain came down in slow, steady rhythms, tapping against the windows like a clock marking time. The living room was dim, the only light coming from the small lamp on the end table beside Darlie's chair. She sat curled up in the armchair, legs tucked beneath her, a book resting half-forgotten in her lap. The soft hum of the rain and the occasional creak of the old house were the only sounds that filled the space.

The front door opened with a groan. Jack stepped inside, rain dotting the shoulders of his coat, briefcase in hand, his posture sagging with exhaustion. He closed the door behind him quietly, as if not to disturb the stillness that had settled over their home like a blanket.

Darlie did not look up at first. She heard him, of course every movement, every sigh. But lately, they had been dancing around each other, orbiting the same space without quite meeting. After a long pause, she raised her eyes to him. They were soft but tired, ringed with the kind of worry that came from weeks, maybe months, of holding everything together alone.

"How did it go today?" she asked, her voice almost a whisper.

Jack dropped his briefcase by the couch and slowly sank into the cushions, his elbows resting on his knees. He didn't meet her gaze. "Same as yesterday," he muttered. "Just more dancing around the truth."

A beat passed. The rain kept tapping.

Darlie closed the book on her lap gently, her fingers lingering on the cover. "Jack..." she began, carefully, as if choosing each word like stepping stones across a river. "We need to talk."

Jack looked up at her then. Really looked. Her face, the one that had watched him chase storms and build models, raise a family and chase impossible dreams, now looked... distant. Not angry. Just distant.

"I know," he said quietly.

She gave a small nod, then said, "I'm worried. Not just about the case. About you. About us."

Jack leaned back, the couch creaking beneath him. "I'm fine," he said, though it was obvious he wasn't.

Darlie shook her head gently. "You're not, Jack. We're not. This lawsuit—it's eating up everything. The savings, your time, your energy. You come home late, and even when you're here, you're still there. Still in that courtroom."

He rubbed his eyes with the heel of his hands. "It's just until this is over. I have to see it through."

Darlie's voice trembled slightly, though she kept it calm. "Do you? Jack, we barely talk anymore. When was the last time we had dinner without it turning into a briefing?"

She stood and walked over to the window, arms crossed loosely, watching the rain. "I know why you're fighting. I admire it. I really do. But I'm starting to wonder if it's worth what it's costing."

Jack's eyes followed her. He didn't speak right away. There was too much between them— unspoken things, fears neither of them had dared say aloud. He didn't want to admit that part of him felt the same that the lawsuit was taking more than he had expected.

But still, he said, "I can't stop now. Not after everything."

Darlie turned to face him. Her expression was unreadable. "And what if everything turns to nothing, Jack? What if you win the case but lose everything else along the way?"

The silence that followed was heavier than before. No shouting, no accusations — just the quiet ache of two people caught in a slow unraveling.

The rain kept falling.

***

Jack didn't speak at first.

He sat there on the couch, elbows on knees, fingers curled into tight fists. The silence between them stretched long and tense, broken only by the soft tick of the wall clock and the hush of rain. Darlie stood by the window, her arms wrapped loosely around herself, waiting.

Finally, Jack spoke — not in anger, but in something quieter. Raw. A little desperate.

"This isn't just about some ride at a theme park, Darlie." His voice was hoarse, tired. "This is my life's work. It's the only thing I have ever done that really mattered."

His words hung in the air. Darlie did not move. Her back was still to him; eyes lost in the rain-slicked glass.

Jack leaned back into the couch cushions, his gaze drifting toward the ceiling. "You remember that trip to Oklahoma?" he asked softly, not waiting for an answer. "That storm I chased with the old team, the one back in the early '90s..."

Darlie turned slowly. She knew the story, of course. Jack had told it a dozen times — but this time was different. He wasn't trying to impress her or relive the glory. He was trying to *remember* something vital. Something pure.

"I was twenty-seven," he went on. "We were crammed in the back of that busted-up van — barely any gas money, the equipment all duct-taped together. We were chasing a supercell near Norman. I remember the dirt under my fingernails, the wind howling so loud I couldn't even hear myself think."

He chuckled, but it was hollow. "That tornado touched down just off the highway. I sketched out a new rotation model on the back of a grocery receipt right there in the van. It was messy and wild and real. And I remember thinking — *this*, this is what I was made to do."

Darlie softened a little. But she said nothing.

Jack continued, slower now. "That kid I used to be... the one who believed science could change the world, this lawsuit, this fight... it's me standing up for *him*, too. I spent years chasing storms, building models, writing papers no one read, just trying to make people safer. And now they want to take it. Twist it. Turn it into a super attraction."

He looked up at Darlie then. His eyes were heavy with emotion. "I'm not chasing fame, Darlie. I don't care about being on TV. I'm trying to protect what I built. What we built."

He paused, swallowing hard. "If I let them use my work without credit — make millions off it, turn it into some flashy thing with no meaning then what was the point? Everything I have worked for, all those years... it will be like none of it mattered."

Darlie's eyes glistened. She walked back toward him slowly and sat down on the edge of the coffee table, facing him. Her voice was soft but steady. "I hear you. I really do. But what about us, Jack?"

He blinked, startled. "What do you mean?"

"I mean *us*," she said. "Our life. Our family. What are *we* building now? Because lately it feels like you are giving everything you have to that courtroom, and when you come home... there's nothing left. You're running yourself into the ground trying to protect your past, but what about our future?"

Jack opened his mouth, then closed it again. For once, he had no answer.

Darlie reached out, her fingers brushing his knee. "I miss you," she whispered. "I miss the man who used to chase storms because he was curious, not because he had something to prove."

Jack's throat tightened. "I don't know how to stop," he said, barely above a whisper. "I've worked too hard for too long to let them erase me. If I back down now, if I walk away... I'll regret it for the rest of my life."

His voice cracked at the end, and he looked away, ashamed of how deeply this fight had burrowed into him.

"I don't want to lose you, Darlie," he said finally. "But I don't know how to *not* fight this."

Darlie didn't speak again right away. She sat with him in the quiet, the storm inside the house mirroring the one outside.

There were no clear answers. Only the weight of two people, both hurting in different ways, trying to understand how they ended up on opposite sides of the same war.

***

The conversation did not end with a slammed door or raised voices. It ended in silence.

A heavy, breathless silence that felt far worse than anger. Jack stood by the window now, arms crossed tightly over his chest, eyes scanning the dark sky as if it held answers. The rain had stopped, but the clouds still hung low and bruised, and somewhere in the distance, thunder grumbled softly like an echo of things unsaid.

Darlie stayed seated on the edge of the coffee table. Her hands were clasped in her lap; her eyes locked on the floor. The space between them wasn't wide, but it felt impossible to cross.

Jack watched the wind rustle the trees outside, his reflection faintly visible in the glass. He looked older than he remembered — lined, exhausted. Not just by the lawsuit, but by something deeper.

Is this what it costs? he wondered. *To protect your life's work... do you have to lose the life built around it?*

He had always thought of Darlie as home. She was the one constant during the chaos of storm seasons and the long nights in the lab. She'd held him together when funding ran dry and papers were rejected. But now... even home felt uncertain. Like walking into a familiar room and realizing the furniture had all been rearranged while you weren't looking.

Jack clenched his jaw. *I'm not wrong,* he told himself. *I'm fighting for something important.* And yet, for the first time, he wasn't sure if he was still fighting alone.

***

Across the room, Darlie looked at Jack the way one might look at a stranger who feels oddly familiar. The man at the window was not the one who used to dance her around the kitchen after dinner or whisper storm facts with childlike wonder under the sheets. That man had been curious, impulsive, brimming with energy and hope.

Now, he looked... frayed. Thinner somehow, not in body, but in spirit. She had loved Jack's passion from the beginning. It had been one of the things that drew her in. But now, that same fire felt like it was burning their life down from the inside.

She wrapped her arms tighter around herself. It wasn't that she didn't understand his reasons. She *did*. She just didn't know how to stand beside a man who refused to look beside him.

Jack didn't say goodnight. He simply turned and walked past her, slow and quiet, the floor creaking beneath his steps. He paused in the hallway, hand resting briefly on the frame of their bedroom door, then turned and entered the study instead.

As Jack's study door clicked shut, the phone rang in the living room.

Darlie hesitated, then picked it up. Her voice softened. "Hi, honey."

It was their daughter, Kathy. Jack could faintly hear Darlie's tone through the thin walls. She tried to sound steady, but there was a tremor there. He couldn't hear the words exactly—just the pauses, the muffled "We're fine," and, "Your dad's... busy."

The word stung. Busy. As if he were some absentee father from years past, still hiding in the lab. He gripped the arms of his chair in the study, listening to the rain tick at the window, feeling a new guilt slip beneath his ribs.

Darlie hung up quietly a few minutes later. She didn't knock on his door, didn't ask if he was listening. She simply walked upstairs, her footsteps fading.

Jack stared at the tornado model on his desk. He thought about his children, Gavin, Kathy and Kevin. For the first time, he wondered if his children—grown now, with their own lives— would only remember him as the man who chose storms and lawsuits over family dinners.

Darlie stayed seated until she heard the soft *click* of the study door closing. A click that sounded too much like a goodbye.

She exhaled, long and low, and stood up. Her legs ached—not from standing, but from holding up so much emotion.

Upstairs, she gently shut the bedroom door behind her.

***

In the study, Jack sat at his desk, staring blankly at a model of a tornado he'd built years ago—a layered spiral of wire, plastic, and data points, frozen in time. It was gathering dust now, just like the part of him that had once built it with excitement, not courtroom desperation.

Outside, thunder rolled again.

The storm wasn't raging anymore. It was quiet now, distant—but still present. Like the silence in the house.

A closed door. A dusty tornado. A scientist unraveling.

There were no dramatic exits or shattered glass. Just two people—brilliant and bruised—sitting in different rooms of the same house, feeling like they were living separate lives. Darlie, aching for connection. Jack, drowning in a battle no one else fully understood.

And neither of them knew how to reach the other anymore.

Not tonight.

Maybe not tomorrow.

13

THE TURNING POINT

The room smelled of coffee, printer toner, and fatigue. Stacks of legal documents were spread across the large oak table in Jack's study, pages rustling under the slow spin of the ceiling fan. It was late, well past midnight—but sleep had become a stranger to Jack these past few weeks. Leonard Briggs, one of the junior associates from his legal team, sat beside him, bleary-eyed and chewing on a pencil. Karen, the lead attorney, stood by the window, staring out into the night as if searching for answers in the dark.

Jack shuffled through another manila folder, barely skimming the pages. Everything blurred together now, contracts, emails, affidavits, technical specifications. Most of it felt useless. Smoke and mirrors. He leaned back, rubbing his temples, frustration swelling.

"This is getting us nowhere," he muttered. "They're going to bury us in bureaucracy."

Leonard said nothing, just passed him another document.

And then—he saw it.

A flash of handwriting caught his eye. Faded ink on yellowing paper. At first glance, it looked like an old lab journal entry, one of dozens he had archived years ago. But something about the date pulled him in: **March 18, 1993**.

His breath caught.

Jack leaned forward, heart thudding. The page detailed an early version of the tornado behavior algorithm; the exact model Universal had replicated for their Twister simulation. Sketched diagrams, equations, artificial tornado photograph, handwritten annotations… and most importantly, a **timestamp** with his signature at the bottom.

Karen turned from the window at the sudden shift in energy.

"What is it?" she asked.

Jack held up the page with trembling hands. "This," he said, voice tight with wonder. "This is it. This is the original prototype—dated, signed, annotated. It proves I was working on this many years before Universal ever came knocking."

Leonard leaned over, his eyes wide. "It's like a patent without the paperwork."

Jack flipped through the rest of the notebook, finding more entries. Correspondence from that time—an old email to a colleague at the university referencing the model's potential. A printed newsletter from a scientific conference where Jack had casually presented an early version of the concept, long before entertainment executives had caught wind of it.

It wasn't just evidence. It was a **timeline**. A clear, undeniable chain of innovation leading straight back to him.

He laughed softly at first, then louder, the sound echoing with a strange mixture of relief and disbelief. "I thought I'd lost this," he said, running a hand over the page like it was made of gold. "It's been sitting here, buried under years of crap... and it might be the one thing that saves everything."

Leonard stepped forward, eyes scanning the notes. "This could be exactly what we need," he said. "It's contemporaneous. Unaltered. Shows intent, process, and authorship. It proves the model came from you, long before it was commercialized."

Jack's hands were shaking now, the adrenaline finally kicking in.

For the first time in weeks maybe months, he felt like he wasn't just reacting. He was fighting back. Not with anger or desperation, but with truth. With real, tangible proof that the ideas Universal had turned into entertainment had been born in his mind, refined through sleepless nights and storm-chasing weekends.

"Let's get this in front of the court," Jack said, eyes sharp with new resolve. "These changes everything."

The mood in the room shifted. Where there had been fatigue, now there was focus. Karen began snapping photos of the pages. Leonard opened his laptop, already drafting a motion for discovery inclusion.

Jack leaned back again, holding the old notebook against his chest like a lifeline.

He didn't have to shout or make a speech. He just sat there quietly, breathing deeply, letting the weight of the moment settle around him.

This wasn't the end of the fight. But for the first time, he could see a path forward — clear and real.

And maybe, just maybe, he would win.

***

The storm outside had finally passed, but inside Jack, a new kind of weather had begun to stir — sharper, more focused.

He stood at the edge of his study, staring down at the aged notebook still open on the table, the yellowed pages spread like a lifeline. The diagrams looked primitive compared to today's simulations, but to him, they were perfect. Each line, each formula a fingerprint from another time. His time.

The house was quiet. Darlie had gone to bed hours ago, though Jack wasn't sure if she was actually asleep or simply too exhausted to keep talking.

Leonard and Karen had left after making digital copies of the documents and high-fiving one another like soldiers who'd finally discovered the map to enemy lines. But Jack didn't celebrate. He didn't smile. He just stood there, both hands gripping the back of the chair, his mind replaying the long road that had led him here.

How many years had he spent chasing storms across desolate highways? How many sleepless nights had he spent writing code, comparing radar data, plotting paths of devastation in the hopes of making the next town safer? How often had he sat alone in dark university labs, watching simulations run on outdated computers, while the rest of the world slept?

This was the proof. This was the culmination of every sacrifice.

And they had tried to take it from him.

Jack's jaw tightened. His reflection in the study window stared back—tired eyes, weathered face, graying at the temples. But there was still fire there. Still fight.

He walked slowly to the desk and closed the notebook with careful hands. Then he pulled out a legal pad and began to write—talking points, references, case numbers, footnotes. He didn't stop to rest. He didn't need to. The weight that had been pressing down on him for weeks now felt lighter. Not gone, but bearable. Contained.

Because now, he had something real.

This wasn't about revenge. It wasn't even about Universal anymore.

It was about recognition. For the years of work. For the science. For the storms he'd chased and the models he'd built when no one else believed in them. For the lonely days when the only thing keeping him going was the hope that maybe—just maybe—he could leave the world better than he found it.

He thought of the students he'd taught. The kids who'd come up to him after lectures with wide eyes and notebooks full of questions. He thought of the communities that had used his tornado model to issue faster warnings. He thought of the night his prototype correctly predicted a touchdown in a small Oklahoma town, giving families enough time to get to safety.

Jack exhaled slowly, his breath fogging the cool glass of the study window.

They could call it theatrical. They could reduce it to spectacle. But he knew the truth. This work had mattered. Still mattered.

He picked up his phone and texted Karen: **"We push forward. No compromise. I want this all the way to verdict."**

And when he put the phone down, Jack didn't feel drained.

He felt ready.

***

Darlie stood quietly in the doorway of the study, one hand curled loosely around a steaming mug of chamomile tea. She hadn't meant to interrupt. She hadn't even planned to check in. But something — some ache of habit or intuition — had drawn her from the dim bedroom to the soft glow spilling under the study door.

Jack was hunched over the desk, surrounded by open folders, old notebooks, and legal pads scribbled with new notes. His brow was furrowed in deep concentration, but his face looked... different.

It wasn't the grim, tight-lipped focus she'd seen so often in the past few weeks. It wasn't the edge of anger or the slump of exhaustion.

There was purpose in him again. A steadiness.

She leaned against the doorframe and waited. When he finally noticed her, he blinked up, surprised like he'd momentarily forgotten the rest of the world existed. His expression softened.

"Did I wake you?" he asked, voice low.

"No," she said. "Couldn't sleep."

A quiet pause passed between them. The kind that once would've felt natural but lately had grown heavy. Tonight, it didn't feel so weighty.

"You found something," she said, gesturing with her chin toward the scattered papers.

Jack nodded, slowly. "Yeah. Something real. Something they can't twist."

She walked further in, placing her tea on the corner of the desk. Her eyes scanned the old research notes—faded ink, rough sketches of tornado cross-sections, margins filled with frantic thoughts only Jack could decipher.

"I remember when you drew this," she murmured, touching the edge of a page. "You came home covered in dust and couldn't stop talking about vortex behavior for three days."

He smiled faintly. "I still think that was the one. The model that changed everything."

Darlie sat on the edge of the couch across from him, folding her hands in her lap.

"I've been angry," she admitted softly. "Not just about the lawsuit. About how far away you've felt. Like I lost you to this thing… and I didn't know if I'd ever get you back."

Jack didn't look away.

"I know," he said. "And I don't blame you."

"But tonight," she continued, "when I saw you in here… you weren't angry. You weren't tired. You looked like the man I married — obsessive, yes," she added with a faint smirk, "but alive. Certain."

She stood again and moved behind his chair, resting her hands on his shoulders. He let out a long breath, the tension slowly easing under her touch.

"I still worry," she said. "About what it's doing to you. About us. But if this really is about your legacy — if this is what you need to finish what you started then I'll stand by you. I just want you to come out of this with your soul intact. Win or lose."

Jack reached up, gently covering her hand with his. For a moment, he didn't speak.

When he did, his voice was low and certain. "I just want the truth to matter."

Darlie nodded. "Then let's make sure it does."

14

VICTORY IN COURT

The courtroom was packed. Every seat was filled. Some by press, some by curious bystanders, and many by people who had followed the trial from the beginning. Cameras were not allowed inside, but that didn't stop the energy from buzzing like static in the air. People leaned forward in their seats, whispering to one another, waiting.

Jack Engle sat at the front, quiet, still.

To his right was Karen, calm as ever, flipping through a final set of papers. On Jack's other side, just behind him in the gallery, sat Darlie. Her hand gently rested on his shoulder. Neither of them spoke. They didn't need to. The past few weeks had been filled with so many arguments, decisions, and moments of doubt. But now, there was only one thing left to hear.

"All rise," the bailiff called.

Everyone stood as the judge entered the room, black robes flowing behind him. His expression was unreadable calm, almost detached. But Jack's heart beat faster. He had played this moment in his mind so many times. Sometimes as a victory, sometimes as a crushing defeat. Now, the real thing was here.

The judge sat. The courtroom settled. Silence.

"This case," He began, his voice firm and measured, "has been presented with complex arguments regarding intellectual property, scientific innovation, and commercial adaptation. It is the opinion of this court—"

Jack held his breath.

"—that Dr. Jack Engle is the rightful owner of the tornado models in question. The court rules in favor of the plaintiff."

It took a second to register. The words landed like thunder in Jack's chest. He blinked.

He heard Darlie gasp softly behind him. Karen leaned forward with a rare smile. Jack slowly sat back down, shoulders slumping under the weight of the news not from defeat, but from the sudden lifting of a burden he'd carried too long.

He had won.

The courtroom filled with murmurs. Universal's team shuffled papers, stiff-backed and silent. Carlton Drake, their lead counsel—offered no reaction, only a small nod to his colleague before packing up.

But Jack didn't look at them. He turned instead to Darlie.

Her eyes were shining. She took his hand.

"You did it," she whispered.

He nodded, too stunned to speak.

***

Later that afternoon, outside the courthouse, reporters swarmed the steps. Flashbulbs went off. Microphones were shoved forward. Jack answered a few questions, but kept it short.

"This wasn't just about me," he said. "It was about standing up for every scientist whose work has been used without credit. It's about reminding the world that behind every model, every invention, every line of data, there's a person. And people deserve to be acknowledged."

***

That night, back home, the house was quiet. For the first time in weeks, Jack didn't head straight to the study. He sat with Darlie at the kitchen table. They ate leftover soup, drank hot tea, and said very little. But the silence was comfortable this time not strained or tired. Just... peaceful.

Eventually, Jack stood and walked to the study anyway. The door creaked open. Inside, everything was as he had left it. Papers. Weather charts. A few unopened letters. And in the middle of the desk, his old tornado model.

He picked it up. The plastic dome was scratched now, the tiny swirling funnel inside slightly crooked. But it still worked. He twisted the knob, and the small vortex spun into life, fragile and beautiful.

This was the thing that had started it all. Not just the lawsuit, but the research. The passion. The questions that had kept him awake as a young man. The thrill of chasing storms. The feeling that nature had a language—and he might be one of the few who could understand it.

He set the model down and stared at it.

He had won the case.

But something told him the real work was still ahead. Protecting his models was one thing.

Making sure they were used with purpose, with meaning, with integrity that was another.

He didn't want his work to end up as just another line item in a corporate portfolio.

He wanted it to matter.

***

Before bed, Jack stood by the window and looked out at the night sky. It had rained earlier. The clouds were breaking now, leaving behind stars and open space.

Darlie stepped in behind him and wrapped her arms around his waist.

"You okay?" she asked.

"Yeah," he said softly. "I think so."

They stood there for a long while.

He was tired, so tired. But he was not broken. He was proud. And more than anything, he was ready to move forward.

The court had given him back his name.

Now, it was up to him to decide what to do with it.

***

Quiet triumph. A man at peace for the first time in years. Not because everything is solved — but because, for once, the world finally heard him.

***

Jack sat alone in the study the next morning, his fingers resting on the edge of a legal folder that Karen had left behind. The courtroom ruling still echoed in his mind. *The court rules in favor of the plaintiff...* It had happened. It was done. But as the initial wave of relief began to fade, a different kind of reflection took its place — one heavier, more complex.

He flipped through the folder. Pages of court transcripts, declarations, and that one critical piece of evidence that had tipped the scale in his favor. His name — **Dr. Jack Engle** — was now officially, irrevocably tied to the tornado models he had spent a lifetime creating.

But as he stared at the legal documents, something gnawed at him.

This win wasn't just personal. It was political. Philosophical. Scientific.

For decades, Jack had lived in the world of academic research, where sharing knowledge wasn't just encouraged—it was expected. He had collaborated, published, peer-reviewed. Scientists built on each other's ideas like scaffolding, climbing toward a higher truth. No one really "owned" a weather pattern. No one could patent the wind.

And yet, here he was—the legal owner of a tornado model.

It felt... strange.

He wasn't sorry he'd won. He was not even uncertain about whether he *should* have fought. But now that the ruling had been made, the path ahead looked blurred. What precedent had he set? Would other researchers now start locking away their discoveries behind legal barricades, fearful of exploitation? Would students and young scientists hesitate before sharing their ideas, worried about ownership instead of impact?

Jack sighed and leaned back in his chair. The law had given him what he asked for. But science? Science didn't always follow courtroom rules. And that dissonance left him unsettled.

He rubbed his temples and looked out the window. What would happen now, when academic work brushed up against commercial ambition? When discovery collided with entertainment? When a weather model could be copyrighted like a screenplay?

For Jack, the answer was no longer theoretical.

He was now the symbol of that question.

15

UNIVERSAL STUDIOS, ORLANDO

The morning air in Orlando was already warm, carrying that faint sweetness of theme park confections and the ever-present scent of sunscreen. But the day hadn't started at the park gates.

It began in a boardroom.

Universal had flown them into a glass-and-steel tower just off the lot, where floor-to-ceiling posters of blockbuster films covered the walls. The room itself felt like a stage sleek conference table, bottled water lined with military precision, a screen glowing with the Twister logo.

Jack and Darlie were greeted by a small team of executives who radiated practiced charm. Handshakes were firm, smiles quick and polished.

To Jack, the whole room smelled faintly of cologne and strategy.

"Dr. Engle," began one of the executives, a man with cufflinks shaped like miniature globes, "what you've created is more than data. It's drama. It's the human struggle against chaos, distilled into pure experience. And audiences, they don't just want to learn, they want to feel."

A woman in a scarlet blazer leaned forward, her tone warm, rehearsed. "We're not just simulating weather; we're telling a story. The sound of a roof tearing away, the panic of headlights flashing through the rain. Those are emotions. And thanks to your tornado model, we can make those moments authentic. Guests will step into the storm and walk out transformed."

Another executive tapped the glossy mock-up of the 50-foot artificial tornado. "Families crave safe danger. They want spectacle. They want something to talk about when they leave. And Twister. Well, Twister delivers."

Jack sat still, hands folded tightly in his lap. He didn't doubt their enthusiasm, it was genuine, in its own polished way. But as they spoke of immersion, synergy, and market share, he felt the distance between their world and his own widen. These people weren't talking about safety, or warnings, or the midnight hours he had spent chasing storms across Oklahoma highways. They were talking about ticket sales.

Darlie watched him closely. She recognized the look in his eyes, the same one he wore after university budget meetings, when grant committees reduced his research to "market viability."

By the end of the pitch, Jack managed a polite thank you. But inside, the unease had already set in.

***

An hour later, a taxi pulled up to the gates of Universal Studios.

Jack Engle stepped out of the taxi first, pulling his worn leather satchel over his shoulder. Darlie followed, her wide-brimmed sun hat shielding her from the blaze of the Florida sun. Around them, the scene could have been pulled straight from a travel brochure, families spilling onto the pavement, children tugging at parents' hands, camera shutters clicking as if trying to capture every ounce of excitement in the air.

But for Jack, there was no holiday thrill here.

This trip had been arranged after weeks of back-and-forth with Universal's legal department. On paper, it was presented as a gesture of goodwill. An invitation to experience the Twister attraction that had, for better or worse, been built on the foundation of his research. In reality, Jack suspected it was a carefully orchestrated PR move, the kind that gave the illusion of cooperation without changing the underlying truth.

Darlie adjusted her sunglasses and glanced at him sideways. "You're awfully quiet."

"Just… thinking."

"About what?"

Jack's gaze swept over the park entrance ahead, where the iconic Universal Studios globe rotated lazily, shining in the morning light. Beyond it, somewhere in that maze of rides and stages, was a manufactured storm built from the bones of his work. "About whether I actually want to see this thing," he said.

A part of him did. Curiosity was too deeply ingrained in his nature to deny. He had spent decades studying the anatomy of tornadoes, decoding their erratic movements, predicting their paths with an accuracy that had once been thought impossible. Seeing those patterns transformed into a three-dimensional, sensory experience could be fascinating, even gratifying.

But another part of him bristled at the thought. The attraction was not designed to educate, not really. It was designed to entertain, to thrill, to make people scream and laugh and then line up again. In the process, the raw, unpredictable danger of tornadoes had been packaged into something marketable. The science, the heart of it — was now buried under flashing lights and fog machines.

Inside the main gates, a young woman in a crisp navy suit approached them with a bright, practiced smile. "Dr. Engle? Mrs. Engle? I'm Marissa, your liaison for the day. Welcome to Universal Studios." She extended her hand, and Jack shook it, noting the faint callus on her palm — a detail that told him she wasn't just an office worker; she spent time around the mechanical guts of the park.

"I'll be taking you behind the scenes of the Twister attraction," Marissa continued. "We wanted you to see exactly how your work was incorporated." Her voice was friendly, but every word was measured, like she was following a script.

They followed her down a side path that cut away from the main crowd. Here, the music and chatter faded, replaced by the industrial hum of service vehicles and the faint smell of machine oil. Darlie, ever observant, glanced at Jack as if to gauge his mood.

"You okay?" she asked softly.

"Ask me in an hour," he said, managing a faint smile.

The Twister building rose ahead, painted to resemble a row of weathered storefronts clinging stubbornly to a storm-battered main street. Props of overturned trash cans, broken shutters, and a flickering streetlamp completed the illusion. Even from the outside, Jack could see how much money had been poured into making chaos look... cinematic.

Inside, the light dimmed, and the temperature dropped a few degrees. A faint, almost invisible rumble played through hidden speakers. Subtle enough that it felt like it was coming from the earth itself. Marissa led them through a "staff only" doorway and into a narrow hallway lined with monitors.

"This is the control room," she explained. "From here, we manage every effect you'll see in the attraction, wind speed, lightning cues, debris movement. The algorithms that control the wind patterns are directly based on your tornado models, Dr. Engle."

Jack stepped closer to one of the screens. There it was—his work. Stripped of its dense mathematical notation, renamed with terms like *Wind Surge 3* and *Funnel Drop Sequence,* but undeniably his. The structure of the simulation was intact, even if the labels were dressed for show business.

It was... impressive. The scale, the precision, the way the machinery mirrored real atmospheric chaos. It all worked. But standing there, watching tourists reduced to mere data points in the simulation, Jack couldn't shake the feeling that something essential had been lost in translation.

They stepped from the control room into the main staging area just as a new audience was filing in. Jack and Darlie stood off to the side, partially hidden by a stack of prop crates. From here, he could see the entire set: the weathered main street façade, the crooked telephone poles, the flickering neon sign of a diner that would soon be "torn apart" by the approaching storm.

A low hum swelled from hidden speakers. Barely noticeable at first, like the earth taking a deep breath. Then, the show began.

The wind machines roared to life, sending newspapers and leaves spiraling down the mock street. Lightning cracked overhead, followed by the deep, guttural roll of thunder that vibrated in Jack's chest. The special effects team had spared no expense, glass rattled in its frames, store awnings flapped violently, and a stop sign shuddered in the gusts.

And then, the funnel appeared.

It wasn't real, of course, but it was eerily convincing. A swirling column of air and mist, lit from within by strobe flashes mimicking lightning. Jack's breath caught. The structure of its movement, the way the wind currents danced and converged into a rotating vortex, he knew that pattern better than he knew his own reflection. This was his model, brought to life on a scale he had never imagined.

Part of him was mesmerized. The scope of the spectacle was overwhelming, dozens of hidden fans, hydraulic systems, and computer-controlled elements working in perfect synchronization. Children gasped, clutched their parents' arms. Teenagers cheered and raised their phones. The crowd was utterly consumed by the illusion, and Jack felt a flicker of pride that his work could hold them in its grip.

But alongside that pride came a hollow ache.

He had built these models to save lives, to give people more warning, more time to seek shelter before the chaos struck. He remembered long nights in the lab, running simulations over and over until the numbers finally aligned. And here, all that effort had been repurposed into a thrill, something to be applauded, not respected.

The attraction was undeniably impressive, but it had stripped away the gravity of what tornadoes truly were. Where Jack saw devastation and hard-earned data, the crowd saw only entertainment.

As the finale hit, a perfectly timed sequence where the diner's façade was "ripped apart" in a burst of wind and flying debris. Jack felt a bittersweet truth settle in.

Yes, the tornado attraction taught people *something*. It showed them the sheer force of a storm, the sensory overload, the danger. But it was a distilled version of reality, wrapped in safety and showmanship. The fear here was designed to thrill, not to warn.

Darlie glanced at him, her expression a question she didn't voice.

Jack managed a small, tight smile. "It's… incredible," he said. And he meant it. But in the space behind the words, where he kept the parts of himself, he couldn't explain, he thought: *And it's not mine anymore.*

16

THE TWISTER ATTRACTION

The heat of a Florida afternoon clung to Jack's skin like a damp cloth. The air was thick with the scents of popcorn, sunscreen, and asphalt baking under the sun. Crowds swirled around him—families corralling excited children, teenagers laughing, camera straps swinging as tourists navigated the winding paths.

Jack and Darlie are about to experience the Twister attraction as ordinary spectators. Darlie adjusted her sunhat, shielding her eyes from the glaring light as they approached the squat, warehouse-like building housing the Twister attraction. Above its entrance, a billboard loomed—an ominous funnel cloud twisting against a lightning-lit sky. Beneath it, bold white letters promised: *"Feel the Fury of Mother Nature."*

Jack slowed, his lips pressing into a tight line. That funnel cloud wasn't just a symbol — it was his. Or at least, it had been built on the bones of his work.

Families funneled into the zig-zagging queue ahead, voices buzzing with excitement. A boy clutched a plastic tornado toy against his chest, whispering to his younger sister, "It's going to feel like a real storm in there!" Two teenagers laughed and dared each other not to scream when the funnel appeared. Nearby, a mother knelt to reassure her daughter: "Don't worry, honey. It's just pretend."

Jack lingered for a moment, listening. Their chatter was filled with anticipation, the thrill of play. For them, this was an adventure, a safe brush with danger to laugh about afterward.

But for Jack, the storm had never been pretend. He still remembered the sickly-green skies of Kansas summers, the metallic tang in the air before a funnel touched down, the freight-train roar that swallowed silence before ripping everything apart. To him, tornadoes were not spectacle. They were survival.

Darlie caught the shadow in his expression and laid her hand gently on his arm. "They don't know, Jack," she said softly. "And maybe they don't need to, not the way you do."

He nodded faintly, though the weight in his chest didn't ease.

They stepped into the cool blast of air-conditioning, the door hissing shut behind them. Fluorescent lights buzzed overhead, reflecting off laminated storm warning posters tacked to the walls. One in particular caught Jack's eye—a replica of an actual warning notice from the late '80s, nearly identical to the ones he'd pored over in research archives.

A low, distant rumble of recorded thunder echoed through the room. The floor beneath them vibrated faintly, a mechanical hum layered beneath the storm soundtrack. Jack's mind immediately began running through the fine details—the fan placements, the mist nozzles, the lighting cues designed to mimic an electrical storm. Someone had taken his science, his life's work, and translated it into this curated spectacle.

Darlie glanced at him, smiling knowingly. "Feels familiar?"

He didn't answer right away, his gaze fixed on the set dressing: a tilted stop sign, its paint dulled and edges rusted; a battered mailbox, its door hanging open; scraps of paper and faux leaves scattered across the floor like debris from a minor windstorm.

It wasn't random. No, these details were specific—down to the precise angles of debris, the denting on the mailbox door. Someone, somewhere, had taken his data sheets and turned them into set design. He inhaled slowly, the faint tang of ozone from the attraction's fog machines pricking his senses. It felt like walking into a theatrical replica of his own career—carefully engineered to thrill, not to teach.

Darlie noticed his silence and nudged him gently. "Jack, are you okay? You seem… a little distant."

He glanced at her, trying to shake off his thoughts. "Yeah, I'm fine. Just… a lot to process, you know? It's strange, seeing all this. I spent years studying these storms—feeling the raw power of them. And now it's all here, turned into a show."

Darlie smiled softly, "I get it. But look at all these people. They're excited. They're seeing something they would never experience otherwise."

Jack nodded but didn't reply. His mind was racing; his thoughts tangled between pride and unease. The idea of turning something as destructive as a tornado into a theme park attraction felt... wrong. It was like turning a natural disaster into a carnival ride.

The lights dimmed, swallowing the crowd's chatter in a sudden hush. A deep mechanical hum came to life somewhere above, vibrating faintly beneath Jack's shoes. A voice—rich and theatrical—filled the space from unseen speakers.

"Imagine," it intoned, "the raw power of nature, the force of a tornado unleashed..."

Wind machines began their slow build, the air shifting against Jack's skin in a steady, rising current. A faint hum deepened into a pulsing roar, and for a moment, Jack swore he could hear the real thing—the freight train rumble of an actual funnel sweeping across the plains.

A fine mist of cool water drifted over his face, settling into the lines at the corners of his eyes. The moisture carried a faint tang, a manufactured echo of the charged air before a true tornado touched down. Jack blinked up at the darkened ceiling as white-hot strobes erupted overhead, freezing the scene in sharp, unnatural flashes.

And then it appeared.

The funnel slid into existence from the darkness above—a twisting, translucent column of vapor, lit from within by ghostly flashes. It churned and narrowed as it descended. The shape and movement were so precise that Jack's breath caught. Every curve, every oscillation, every subtle shift in the spiral was his. Not his hands on the controls this time, but his fingerprints were there all the same—born in a Kansas lab decades ago, now magnified and projected for a theme park audience.

Jack's heart thumped, an uneven beat of pride and disbelief. It was dazzling, in its way—a conjured storm obeying the hand of human design. But the absurdity of it was undeniable. Years of equations, trial runs, failures, and breakthroughs— all condensed into a five-minute spectacle, complete with sound effects and safety railings.

He gripped the bar in front of him, caught between admiration for the craft and a gnawing sense that somewhere along the line, the storm had stopped being his.

The funnel swelled, widening and stretching, its vapor walls churning faster until the air itself seemed to shiver. A deeper, more guttural roar filled the chamber, and a sharp gust of wind rattled loose fabric and tugged at hats. A chorus of gasps and startled laughter rippled through the crowd.

Jack didn't move.

Somewhere inside him, two versions of himself collided. The scientist cataloged every detail — the calibration of the wind machines, the precise lighting angles that gave the funnel its ghostly presence, the subtle turbulence patterns mimicking his old wind-tunnel tests. It was textbook engineering brilliance.

But the purist in him — the man who'd stood in wheat fields with his heart hammering as the sky twisted into something alive and dangerous — bristled at the performance aspect. Here, the chaos was contained. Sanitized. Packaged for consumption.

From the corner of his vision, he caught Darlie watching him. Her smile was soft, knowing. She didn't need to ask what he was thinking; she could read it in the set of his shoulders, in the way his eyes refused to leave the vortex. She knew he was both impressed and unsettled.

Darlie leaned in closer, her voice soft, but teasing. "I can almost hear you thinking. Is it better than you expected, or worse?"

Jack let out a quiet laugh, though it didn't reach his eyes. "It's… something, all right. It's just hard to watch something I worked on for so long turned into a show."

"I understand," she said, nodding. "But, Jack, you've always said the goal was to help people understand storms. To predict them. This is just another way of sharing what you know. People are seeing it, feeling it."

Jack paused, rubbing his jaw. "I've always wanted people to understand the science, the true nature of tornadoes, not just… this. There's a huge difference between watching an artificial storm from a safe distance and standing in its path. The destruction, the fear, the danger—it's real. And this? This is just… a performance."

Darlie's voice softened, "But maybe that's okay. Not everyone needs to live through it to understand it. A little bit of awe can go a long way, Jack. The feeling they have right now—maybe that will be enough to make them want to know more. To care."

Jack exhaled slowly, considering her words. The idea of planting a seed, of inspiring curiosity without needing to deliver the full weight of a storm's reality, was something he hadn't fully allowed himself to think about.

"Maybe you're right," he said finally. "But it's hard to let go of the fear. The real storm… you can't fake that."

Darlie smiled and squeezed his hand. "I know. But maybe sometimes, it's not about scaring people. Maybe it's about sparking their curiosity, showing them that even the most terrifying forces of nature can be understood—and maybe even controlled."

Jack looked over at her, a small smile tugging at the corner of his lips. "You're a lot more optimistic than I am."

She shrugged playfully. "Someone has to be."

As the next group of visitors filed into the attraction, Jack stayed behind for a moment longer, deep in thought. The sounds of the crowd drifted around him—laughter, excitement, the chatter of tourists eager to experience the thrill of the storm. He closed his eyes for a second, trying to push away the tightness in his chest.

"Jack?" Darlie's voice cut through his thoughts again.

"Yeah?" he asked, looking up at her.

She smiled. "You know, sometimes it's not about the full story. Sometimes, it's about the feeling.

Maybe this is just the beginning. Maybe these people won't forget this moment. And maybe that's enough for now."

Jack nodded slowly. "Maybe you're right."

He stood up straighter, taking one last look at the attraction, at the crowd rushing in and out, their faces full of excitement. Maybe he couldn't control how his work was used, but if it sparked even the smallest interest in someone's heart, that would be enough. And in that way, his storm — his legacy — had traveled far beyond the classroom, the lab, and the research papers.

Darlie squeezed his arm gently. "Come on, let's grab something to eat. You've had enough of the storm for one day."

Jack smiled, the weight in his chest lifting just a little. "Yeah, let's go."

As they walked away from the Twister building, Jack knew one thing for certain: no matter how his work was remembered, it would always be a part of something larger, something that had the power to move and inspire. And that, for all its complexities, was enough.

17

BACK TO KANSAS

The flight home had been uneventful, but the drive from the airport was something else entirely. Out here, the road stretched in a straight, unbroken line through a sea of gold. Wheat fields rolled on for miles, swaying under the lazy push of a warm prairie wind. The hum of cicadas filled the air, their steady drone a familiar summer soundtrack.

The silence was almost physical — not the absence of sound, but the kind that settled into your bones. After the riot of noise in Orlando, the music loops, the recorded thunder, the chatter of crowds, this was a different kind of world.

Jack kept one hand on the wheel, the other resting on his thigh until Darlie's hand found it, her fingers curling gently over his knee. She didn't say anything; she didn't have to.

He glanced at the horizon, where clouds piled soft and white against the endless blue. Every storm, he thought, started like this in quiet. Calm on the surface, the real work happening in the unseen layers above.

The highway stretched on, and Jack breathed in the scent of dry grass and sun-warmed earth, feeling the knot of the past week begin to loosen.

***

They pulled into a roadside diner just outside Lawrence, a low-slung building with a flickering neon sign that read EAT. Inside, the air smelled of coffee, bacon grease, and lemon cleaner, the kind of place where time ran on refills and the booths had molded themselves to generations of tired drivers.

Jack and Darlie slid into a vinyl booth near the window. A waitress with tired eyes and a friendly smile brought two mugs of coffee without needing to be asked.

As Jack stirred in a packet of sugar, a man in a seed company cap at the counter turned, squinting at him. "Say — aren't you that tornado guy?"

The words carried easily across the diner. A couple of other patrons looked up, curiosity piqued. Jack froze for a fraction of a second, the spoon clinking softly against the side of his mug.

Darlie answered for him, light and polite. "He studies storms, yes."

The man grinned. "Saw you on the news. And that tornado inside a building down in Florida! My niece went last summer. Said it was somethin' else. You really built all that?"

Jack cleared his throat, shifting in the booth. "I… worked on the science behind it. And yes, I built the first artificial tornado in a room and not in a box."

"Well, shoot," the man said, slapping the counter with his palm. "That's somethin' to be proud of. You're makin' Kansas famous."

The room hummed again with small talk and the scrape of forks on plates, but Jack couldn't quite shake the weight of those words. Proud. Famous. They fit awkwardly against the truth he carried inside: that his work had been meant to warn, not entertain.

Darlie's hand found his under the table, giving it a reassuring squeeze. He gave her a faint smile, but the unease lingered. He had returned to Kansas, but the shadow of Florida had followed him here, tucked into strangers' recognition and casual admiration.

By the time Jack pushed open the door to his office later that afternoon, the scent of paper and old coffee greeted him like a familiar handshake. The place hadn't changed in his absence. Stacks of research papers still leaned at precarious angles on the edge of his desk, weather charts curled slightly at the corners, and a half-dozen battered reference books lay open as if waiting for his return.

He eased into his chair, running a hand over the blotter as if to reassure himself that this was still his world. Outside the open door, footsteps passed in the hallway, followed by the sound of a familiar voice.

"Hey, Jack!"

He looked up to see Vince from down the hall, a grin stretched across his face. "You're a household name now," Vince said, stepping in with the easy swagger of someone bringing good news.

Jack huffed a laugh, shaking his head. "Never thought I'd get there by making a tornado in a theme park."

Another colleague leaned in the doorway, offering a congratulatory nod. "You brought meteorology to the masses, Jack. That's no small thing."

The words landed in that complicated place inside him, part pride, part unease. His charts, his equations, his quiet, methodical work now distilled into something you could buy a ticket to see.

Still, he smiled, grateful for the welcome. The papers and charts seemed to be watching him from the desk, as if waiting to see what he would do next.

When the last well-wisher drifted away and the hallway returned to its usual muffled quiet, Jack settled into his chair. The congratulatory words still echoed faintly, their warmth dulled by an undercurrent he couldn't quite shake.

He knew the truth. The sudden attention wasn't just for the science. It was for the show, the spectacle, the storm wrapped in flashing lights and souvenir T-shirts. The headlines didn't read Engle Advances Tornado Modeling; they read Theme Park Twister Wows Millions.

On the desk before him lay a chart, still half-covered by the papers he'd left before the trip. He slid it free, smoothing the edges. Lines and figures detailed storm damage probabilities across the Midwest—cold numbers with warm implications.

This was the work that mattered, the part that could warn a town in time, that could save lives.

His eyes traced the chart's neat columns, but in his mind's eye, he saw the swirling funnel in Orlando, perfectly safe, perfectly packaged.

Would this chart, this real work, outlast the Hollywood version? Would anyone remember the equations once the applause faded?

The only answer was the steady ticking of the clock on the wall.

Jack leaned back in his chair, the chart still spread before him, his pen resting idle in his hand. A faint shift in the light caught his eye, pulling his gaze to the office window.

Far on the horizon, the sky had begun to darken. Low, heavy clouds were stacking themselves in slow, deliberate layers, the kind that spoke of changes brewing miles away.

He watched in silence, the familiar anticipation stirring somewhere deep inside. Out there, the real thing was gathering — no stage lights, no rehearsed thunder, no ticketed entry.

The clouds didn't care who was famous or forgotten. They had their own schedule, their own rules.

Jack sat still, listening to the quiet hum of his office, until a faint roll of thunder reached him, distant but sure.

18

THE BIGGER PICTURE

The study smelled faintly of old paper and lemon oil from Darlie's recent dusting. Evening light slanted in through the half-drawn curtains, painting the room in long golden stripes. Outside, the cicadas had begun their slow chorus, the sound muffled by the glass but still steady enough to remind Jack of summer evenings long past.

His desk was crowded. Not chaotically, but with the purposeful disorder of a man who knew exactly where everything was. Spiral-bound notebooks sat half-open, their margins filled with his looping, compact handwriting. Stacks of printed satellite images leaned against one another like old friends; the edges slightly curled from handling. A coffee mug, half-full and cooling, rested perilously close to a folder labeled *Midwest Risk Assessment – 2005– Present*.

The television in the corner was on low, a local news broadcast flickering in muted tones. Jack hadn't been watching it closely; it was there for background noise, something to keep him company while he sifted through data sets and weather models.

But a particular phrase caught his attention, pulling him out of the numbers.

"…and thanks to advances in tornado modeling and public safety awareness, residents in high-risk areas now have an average of ten minutes of warning before a storm hits — nearly double the time they had a decade ago…"

Jack's pen froze above the paper.

The anchor continued, speaking over footage of radar screens, emergency sirens, and schoolchildren in a safety drill. There was no mention of his name, no smiling photograph in the corner of the screen, but Jack knew the numbers, the algorithms, the models behind that statement. He knew the patterns they were showing and he recognized the fingerprints of his work.

He leaned back in his chair, letting the pen drop.

The folder before him suddenly seemed heavier, not because of the paper, but because of what it represented. Years of early mornings and sleepless nights, equations scribbled on napkins in diner booths, arguments with colleagues over coffee, and the steady, stubborn belief that they could make a difference.

And they had.

Not in the dramatic, applause-filled way of theme parks or talk shows, but in the measured, unseen moments that stretched the space between sirens and storms the space where lives were saved.

He reached for his coffee, took a slow sip, and let the truth of it settle over him.

Jack set the coffee mug down and let his gaze drift away from the desk. He wasn't thinking about numbers now, or even about the new models waiting to be tested. He was thinking about places.

Small towns tucked along county highways, where the sirens used to wail only minutes before the sky dropped its fury. Neighborhoods with tree-lined streets and backyard swings, where mothers once had to choose between grabbing the photo albums or gathering their children.

He pictured a school gymnasium in Oklahoma, the kind with faded basketball lines and a smell of dust and sneakers. He imagined a teacher ushering a line of students toward the shelter, her voice calm but brisk, knowing they had ten extra minutes now, ten minutes they wouldn't have had years ago.

Ten minutes could be the difference between standing in your kitchen and standing in the basement, between being caught on the road and making it to a neighbor's cellar. Ten minutes could mean everything.

On the edge of his desk sat a folder of correspondence — letters and emails that had trickled in over the years. Most were from colleagues, some from students, but one stood out. He reached for it now, unfolding the creased paper.

"Dear Dr. Engle," it began, in neat, deliberate handwriting. "I don't know if you'll ever read this, but I needed to say thank you. Last spring, when the sirens went off, we had just enough time to get our kids to the cellar. The tornado hit our house dead on. We lost the roof, the porch, half the living room. But we didn't lose each other. We had ten minutes. That was the difference. We will never forget that."

Jack held the letter quietly, his thumb resting on the final line. He had read it before, but tonight it felt heavier. The numbers on his charts had always been about probabilities, margins, averages. But this — this was flesh and blood. A family alive because of those extra minutes. The models weren't just theory; they were survival.

Jack thought of the countless families who would never know his name, never know that a man in Kansas had spent decades shaving seconds, then minutes, off the warning gap. To them, the sirens were just there when they needed them.

And maybe that was how it should be.

The true measure of his career wasn't the applause in a theme park or the headlines in a newspaper. It was the quiet, invisible work, the safety of strangers he would never meet, in towns he would never visit, on nights when storms would pass without taking what mattered most.

That, he thought, was worth every chart, every equation, every hour bent over a desk in the glow of a single lamp.

***

Jack swiveled slightly in his chair, his eyes catching on the muted television screen again. A commercial break was running now bright colors, quick cuts, music engineered to stick in your head.

It reminded him, strangely, of the "Twister" attraction. Flash, sound, motion, all designed to pull people in.

He had spent months resenting that spectacle, telling himself it cheapened the work, hollowed it out into something that could be bought and consumed between rollercoasters and souvenir stands. And yet…

His mind drifted back to the little boy he'd heard outside the Twister building, tugging his mother's hand, declaring he wanted to be a tornado scientist.

Maybe that mattered more than he'd let himself admit.

Yes, the show dramatized storms, made them safer, neater, without the gut-knotting uncertainty of the real thing. But it also planted seeds. It put tornadoes in the minds of people who might never have thought about them, or who only saw them as random chaos instead of forces that could be studied, understood, predicted.

Maybe the spectacle wasn't the enemy after all. Maybe it was just the delivery system.

The science had always been his language. Theatrics weren't. But if a staged twister could carry that science into millions of homes, into the imaginations of children who might one day take up the work maybe the two worlds weren't so far apart.

A faint smile tugged at the corner of his mouth. He turned back to his desk, the old and new worlds sitting there together in the quiet glow of the study lamp.

Jack leaned back, lacing his fingers behind his head, and stared at the ceiling for a moment. He had spent most of his career thinking of science as a precise, careful thing — a discipline built on peer-reviewed papers, data tables, and the kind of language that only other scientists could fully appreciate.

In graduate school, he had once believed that the highest form of success was to have a model cited in a respected journal, to have his equations debated at conferences where the coffee was bad and the rooms were cold but the minds were sharp. Back then, the idea that his work might one day be turned into an amusement park attraction would have seemed absurd, even insulting.

But time and perhaps a little perspective had shifted something in him.

Science, he realized now, was never meant to sit forever on a library shelf or live only in the heads of a handful of specialists. Knowledge had to travel. It had to cross borders, climb over walls of jargon, survive being simplified, and sometimes even endure being over-simplified, if it was ever going to reach the people who needed it most.

That journey was rarely neat. Sometimes it meant that the data he had obsessed over for years was condensed into a few flashy sentences for a news segment. Sometimes it meant that his meticulously calibrated tornado models were dressed up with strobe lights and fog machines in a theme park, their danger contained, their edges smoothed.

But maybe that was just another kind of storm path — unpredictable, twisting, messy yet still moving forward.

A tornado didn't always travel in a straight line. It veered, it wavered, it sometimes doubled back on itself before pushing ahead again. Why should the path of science be any different?

He thought about how his models had traveled: from scratchy pen-and-paper sketches in his Kansas office… to digital simulations running on clunky early computers… to academic citations… to safety protocols in schools… to the "Twister" attraction, where children stood wide-eyed, gripping railings as the floor shook beneath them.

It was a strange trajectory, but a trajectory nonetheless. And in the end, the destination mattered more than the route. If the public walked away with even a fraction of the respect maybe even awe for the forces of nature that he had carried since boyhood, then perhaps it was worth the compromises along the way.

Science wasn't just about precision. It was about translation shaping ideas into forms the world could hear, understand, and feel. And if that meant his work sometimes wore a costume to get in the door, so be it.

***

The air outside was warm, the kind that wrapped around you like a familiar quilt. Jack stepped onto the porch, the old wooden boards groaning softly under his weight.

The Kansas sky was putting on its own quiet show. The horizon glowed in broad strokes of orange, fading upward into deep violet, a palette only summer could mix. Cicadas buzzed in the tall grass, their rhythm steady and unhurried, and somewhere in the distance a lone meadowlark called out into the falling light.

He leaned against the porch railing, breathing it in. The smell of cut hay, the faint tang of earth after a day's heat.

Then he saw it.

Far off to the east, a bank of clouds loomed, stacked high and full. Every few seconds, they pulsed from within, as if some invisible hand were striking a match inside them. Heat lightning silent, but alive with promise.

Jack's lips curved into a small, private smile.

It didn't matter whether the storm was born in a Kansas wheat field, in the sterile hum of a lab, in the echoing chambers of a courtroom, or inside a child's imagination after stepping off a theme park ride. Storms had a way of calling to him, no matter the form they took.

And he knew, without question, that he would always answer.

19

THE PRICE OF FAME

The living room had settled into the soft, layered quiet of a Kansas evening. Outside, the crickets were already tuning their instruments, filling the gaps between the occasional creak of the old farmhouse's wooden frame.

A single lamp in the corner bathed the room in a pool of warm amber light, throwing long shadows over the familiar clutter of a life well-lived, the quilt folded neatly over the back of the couch, the bookshelf sagging under the weight of meteorology journals and old paperbacks, the dented coffee table that had survived decades of elbows, mugs, and grandchildren's toy cars.

On the low table, beside a half-empty sugar bowl and two cups of tea that had long since cooled, lay an untidy stack of mail. The pile looked deceptively domestic, but its contents told a different story. Thick envelopes from media outlets. Glossy invitations embossed with silver foil — keynote speaking engagements, guest appearances, charity fundraisers. Handwritten letters from storm chasers, science students, even a school in Oklahoma that had painted their tornado shelter with his name. And somewhere near the middle of the stack, a proposal from a cable network for a reality series: *Storm Man.*

Jack sat in his recliner, the leather worn smooth where his hands rested on the arms. He wasn't looking at the mail now. Instead, a glossy magazine lay open in his lap, the paper cool under his fingers. His own face stared back at him from the page, a candid shot taken outside the Universal Studios "Twister" attraction, his smile caught halfway, the wind from the overhead fans ruffling his hair.

The article headline read:
"The Man Who Put Tornadoes on the Map."

Jack's eyes scanned the first paragraph for the fifth time, but the words swam, refusing to settle. The journalist had gotten the facts mostly right, his background, his work in tornado modeling, his "partnership" with the theme park but the tone felt off. It was slick. Showy. It made him sound like some kind of science celebrity, a man who'd sought the spotlight rather than one who'd been dragged into it.

From the kitchen, the faint clink of porcelain broke the silence. Darlie was rinsing dishes they hadn't eaten much from. Supper had been a quiet affair; neither of them had seemed eager to fill the air. The smell of her chamomile tea still lingered, though she hadn't taken more than two sips before setting the cup aside.

Jack shifted in his chair, the magazine bending slightly in his hands. He thought about the years before all this, before the letters, the camera flashes, the Hollywood executives with their fast talk and faster contracts. Back then, his name meant something in the meteorology community and almost nothing outside of it, and that had suited him fine.

Now, here he was, part scientist, part public figure.

And though he wouldn't yet admit it out loud, that balance was wearing him thin.

***

The phone rang again.

It had been doing that more and more lately — sometimes three or four times in an evening, even after supper, even when the sun was sliding low and most of Kansas was winding down. The ring used to be a neutral sound, just another part of the house's background noise, like the hum of the refrigerator or the creak of the porch steps. Now it carried a weight, a slight jolt of expectation each time it pierced the air.

Jack didn't move to answer it.

From his recliner, he let it ring until the machine picked up, the tinny click followed by his own recorded voice. There was a time when that voice had felt like it belonged to him. Lately, it sounded like someone else's.

In the corner of the room, Darlie looked up from her knitting. She didn't say anything, but her eyes lingered on him a moment longer than usual, watching the way his shoulders stayed tight even after the ringing stopped.

He sighed, pushing a hand through his hair, and let his gaze fall to the magazine article still open on his lap. His own face smiled back at him but it wasn't the kind of smile he remembered giving. It was the sort of smile you learned to hold during photo ops, polite and faintly guarded.

Recognition had crept into his life in ways he hadn't anticipated. At the grocery store last week, a woman in the produce aisle had stopped him mid-reach for a bag of apples. She'd tilted her head, squinting, and then snapped her fingers like she'd just remembered a long-forgotten name.

"You're that tornado guy!" she'd said, loud enough for half the store to hear.

He'd nodded, given her the small, practiced smile, and listened as she recounted how her nephew had visited the "Twister" at Universal. She'd never mentioned his research, only how real the special effects had looked.

At the post office, the clerk had slipped his package across the counter with a grin. "Hey, saw you on the news last night. You're getting famous, Jack."

And at the university… the change there was the most disorienting.

Some colleagues, the ones he'd spent decades trading research papers and field notes with, now seemed to measure their conversations with him in soundbites. Meetings that had once been about shared curiosity now came peppered with lines like, "This'll play great in the press" or "We could pitch that for next year's public outreach program."

It wasn't that he minded public outreach, he'd always believed in educating the public. But there was a difference between engaging people and becoming a product. Sometimes he wondered if they were talking to him as a peer anymore, or as a brand they could leverage.

The house was quiet again, save for the soft, rhythmic click of Darlie's knitting needles. She'd switched to smaller needles lately; he knew that sound as well as he knew the sound of rain on the roof.

"You've been on the road more than home lately," she said without looking up.

He glanced at her, then away again. "It's part of the deal, I guess."

"Is it worth the deal?"

The question landed in the space between them, soft but heavy.

He tried to laugh it off, but the sound came out thin. "We've had some nice dinners in nice cities. You've met a few movie people."

"I'm not asking about dinners, Jack." She finally looked up, her eyes steady. "I'm asking if *you* think it's worth it."

He didn't answer right away. His gaze drifted to the stack of mail again, the invitations, the contracts, the personal notes from people he'd never met. Once, his work had been about the sky above Kansas and the unpredictable forces that moved through it. Now it felt like it was about schedules, press calls, and flights that all blurred together.

He leaned back in the recliner, rubbing the bridge of his nose. "It's… complicated."

Her needles paused mid-click. "It's not a trick question."

"I know."

For a moment, neither of them spoke. The distant hum of the refrigerator filled the gap. Outside, a semi-truck rumbled down the highway, the sound fading into the prairie night.

"It's not like I planned for this," he said finally. "One day I'm in the lab, the next I'm in Florida watching a tornado I didn't even build steal the show."

"But it's still your work," she said gently.

"Some days I'm not sure it is anymore." He tapped the magazine page with one finger. "This version of me — the one people clap for, the one they put on TV — that's not the same guy who stayed up all night running simulations in the lab."

"You can be both," Darlie said, her voice quiet but firm.

"Maybe." He hesitated. "But the first one, the scientist, he didn't have to wonder who he was doing it for. The second one? I'm starting to think about that too much."

Her knitting resumed, the soft click-click filling the air again. "Just don't forget which one came first."

Jack nodded slowly, but the knot in his chest didn't loosen.

***

The truth was, recognition wasn't a single event. It was a series of small shifts, like the air before a storm, a gradual thickening, a change in pressure. He'd thought he could adapt to it, but adaptation came with its own cost. Somewhere in the middle of all the interviews, the smiling photos, the polite conversations with strangers in the frozen food aisle, he'd started to feel like a shadow of himself was doing the public work while the real him was waiting in the wings, quietly keeping score.

***

Jack had always thought of recognition as a distant, almost mythical thing, something that happened to politicians, movie stars, and the occasional Nobel laureate. He'd never considered that his own name might end up on the lips of strangers in airports, or that his inbox might swell with invitations to conferences that had nothing to do with advancing science and everything to do with drawing crowds.

At first, it was flattering.

There was a strange novelty in being ushered to the front of a line, in being introduced on stage with applause, in having people lean in with genuine curiosity when he talked about vortex dynamics. But novelty, he was learning, has a short shelf life.

Now, weeks into this new chapter, it was something else entirely exhausting.

His days no longer belonged to him. They belonged to whoever had managed to wedge their meeting, call, or interview into his schedule. His phone calendar, once a quiet list of lab hours, lectures, and a scattering of faculty meetings, was now a color-coded minefield. Red blocks for travel. Blue blocks for "public appearances." Yellow blocks for interviews with names he didn't recognize but was told were "important for brand presence."

Brand presence. The first time he'd heard that phrase in a meeting, he'd looked around the table, waiting for someone to smirk or correct the speaker. No one had.

Even his research, the core of who he was, had become collateral damage in the war for his attention.

The lab felt different now. It was harder to slip into that deep focus he used to love, where hours would pass unnoticed as he tweaked models and adjusted variables. Instead, every forty-five minutes or so, someone would knock on his office door to remind him about the next call, or a publicist would email "just to check in" about an upcoming event.

And then there was the constant shadow of the Universal Studios partnership.

It was everywhere. In interviews, journalists inevitably circled back to it, as if his entire career could be summed up by a Twister attraction in Orlando. At conferences, introductions now included it as a kind of badge: *"Ladies and gentlemen, the man behind the tornado at Universal Studios!"* — as though his contribution to meteorology was measured in ticket sales and popcorn revenue.

There was a part of him, the part that still thrilled at a clean simulation run or a well-plotted damage probability curve that found this maddening. Tornadoes were not a toy. They were unpredictable, destructive, capable of reshaping entire communities in minutes. He had spent decades trying to understand them so that people could survive them.

And yet… the spectacle had eclipsed the science.

He found himself thinking about that more and more: *Am I serving the science… or the spectacle?*

Some days, the question gnawed at him from the moment he woke. He would sit at the kitchen table, coffee cooling beside him, scanning the day's itinerary and wondering when his work had become a performance.

Science had always been his anchor. It was quiet, methodical, and immune to the whims of public opinion. Equations didn't care if they were marketable. Data didn't need a press release. But now, everything he did seemed to be filtered through a lens of presentation. Even technical discussions with sponsors veered toward questions like, *"How will this look in the press materials?"*

That morning, in the lab, he'd been interrupted three times before lunch. The last time, a young staffer had poked her head in to remind him of a "quick media hit" scheduled for 1:15. She'd used the word "hit" like it was a marketing victory. Jack had stared at her for a moment before nodding, but inside, he'd wanted to tell her that every fifteen minutes spent in front of a camera was fifteen minutes not spent improving the accuracy of the next storm model.

It wasn't just about time; it was about momentum. Science thrived on continuity, on long, uninterrupted stretches where your brain could settle into the work. These days, his brain felt like it was constantly being yanked out of gear.

And yet... he wasn't sure he could walk away from it.

That was the most unsettling part.

There was a strange intoxication to the attention. People *listened* to him now. When he gave lectures, the rooms were packed. When he proposed funding for a new project, it didn't take months of pleading — a few phone calls and it was approved. The visibility gave him reach, resources, influence. And he couldn't deny that, in the right moments, it could do good.

But at what cost?

In quieter moments, he caught himself calculating the trade-offs. How many hours of raw research had been lost this month? How many potential breakthroughs had slipped away while he was on a plane or smiling in front of a backdrop?

Darlie had noticed the change in him.

"You used to come home talking about experiments," she said one evening over dinner. "Now it's always about the next trip, or who you met, or something the press got wrong about you."

He'd bristled, though he knew she was right. "That's just the way things are right now," he'd said, but even to his own ears it sounded like an excuse.

Her look had been steady, unblinking. "Is it the way you *want* them to be?"

The question had hung between them for the rest of the meal.

That night, after Jack had gone to bed early, Darlie lingered in the quiet. The house felt too big sometimes, even with him in it, because his mind was elsewhere. She opened her old journal, the one with a cracked leather spine, and began to write in her looping, patient hand.

Some days, I hardly recognize him. The man who used to race in from the lab, hair wild from the wind, eager to explain his latest finding, now comes home tired, distracted. He smiles, but it doesn't reach his eyes. The children see it. I see it. Even he must see it, though he won't admit it. I try to remind myself this is a season — that storms pass, that fame too will pass. But what if it leaves behind damage we can't repair? I love him, and I know his work matters. But I miss the man who belonged more to the sky than to the cameras. I miss my Jack.

She closed the journal softly and set it aside, extinguishing the lamp before slipping into bed beside him. He stirred but didn't wake. Darlie lay there in the dark, staring at the ceiling, wondering whether the storm they were in now could be forecast, or if it would have to be endured.

Jack, meanwhile, found himself restless in the nights that followed. He thought about the boy he once was, standing in a Kansas wheat field, eyes wide with wonder at the first funnel cloud he'd ever seen. That boy had chased storms for answers, not applause. Somewhere along the way, the chase had changed.

"I never asked for all this," he said quietly one evening.

"I know you didn't," Darlie answered. "But it found you anyway. And you let it in."

Her words weren't an accusation, just a fact. And facts, he knew, were harder to argue with than opinions.

The silence that followed pressed heavy, broken only by the ticking of the mantle clock. Finally, Jack whispered: "I don't want to lose us, Darlie. I don't. But I don't know how to stop this train now that it's moving."

Darlie reached for his hand. "Maybe the real question isn't whether you can stop it. Maybe the question is whether you can survive it — and whether we can, too."

Together they stood at the window, looking out at the restless Kansas night. The wheat bent and shifted under an invisible hand, whispering of storms yet to come.

"That's where it started," Jack murmured, his voice rough. "Out there. Just me and the sky. No cameras. No contracts. Just questions I wanted answers to."

"Maybe that's where you'll find your answer again," Darlie said. "Not in boardrooms or interviews. Out there."

For a long moment, neither spoke. The darkness beyond the glass was endless, but somewhere inside it, thunder was rolling.

Jack squeezed Darlie's hand. "I'll try."

"That's all I'm asking."

Later, long after Darlie had fallen asleep, Jack remained at the window. The wind sighed through the fields. Somewhere far off, a storm was building — not in the clouds, but in his own life. And like every storm before, he knew it would demand something of him.

Later that night, lying in bed, he'd stared at the ceiling and replayed the day in his mind, the handshakes, the photographs, the polished talking points. Somewhere in the middle of it, he'd remembered a field trip from years ago, standing in the middle of a Kansas wheat field with a graduate student, both of them watching a supercell churn on the horizon. That was the work he loved: direct, unfiltered, grounded in the raw reality of the storm.

Now he was watching his storms under fluorescent lights in a theme park.

It wasn't that the attraction was bad — in fact, he'd been quietly impressed with its engineering. But it had become a symbol for the shift in his life: controlled, packaged, sold in thirty-minute intervals.

The thought came again, sharper this time: *Am I serving the science… or the spectacle?*

He didn't have an answer.

What he did know was that the question wouldn't leave him alone. It followed him into meetings, whispered at the edges of conversations, pressed against him in the stillness of the early morning before the phone started ringing again.

It was the kind of question, he realized, that could define the next chapter of his life — or end it.

***

The living room was quiet except for the ticking of the old mantle clock and the faint rustle of paper as Darlie sorted through the day's unopened mail. Most of it was addressed to Jack: invitations, requests for interviews, letters from fans. She stacked them neatly on the coffee table, her lips pressed in a thin line.

Jack sat opposite her, magazine still open on his lap though his eyes hadn't touched the words in half an hour. His gaze wandered to the muted television across the room, where a rerun of the local weather flickered. A meteorologist traced a cold front sweeping across the plains, his voice tinny and unimportant in the silence of their home.

Finally, Darlie broke it. Her tone was soft, but the softness carried weight.

"Jack," she said, setting the stack of envelopes aside. "When does it stop?"

The question hung in the air like a thunderhead forming on a hot afternoon — heavy, inevitable, sparking with tension.

Jack blinked, as if pulled out of a trance. "What do you mean?"

"You know what I mean." She leaned forward, folding her hands in her lap. "The travel. The interviews. The cameras following us at the grocery store. The constant phone calls. When does it stop?"

Jack opened his mouth, then shut it again. He shifted in his chair, suddenly aware of the ache in his shoulders, the tightness in his jaw. "It's... it's part of the deal, I guess," he muttered.

Darlie tilted her head. "Is it worth the deal?"

The words cut deeper than he expected. He ran a hand across his face, buying time. His mind flickered through images: conference halls filled with applause, newspaper headlines calling him *the Tornado Whisperer*, executives at Universal smiling as they shook his hand. Then other images intruded — Darlie sitting alone at the kitchen table, the grandchildren asking why Grandpa wasn't home again, the empty quiet of his office when he returned too late to get any real work done.

He sighed, leaning back. "I don't know," he admitted. "I honestly don't know."

Darlie studied him for a long moment, her eyes searching his. "You always used to know. About storms, about teaching, about what mattered. Now..." She shook her head. "Now it's like you're caught in someone else's whirlwind."

The irony wasn't lost on him. He almost smiled at the metaphor, but the weight of it pressed too hard. "It's not that simple," he said, his voice low. "The funding we've gotten since the Universal deal — it's allowed us to expand the lab, buy new equipment, hire more staff. We're making progress we couldn't have dreamed of five years ago."

Darlie nodded slowly. "I know that. I see the difference it makes. But at what cost, Jack? You're gone more than you're here. When you are home, you're exhausted, your mind still somewhere else. We used to have evenings together. We used to take walks after supper. Now it's like I'm living with a ghost who occasionally sits in that chair."

Her words stung because they were true. He tried to summon a rebuttal, but all he found was silence.

She went on, her tone still gentle but firm. "You've given your life to storms. I accepted that a long time ago. But now it's not just storms. It's... fame. It's appearances. It's playing a role that doesn't even look like you anymore. And I'm worried, Jack. I'm worried we're losing something we can't get back."

Jack stared at his hands, rough and weathered, folded in his lap. He thought about the boy he once was, standing in a Kansas wheat field, eyes wide with wonder at the first funnel cloud he'd ever seen. That boy had chased storms for answers, not applause. Somewhere along the way, the chase had changed.

"I never asked for all this," he said quietly.

"I know you didn't," Darlie said. "But it found you anyway. And you let it in."

Her words weren't an accusation, just a fact. And facts, he knew, were harder to argue with than opinions.

He looked up, meeting her gaze. "What do you want me to do? Walk away? Turn down every request? Cut ties with Universal? That's not realistic, Darlie. There are contracts. Obligations. People depending on me."

"And what about me?" she asked softly. "What about your family? Don't we count in that equation?"

The silence after her question was long and heavy. Jack shifted, restless, as though the recliner had suddenly become too small for him. He wanted to say of course they counted, that they always had. But he also knew that in practice, the balance had shifted. Science and family had always coexisted uneasily, but now fame had tipped the scales even further.

Finally, he spoke, his voice raw. "I don't want to lose us, Darlie. I don't. But I don't know how to stop this train now that it's moving. Every time I think about saying no, I hear another voice telling me it's too important, that too much is at stake."

Darlie leaned back, sighing. "Maybe the real question isn't whether you can stop it. Maybe the question is whether you can survive it — and whether we can, too."

Jack felt the truth of that settle into his chest. He thought about his father, a farmer who had measured success in acres planted and harvests brought in, who had never cared whether anyone outside their county knew his name. He wondered what his father would think of all this — of a son who studied storms, who ended up on billboards and in magazines because of it. Pride? Confusion? Maybe both.

The clock ticked on, each second a reminder that time was moving whether he had answers or not.

Darlie rose and crossed to the window, pulling the curtain aside. Outside, the Kansas night stretched wide and endless. The wheat fields swayed under the touch of a restless breeze. The sound was soft but insistent, a whisper of the power that always lurked just beyond the horizon.

Jack joined her, standing close enough to feel the warmth of her shoulder against his. Together they looked out into the dark, listening. The wind carried with it the scent of earth, the promise of storms not yet formed.

"That's where it started," Jack murmured, more to himself than to her. "Out there. Just me and the sky. No cameras. No contracts. Just questions I wanted answers to."

Darlie turned her head, watching him. "And maybe that's where you'll find your answer again. Not in boardrooms or interviews. Out there."

He swallowed hard, his throat tight. "I don't know if I can go back to that."

"Maybe you don't need to go back," she said gently. "Maybe you just need to remember."

The words struck something deep in him — a reminder that storms, like life, were cycles. They formed, they raged, they passed. What lingered was how you weathered them.

For a long time, they stood in silence, side by side at the window. Jack felt the weight of everything pressing down — the fame, the obligations, the contracts, the family he loved. He didn't have an answer to Darlie's question. He didn't know when, or if, it would stop.

But in the whisper of the wheat and the restless sigh of the Kansas wind, he felt the beginning of something — not resolution, but awareness. A storm was building, and this time it wasn't in the clouds.

He laid a hand gently over Darlie's, squeezing it. "I'll try," he said simply.

She squeezed back. "That's all I'm asking."

Later that night, long after Darlie had gone to bed, Jack remained at the window, staring out into the dark. The fields shifted and bent with the wind, endless and patient. Somewhere far off, a faint roll of thunder echoed, distant but inevitable.

Jack closed his eyes and listened, the sound carrying him back through years and storms, back to the boy who had once felt nothing but wonder. He wasn't sure if he could ever return to that boy's purity of purpose. But as the thunder rolled again, he knew one thing for certain: the storms would always be there, waiting.

And maybe, just maybe, the answers would be too.

20

FAMILY TIES

The Kansas wind was restless but kind that Saturday afternoon, bending the tall grass at the edges of Jack's backyard into waves that shimmered in the light. The sun sat high and golden, softened by passing clouds that rolled like slow ships across the sky.

On the picnic table beneath the old elm tree, Darlie had laid out a spread that smelled like every summer afternoon Jack had ever cherished: thick ham sandwiches on fresh bread, pitchers of lemonade sweating in the heat, a bowl of potato salad that glistened under its dusting of paprika, and, waiting like the crown jewel, Darlie's famous lattice-topped pie, blackberry this time, the crust golden and splashed with sugar.

The children and grandchildren had spilled across the yard, laughter rising and falling like birdcalls. His son, Gavin, stood barefoot in the grass, tossing a bright yellow Frisbee toward Jack's oldest grandson, Jason, whose clumsy catch sent him tumbling backward in mock dramatics. The younger ones shrieked with delight, clapping their hands and demanding their turn.

Jack sat back in a lawn chair at the edge of it all, a glass of lemonade cools in his hand. The ice cubes clicked against the rim as he swirled it absently, watching the game unfold. The breeze carried the mingled scents of fresh-mown grass and Darlie's pie cooling on the table. Somewhere nearby, cicadas droned, their chorus steady and ancient.

It had been too long since the house had sounded like this full of chatter, footsteps, the unself-conscious laughter of children. For months, his days had been ruled by schedules, travel, and the sterile hum of hotel lobbies. But now, for this moment, he was home. He could feel it in his bones, in the way the chair sagged comfortably under his weight, in the way Darlie's hand brushed his shoulder when she passed to refill a plate.

"Your aim hasn't improved," Jack called out as Gavin launched another crooked throw.

Gavin shot him a grin over his shoulder. "Guess I inherited your arm, Dad."

That earned a chorus of laughter from the younger ones. Jack smiled, shaking his head, but inside he felt the warmth of something steadier than amusement, pride.

Darlie lowered herself into the chair beside him, smoothing her skirt. She watched the scene unfold with the quiet satisfaction of someone who had orchestrated many such afternoons over the years. "They're good together," she said softly.

Jack nodded. "Better than I ever was with my cousins. All we did was fight over who got the last slice of pie."

Darlie chuckled, her eyes sparkling. "Don't think you've grown out of that."

Their banter was easy, familiar, but beneath it Jack felt a tug — a reminder of how fleeting these moments were. He leaned forward, elbows resting on his knees, watching as his granddaughter Leda scooped up the Frisbee with both hands and, with great ceremony, attempted to throw it. It fluttered like a wounded bird and landed a few feet away, but she squealed with delight all the same.

The sound burrowed into Jack's chest, settling somewhere tender. He thought about how different her childhood was from his own, hers threaded with laughter and safety, his shadowed by storms and the unrelenting pull of unanswered questions. And yet, here they were, connected by invisible threads of legacy.

"Grandpa, catch!" Jason shouted suddenly.

Jack blinked, startled out of his thoughts, as the yellow Frisbee sailed toward him in an uneven arc. He set his lemonade down and raised both hands. The disc slapped against his palms with surprising force, wobbling but held. The children cheered, and Jack laughed, a real laugh, unguarded and deep, shaking loose some of the tension that had built up in him these past months.

He stood, feeling the creak in his knees but ignoring it, and tossed the Frisbee back toward Jason. His throw curved wide, sending the boy running to catch it. Another cheer erupted.

For several minutes, Jack let himself be pulled into the game. He passed the disc, bent to let a wayward throw sail overhead, even jogged a few steps across the lawn to scoop it off the ground. His laughter mingled with theirs, and for once he wasn't thinking about interviews or storm models or the next trip on his calendar. He was just Jack, father, grandfather, a man in his yard on a Saturday.

Eventually, breathless and smiling, he returned to his chair. Darlie handed him his glass again, her eyes crinkling at the corners.

"You look ten years younger," she teased.

"Feels like twenty," he admitted, taking a long sip of lemonade.

The children crowded around the table soon after, appealing for food. Darlie moved gracefully among them, serving sandwiches and pie, cutting slices with practiced precision. Jack stayed seated, watching the way they devoured everything with the gusto only children could summon. Crumbs scattered across the table, laughter spilled in waves, and the pie disappeared almost faster than Darlie could cut it.

Jack felt something shift inside him then, not a dramatic epiphany, but a steady recognition. This was legacy, too. Not in journals or rides or interviews, but in the faces of those who bore his name, in the laughter echoing across his yard.

His youngest granddaughter, Leda, climbed onto his lap with sticky fingers and berry-stained lips. "Grandpa, can we have another picnic tomorrow?" she asked, her voice small but earnest.

Jack chuckled, pressing a kiss to the top of her head. "We'll see, sweetheart. We'll see."

She leaned against him, already distracted by the sound of her cousins arguing over the last cookie. Jack held her close, the weight of her small body grounding him. He thought again of the storms, of the long nights in labs, of the weight of fame pressing on him like a storm front. But here, in this moment, he felt none of it.

Darlie caught his eye across the table. Her expression was calm, knowing. She didn't need to say it aloud she could see it too. The children didn't care about theme parks or research grants. They cared about this: afternoons filled with sunshine, pie, and the presence of their grandfather.

Jack reached for his glass again, raising it slightly in a quiet toast to Darlie. She raised hers back, the corners of her mouth turning up.

The breeze swept through the yard again, rattling the leaves of the elm, carrying with it the scent of warm earth and summer. Jack breathed it in, letting it fill him, letting it remind him of what mattered most.

***

The yellow Frisbee wobbled through the air, a clumsy arc thrown by one of the younger boys, and for a heartbeat Jack thought it was going to nosedive into the grass. But something stirred in him, a flicker of the boy who once ran barefoot through Kansas fields, chasing storms instead of discs. He pushed himself up from the chair, knees protesting, and took off at a slow jog across the yard.

"Grandpa's running!" Jason shouted in mock amazement.

The children squealed, their voices bright against the drone of cicadas. Darlie, standing near the table with her hands still dusted in flour from the pie crust, paused to watch, her smile tugging wider as Jack closed the distance.

At the last second, he stretched his arms and with surprising precision caught the Frisbee before it could kiss the dirt. The children erupted in cheers, clapping and bouncing with glee.

"Nice save, Grandpa!" Leda cried, spinning in a circle as though she had witnessed a miracle.

Jack laughed, really laughed, the sound bursting out of him unguarded, shaking loose the weariness that had weighed him down these past few months. It was not the polite chuckle he gave to journalists or the reserved smile he offered colleagues. This was different. This was the laugh of a man who, for a moment, had forgotten about deadlines, obligations, and fame.

He held the disc aloft like a trophy, then whipped it back toward Jason with as much force as he dared. It sailed farther than anyone expected. Jason sprinted after it, his little brother on his heels, both of them colliding in the grass as they tumbled after the disc.

The grandchildren roared with laughter, and Jack joined them, bending forward with his hands on his knees, his chest heaving with both exertion and joy. Darlie shook her head fondly, calling out, "Don't go breaking anything out there, old man!"

Jack waved her off, still grinning. For the next half hour, he let himself remain in the game. He stumbled, chased, even managed a few decent throws, each one rewarded with whoops of approval from the children. By the time the sun dipped lower, painting the sky in streaks of orange and violet, Jack was flushed and breathing hard, but lighter than he'd felt in years.

Finally, Darlie corralled everyone back toward the picnic table. "Alright, everyone, pie before it disappears," she announced.

The children needed no convincing. They crowded around, jostling for spots, their cheeks pink from play and their hands eager. Darlie cut generous slices of her blackberry pie, the crust crackling as the knife slid through. Plates were passed, forks distributed, lemonade glasses topped off.

Jack sank back into his chair, the cool wood pressing against his back, and accepted a slice. The pie was warm, tart, and sweet all at once, the taste carrying him back through decades of summer afternoons much like this one.

It was Leda who broke the calm first, her fork paused midair. "Grandpa, is it true you were on TV?"

The question hung for a moment, and all eyes turned to Jack. His son Gavin grinned. "They've been talking about it since we got here. They saw a clip about you and the tornado attraction."

Jack chuckled softly, setting down his fork. "So, the news made it all the way here, did it?"

"Of course it did!" Jason piped up, his mouth still full of pie. "My friends at school said they saw you standing next to a real tornado in California. Was it scary?"

Jack's lips twitched at the exaggeration. "It wasn't a real tornado, Jason. It was a simulation. An artificial tornado at a theme park."

"But it looked real," Leda pressed. "Mom showed us the commercial. There was thunder and everything!"

The table buzzed with excitement. Questions tumbled out of the children in overlapping waves, Did he make the tornado himself? How did they keep people safe? Could anyone touch it? Was it fun?

Jack raised his hands in surrender. "One at a time, one at a time." He leaned back, letting their enthusiasm wash over him. There was no skepticism in their voices, no debate over commercialization or fidelity to science. To them, the tornado wasn't a dilution of decades of work, it was magic. And that realization softened something inside him.

"It was... impressive," Jack admitted, choosing his words carefully. "They built it using the model

I worked on years ago. So, in a way, yes, I helped create it."

The children gasped as though he had just confessed to inventing a rocket ship. Leda's eyes widened. "So, you're, like… famous?"

Jack hesitated. "Well, I don't know about that."

"Yes, you are!" Jason declared, pounding the table with a sticky fist. "Grandpa makes tornadoes for the whole world to see!"

The adults laughed at the boy's conviction, but Jack caught Darlie's gaze across the table. Her smile was warm, but her eyes held something deeper, an acknowledgment of the truth behind the children's innocent excitement.

That was when Kevin., his youngest son, leaned back with a faint smirk. "Come on, Dad. Let's be honest, most people know you now because of that theme park tornado. Not your papers, not your charts. The tornado attraction."

The air shifted, just slightly. Jack set his fork down, his eyes steady on his son. "The tornado attraction exists because of my development of artificial tornadoes. Because of decades of work you never saw, work that has saved lives. If

Hollywood wants to package it in flashing lights, that doesn't erase the truth underneath."

Gavin shrugged. "I'm just saying, the world remembers the spectacle, not the science."

Jack's voice was calm, but there was steel in it. "Maybe so. But the spectacle wouldn't exist without the science. And one day, when the storms come, not the pretend ones, the real ones, people will be grateful for warnings, not rides."

A silence followed, broken only when Leda piped up again, her voice small but firm: "I think Grandpa's storms are better than Orlandos."

The tension eased, laughter rising again around the table. But the moment lingered with Jack, reminding him that legacy was never simple, it was always contested, always refracted through the eyes of different generations.

Jack *was* famous now, in ways that still felt strange to him. And here was the proof: his own grandchildren speaking of him not just as their grandfather, but as a figure others admired.

He took another bite of pie, chewing slowly. The tartness of the berries lingered, grounding him. "What matters," he said finally, "isn't being famous. It's that the tornado attraction might help people learn about storms, what they look like, what they sound like. Maybe it'll even make some folks take warnings more seriously."

"Like a science lesson?" Leda asked.

"Exactly," Jack said.

The children nodded solemnly, digesting this as though it were as important as the pie itself. Gavin, sitting back with his arms crossed, gave his father a thoughtful look. "You know, Dad, I think they're proud of you in their own way. They may not understand the science, but they see the excitement. They see you."

Jack felt his throat tighten, unexpected emotion rising. He looked around the table — at the grandchildren smeared with berry stains, at his grown children smiling, at Darlie pouring more lemonade. For the first time in a long while, he felt the threads of two worlds knot together: the public image, the scientist, and this private circle of family.

It was Jason who broke the quiet, lifting his fork like a sword. "When I grow up, I'm gonna make tornadoes too!"

The table erupted in laughter again, but Jack didn't laugh this time. He only watched the boy, a smile tugging faintly at his lips, and wondered what seeds were being planted at this very moment.

***

After the pie plates were scraped clean and the Frisbee lay abandoned in the grass, the family began to scatter in the easy rhythm of a summer afternoon. Some of the grandchildren wandered off to chase fireflies starting to blink in the dusk, while others sprawled across the porch steps, their chatter drifting with the breeze.

Jack lingered by the picnic table, his coffee cooling in his hand, watching them. The laughter of his grandchildren carried something familiar, the same wide-eyed energy he had once felt chasing storms across Kansas fields. It stirred a memory, sharp and insistent, and before long he found himself rising from his chair.

"Come on," he said suddenly, his voice cutting through the hum of cicadas. "I want to show you all something."

The children perked up instantly. Kara, the eldest granddaughter, tilted her head curiously. "What is it, Grandpa?"

"You'll see," Jack said with a conspiratorial smile. He waved a hand toward the garage.

They followed him in a small parade. Leda leading the way, Jason and his younger brother, Trey, darting ahead like scouts, and the others trailing behind with Darlie shaking her head fondly. The garage was dim, smelling faintly of motor oil and cardboard, its corners cluttered with decades of odds and ends. Jack rummaged through a tall metal cabinet, the kind that rattled when you pulled the drawers. After a moment, he withdrew a long, rolled-up tube, yellowed at the edges.

"What's that?" Jason asked, bouncing on his toes.

Jack carried it carefully to the workbench, unrolling it with deliberate care. The paper crackled as it spread across the surface, revealing a hand-drawn weather chart, the ink faded but still legible. Contours of pressure systems sprawled across it, dotted with notations in Jack's meticulous handwriting.

"This," Jack said, smoothing the edges with his palms, "is one of the first storm charts I ever made. I drew it in graduate school, long before computers did all the plotting for us."

The children gathered around, their faces glowing in the faint light of a single bulb overhead. Leda leaned in closest, tracing the lines with her eyes.

"It looks like a treasure map," she whispered.

"In a way, it is," Jack said. "A map of the sky. Each line here tells us how the air was moving that day — warm fronts, cold fronts, low-pressure systems. Put them together, and they can tell you if a storm is coming."

Jason's brow furrowed. "So... this helped you see tornadoes before they came?"

Jack nodded slowly. "Not exactly see, but predict. Charts like these were the start of learning how to give people warnings - warnings that meant they had minutes to find shelter instead of seconds."

The children's eyes widened. Darlie, standing in the doorway with her arms folded, watched silently, her expression soft.

Leda looked up at him, her voice hushed. "So, you save people's lives?"

The words landed heavier than he expected. He had heard accolades from colleagues, seen awards hung on his office wall, endured journalists reducing his decades of work into neat sound bites. But none of it had pierced him like this simple question from his granddaughter.

He cleared his throat. "Sometimes," he said carefully. "I like to think the work I've done has given people a better chance. If families make it to their shelters in time, if they choose the northeast instead of the southwest location, if children get home safe from school before a storm — then yes, maybe it has saved lives."

There was a silence in the garage, broken only by the distant trill of a cricket. Leda's gaze didn't waver. For the first time, Jack saw in her eyes not just childish curiosity, but something deeper, a dawning understanding of what it meant to dedicate one's life to something bigger than oneself.

Jason piped up again, less solemn but no less earnest. "Grandpa, if you know when storms are coming, can you make them stop?"

Jack chuckled, shaking his head. "No, buddy. No one can stop a storm. Nature's too powerful for that. But we can learn from it. We can try to outsmart it, give people enough time to get out of its way."

The boy frowned, unsatisfied, but Leda nodded gravely as though she understood.

Jack's eldest son, Gavin, stepped closer, folding his arms as he studied the chart. "I remember you drawing these when we were kids," he said quietly. "I never understood half of it. But I remember the way you'd stay up all night, hunched over a desk, chasing lines and numbers. I thought you were crazy back then. Now… I guess I get it."

Jack looked at his son, a grown man now, with a family of his own and felt a pang of something bittersweet. Legacy wasn't just about what you left to the world; it was about what carried through your blood, what your children witnessed and remembered even when they didn't understand.

He tapped the chart gently. "This kind of work isn't glamorous. It's slow. It's messy. Half the time, it feels like guesswork. But every improvement, every model, every warning system builds on the last. That's how science works, step by step, until one day, those steps make a difference."

Leda tilted her head. "And your steps made a difference?"

Jack met her eyes. "I hope so."

The children fell quiet, the weight of the moment settling over them. For once, they weren't giggling or bouncing on their feet. They were listening, really listening. And Jack realized, with a sudden swell of emotion, that this was the audience he cared about most. Not tourists in a theme park, not executives in suits, not reporters holding microphones. These children, his family were the ones who would carry his story forward in ways no book or ride ever could.

He rolled the chart back up carefully and handed it to Leda. "Keep this safe for me," he said. "It's part of where we came from."

Her hands trembled slightly as she took it, cradling it as though it were indeed a treasure map.

Later, back at the picnic table, the conversation flowed more easily. The grandchildren showered him with questions about the biggest storm he'd ever seen, the scariest, the most beautiful. Jack answered each with honesty, weaving stories of his fieldwork, his mistakes, his triumphs. He spoke not as a celebrity or a scientist, but as a grandfather sharing stories by the firelight.

At one point, Darlie caught his eye and mouthed the words, *Look at them.*

He did. And what he saw stunned him: children leaning forward, hanging on his every word; his adult children nodding with pride; even Darlie, after all these years, gazing at him with the same mixture of admiration and love.

For decades, Jack had measured his worth in data, publications, models, and warnings. Tonight, for the first time, he understood legacy differently. It wasn't ink on paper or simulations in a lab. It was this, the widening of a child's eyes, the awe in a granddaughter's voice, the pride of a son remembering his father's devotion.

As the stars pricked the Kansas sky, Jack leaned back in his chair, listening to his family's laughter mingle with the distant hum of the night. A realization settled into him, gentle but firm: his life's work wasn't confined to academia or even to the broader public. It lived here, too, in this backyard, carried forward by those who would remember him not only as a scientist, but as a man who had tried — in his own way — to wrestle meaning from the storms.

And maybe, just maybe, that was the truest kind of legacy.

***

The evening had begun its gentle descent into night by the time the laughter and shouts began to taper off. The Frisbee lay forgotten under the picnic table. Empty plates, stained napkins, and half-drunk cups of lemonade stood as the day's artifacts. Fireflies blinked lazily in the yard, their quiet rhythms replacing the excited energy of the children who had finally begun to tire.

Darlie stood at the porch rail, her apron dusted faintly with flour from earlier, hands folded lightly in front of her. The yard before her was alive with motion, grandchildren darting, chasing one another in uneven circles, while her own children corralled them with practiced patience. But her eyes were not on the chaos. They were on Jack.

He was seated in his chair near the table, leaning back with his coffee cup balanced against his palm. His posture had softened in a way she rarely saw anymore, his shoulders unknotted, his face unguarded. Even across the yard, Darlie could see the faint flush of his cheeks from running earlier, and the trace of a smile still tugged at the corner of his mouth as he watched the children wrestle in the grass.

Darlie's heart swelled. Fame had brought with it a shadow, a distance in Jack's eyes she sometimes struggled to reach through. He had always been a man devoted to storms, but in recent years, the obligations tied to that devotion had grown heavier, reshaping him into someone she worried might forget who he was beneath the accolades. Yet here, under the glow of fireflies and the fading sun, she saw him as he once was: the man who used to return home from fieldwork covered in dust and rain, laughing at himself, alive with stories of the sky.

The sound of her daughter, Kathy's voice, carried over, breaking into her thoughts. "Dad, we should probably get these kids packed up before they collapse on the drive home."

Groans of protest rose from the grandchildren, but coats were fetched, shoes wrestled on, and the slow process of leave-taking began. The yard filled with the bittersweet rhythm of goodbyes, hugs exchanged, promises of another visit soon, children clinging for one more round of Frisbee that wouldn't come.

Leda, clutching the rolled-up weather chart Jack had entrusted to her earlier, hugged him tightly before climbing into the car. "I'll keep it safe, Grandpa. I promise."

Jack chuckled, resting a hand on her shoulder. "I know you will."

One by one, the vehicles rumbled down the gravel drive, their headlights cutting through the twilight before fading into the distance. The cicadas grew louder in their absence, filling the silence left behind.

And then it was just the two of them.

Jack stood in the yard, his gaze following the last set of taillights until they disappeared beyond the bend. His hands slid into his pockets as he exhaled, a long, thoughtful breath. Darlie stepped down from the porch to join him, her sandals crunching softly in the gravel.

For a while, neither spoke. The yard felt impossibly still compared to the clamor of moments before. The wheat fields in the distance rustled faintly in the evening breeze, a sound like whispered secrets. Above them, the first stars had begun to prick the sky, faint but steady.

Darlie slipped her hand into his. His fingers closed around hers almost automatically, though she felt the weight in them, the heaviness he carried when the world demanded too much. She squeezed gently, grounding him.

"You looked happy out there today," she said softly.

Jack gave a half-smile. "Haven't run like that in years. My knees are reminding me now."

She chuckled, shaking her head. "You caught that Frisbee like you were twenty again. The kids will be talking about it for weeks."

"They make it easy," Jack murmured. His voice had quieted into something thoughtful. "For a while, I forgot... everything else. Just playing, laughing... it felt good."

Darlie studied him. The lines at the corners of his eyes seemed deeper tonight, not from exhaustion but from smiling. She reached up, brushing a fleck of grass from his shirt. "That's why you do it, isn't it? Not for the interviews or the theme parks. For them. For families like ours."

Jack hesitated. His gaze drifted toward the fields, where the horizon had darkened into a band of indigo. "Sometimes I wonder if I've lost sight of that. If I've let all the noise drown it out."

"You haven't," Darlie said firmly. She shifted closer, her shoulder brushing his. "I've seen you. The real you — the one who paces the kitchen at three in the morning because you're worried about a storm two states away. The one who spends hours explaining clouds to kids who barely know their multiplication tables. That man hasn't gone anywhere."

He looked at her then, really looked, and the flicker of doubt in his eyes softened. "You always know what to say."

"It's not about knowing," Darlie replied. "It's about remembering. And I'll remind you as many times as it takes."

The breeze picked up, carrying with it the earthy scent of wheat and dust. Jack tightened his hold on her hand, drawing strength from its familiar warmth.

"I used to think my legacy would be papers published, charts drawn, models built," he said slowly. "But seeing Leda's face today… hearing her ask if I save lives… It hit me differently. Maybe that's what it's all about. Planting the seed. Inspiring them to see the world a little differently."

Darlie nodded, her eyes glistening in the fading light. "That's always been the heart of it. Not storms or data, but people. You've never been chasing tornadoes, Jack. You've been chasing ways to keep people safe. And they know it — even if the world sometimes forgets."

They stood in silence after that, listening to the symphony of the night settle around them. The house behind them glowed softly, a beacon of warmth against the wide Kansas dark. Jack felt the weight in his chest ease, just a little, as he leaned into the familiar comfort of Darlie's presence.

Finally, he exhaled, almost a whisper. "Thank you."

"For what?" she asked, tilting her head.

"For reminding me why I started. For holding me steady when the storms get too loud."

Her smile deepened, lines etched by decades of shared life. "That's what we do, Jack. You chase the storms. I hold the anchor."

They stood there for a long while, hand in hand, until the night grew cool and the stars sharpened overhead. It wasn't a grand ending, no fanfare or applause, just two people, side by side, watching the sky together.

And for Jack, that was enough.

21

THE ENGLE BAND

Dr. Jack Engle had spent most of his life chasing storms. He knew the sound of a tornado before most people even registered the sudden hush of a dying wind. He built models of them, studied their spiraling violence, and lectured about their mysteries at universities and weather conferences. But now, at this stage in his life, a new storm was taking shape—a storm of rhythm, melody, and family.

It all began one Sunday afternoon in his living room. The sun dipped low through the curtains, splashing gold across the oak floors. Jack tuned his well-worn acoustic guitar; the one that he had made and strummed between chases on lonely motel nights in Oklahoma and Kansas. Across from him, his grandson Trey leaned against the couch, humming half-formed lyrics into a notebook.

"You know, Grandpa," Trey said, tapping his pencil against the page, "we've got enough songs here to actually do something with. We don't just have scraps anymore."

Jack looked over his glasses and grinned. "You think so? I've been writing songs since before your dad could talk, but I never thought about doing more than singing them to myself."

"Well, maybe it's time," Trey said. "We've got the players. Dad can shred a solo like nobody else. Stan's been itching to plug in his electric. Leda can keep the bottom end steady. And I can sing harmonies with you. Why not?"

Jack chuckled, his voice carrying both the gravity of age and the excitement of possibility. "A tornado scientist turned recording artist. Now that's a headline."

"Better headline than 'Retired meteorologist yells at clouds,'" Trey teased.

That afternoon turned into a tradition. Every Sunday, the Engle family would gather in Jack's living room, instruments in hand, snacks on the coffee table, and a stack of handwritten lyrics waiting to be tested.

The First Rehearsal

Gavin, Jack's son and longtime guitarist, arrived carrying his Fender Stratocaster, slung over his shoulder like an old friend. Stan followed with his own guitar case, eyes gleaming with the fire of someone ready to prove himself. Leda trailed behind, bass strapped across her back, confident but quiet.

"All right, Dad," Gavin said, plugging into the small amp by the wall. "What's first on the list?"

Jack thumbed through the stack of lyrics. "We'll start with the one that's been running through my head all week— 'Kansas Tornado.' It's got the energy we need. Think of it like the opening salvo of a storm."

Trey leaned forward, already humming. "Yeah, the chorus is catchy. Everyone's gonna remember it."

Jack tapped his foot, strummed a few opening chords, and the room slowly came alive. Gavin slid into a sharp riff, Stan answered with rhythm fills, and Leda thumped a steady bass line that tied it all together. Trey closed his eyes and sang a rough first verse.

The sound was messy, uneven—but it was alive.

"Hold up, hold up," Jack said, raising his hand after the first run-through. "We're rushing the chorus. Slow it just a beat so it hits harder when it lands."

Stan rolled his eyes but nodded. "Okay, but if we drag it, it'll lose the punch."

"No," Gavin corrected, "Dad's right. A tornado doesn't just appear—it builds. You've gotta feel the tension."

Leda smirked. "Listen to the storm chasers trying to talk about music. Can we just play?"

They all laughed, then dove back in. This time, it clicked. The chords wrapped around each other like wind in rotation. Trey's voice rose strong and clear, blending with Jack's deeper tones, and for a moment, the family forgot everything else.

When they stopped, the room buzzed with silence.

"That," Trey whispered, "felt like the real deal."

Jack leaned back, wiping his brow though the room wasn't hot. "One song down. Eleven to go."

Building the Album

Over the weeks, the Engle family turned their Sundays into sacred time. They worked through songs with titles like *Where the Wind Goes, Chasing Storms, Lightning Strikes Twice,* and *Still Standing.* Each piece carried Jack's weather-stained fingerprints — lyrics born from nights on the plains, metaphors of storms and survival.

"Grandpa," Leda said one afternoon after nailing a tricky bass line, "you realize every song mentions wind, rain, or tornadoes, right?"

Jack laughed. "Well, when your life revolves around storms, they tend to sneak into your metaphors. But people connect with storms — they've been scared by them, amazed by them, survived them. That's what music's about: connection."

Stan leaned over his guitar. "I like *Where the Wind Goes.* That solo section is fire. We should feature it."

"Spoken like a true lead guitarist," Gavin said, giving him a playful nudge.

Bit by bit, the songs tightened. Trey recorded rough demos on his laptop, experimenting with harmonies and effects. Leda worked with Gavin on timing, while Stan added riffs that pushed songs into modern rock territory.

And Jack — Jack simply glowed. For years he had lived in the adrenaline of chasing storms. Now he was chasing sound, and it thrilled him just the same.

The Recording Studio

When the twelve songs felt polished enough, Gavin made the call. A friend from college owned a modest recording studio in Wichita, and he booked them an all-day session.

Walking into the studio was like stepping into another world. Foam panels lined the walls, cables snaked across the floor, and behind the glass window, a sound engineer gave them a thumbs-up.

"Okay, family," Jack said, strapping on his guitar. "Let's make history."

The first track they laid down was *Kansas Tornado*. Trey and Jack sang side by side, headphones clamped over their ears, watching each other's timing. Gavin and Stan locked into a dueling guitar section, their fingers flying. Leda's bass thudded steady as a heartbeat.

When the last chord rang out, the engineer's voice came through the intercom. "That's a keeper. You guys really have something here."

Jack turned to his family, eyes shining. "Hear that? A storm in a bottle."

Release Day

Weeks later, the finished album landed on Spotify, Apple Music, and every major streaming platform. The family gathered once again in Jack's living room, but this time the music wasn't coming from their instruments—it was coming from the speakers.

The opening riff of *Kansas Tornado* roared to life, crisp and polished. Jack closed his eyes, listening to his own voice echo back at him. Trey sang along, laughing with disbelief. Stan air-guitared his solo. Leda shook her head, grinning.

"We actually did it," Gavin said softly.

Jack looked around the room—the guitars leaning against chairs, the notebooks filled with lyrics, the family bound together by both blood and music.

"You know," he said, "storms are powerful, but they pass. Music—this—is the kind of storm that lasts."

And as the chorus of *Kansas Tornado* thundered through the speakers, the Engle family knew they had started something that was bigger than themselves.

22

FAMILY DAY AT THE PARK

The Florida sun was doing what it normally does, illuminating Orlando; a brightness that made the concrete walkways glimmer, and the palm fronds wave in the light breeze. Universal Studios was buzzing with excitement. The mix of sweet churros with a generous coating of cinnamon, buttery popcorn, and fried goodness from stalls added to the din of excited screaming from the rollercoasters and raucous laughter of families making their way through the park.

Jack took his time, hand in hand with Darlie, as their children and grandchildren sped off in front of them. The kids ran from one bright thing to another, their voices rising with exasperation — "Grandpa, look at that one!" — and the adults were trying to keep everyone loosely as a team, with bodies all around.

Jack was not accustomed to a place like this, just fun. Most of his life had revolved around crazy storms, and science, and of late, courts and lawyers. But this time he was just another grandfather in the arms of a very busy park in Orlando with families. That fact was both comforting and disturbing.

His youngest grandson, Mike - an endlessly hyperactive boy - grabbed Jack's sleeve. "Grandpa Jack," he said, "can we do the Twister ride? Please? They say it is the best!" The little kid's eyes were wide and kept pulling on Jack's arm as if the ride would close any second.

Jack paused. He had been aware that this moment was destined to arrive from the moment they stepped through those gates, but there it was, the vouched-for request, and he felt it wash over him. Twister. Just the name made something tighten in his chest. It wasn't just a ride, it was a phenomenon that came from his work, his models, his obsession. It had now become a theme park ride along with mickey ears and costumed characters.

Darlie met his knowing glance. She smiled a small smile, put her hand lightly over the top of his. "You knew they would ask," she said quietly. "And you can't be the one to let them down."

Jack exhaled and glanced over to his grandchildren—so excited and impatiently bouncing from one foot to the other. For them, it was not about a legacy or intellectual property. It was about adventure. It was about stepping into a storm and emerging with a memory to share for weeks.

"Okay." Jack finally said, his tone filled with a mixture of exasperation and fondness. "Let's go see the storm."

The children squealed with delight, and in a flurry of energy, took off through the crowd in the general direction of the attraction. Jack walked at a more conservative pace, Darlie beside him, already gathering all the emotions he knew would wash over him while riding the attraction.

***

The line for the Twister attraction snaked forward in its slow, steady crawl, but Jack barely noticed the time. His grandchildren kept him distracted with their chatter, pointing out the posters of storm chasers on the walls, the hanging television screens that played clips of roaring tornadoes, and the ominous rumble of thunder that pulsed through the speakers every few minutes. It was part of the pre-show design—Universal's attempt to build suspense. To the kids, it was thrilling. To Jack, it was unsettlingly familiar.

As they finally stepped through into the darkened staging area, that's when the real action began. The lights dimmed to a dappled darkness that cast long shadows across the room. A low grumbling hum began to vibrate under their feet and the hiss of air duct system activating pre storm began to flow through the audible spectrum. Jack felt the soft vibration running upward through the soles of his shoes and through his bones. The ride designers really did their homework.

"Here it comes!" his granddaughter shouted holding the rail with two hands. She was small, maybe nine years old; but her eyes danced with the thrill of danger that was manufactured safely.

Jack forced a smile at her enthusiasm, though his own chest was tight. He knew what was coming: the simulated funnel, the orchestrated chaos of sound and light. He had watched real tornadoes form in Oklahoma fields, raw and unfiltered. This version was different—slick, choreographed, entertainment packaged with a bow. Yet, as the lights above began to flicker and the floor gave a subtle, jolting tremor, he couldn't deny the craftsmanship.

Wind whooshed past them, sudden and sharp, like a breath drawn straight from the sky. A metallic crash echoed from one corner of the stage as a mock streetlight toppled. Sparks flew from hidden wires. Jack's granddaughter shrieked—but it was the shriek of delight, not fear. She laughed and buried her face against the railing before peeking out again, daring the storm to come closer.

Jack's eyes softened. For her, this was magic.

The simulated storm intensified with the kind of accuracy only engineers and performers could conjure. A crack of thunder! Pounding through the roof. The displace floor trembled like a ski lodge after an avalanche. Hidden machines blasted wind through hidden openings, slapping hair into faces, stripping shirts from shoulders. The sound system opened the depths of the space with the layered roars of a funnel cloud, especially recognized by Jack as the freight-train growl he was so familiar with. Then, in a burst of strobes and swirling smoke, the funnel itself appeared.

The funnel dropped like a living object from the rafters—jumping, twirling, grabbing the stage below. The audience was stunned. It was indescribably real somehow a vortex created through mist, light & technique. The children screamed again, lean over the stair railing without hesitation. Darlie, at Jack's side gripped his hand. He felt her squeeze—steady, firm, reassuring, although he could not read her expression during the storm's chaos.

Jack's granddaughter's laughter rang out again, pure and unguarded. She leaned forward, her knuckles white on the rail, eyes reflecting the swirling light of the funnel. "Grandpa! Look! It's real—it's really real!"

Her words hit him harder than the simulated winds. She believed it, believed in the storm as only a child could, without cynicism, without awareness of the mechanics hidden in the walls. For her, it was not a trick. It was an adventure.

Jack's throat tightened. He thought back to his own childhood, chasing storms in his imagination before he ever chased one across the plains. He had felt the same awe, the same sense of standing at the edge of something larger than himself. That awe had driven him into science, had fueled years of lonely research, had cost him nights at home and holidays missed. To see that wonder reborn in her eyes—it was both beautiful and agonizing.

Because she was seeing it here. In a theme park. Packaged, sold, and consumed like popcorn.

As the staged tornado reached its peak, the floor shook more violently. The truck—a topple truck; the crew cleverly rigged it so that it would collapse forward—came right onto the set. Flames shot up briefly from the hidden gas lines and licked the air in a shallow, controlled explosion. The audience gasped and cheered. Jack's grandson was clapping and squealing, his little hands smacking together with the reverberations of the ground as the thunder continued to roll. To them, this sight was thrilling and dangerous.

Jack felt torn in two. The scientist in him wanted to laugh, to remind them that tornados do not have harnesses or emergency shutoff switches. That the destruction he had studied, and the lives that were lost, was not something to package as performance art. But the grandfather in him—looking at their wide, sticky faces, with flush cheeks—knew that performance, spectacle, was indeed what made it meaningful. For the first time, they saw what it felt like to be in a storm, even if only its shadow. And maybe—just maybe—that was enough for them to regard the real thing.

He leaned down toward his granddaughter, raising his voice over the roar. "Pretty amazing, isn't it?"

She beamed up at him, her hair flying wild in the artificial wind. "The best ever!" she shouted.

Her joy broke something loose inside him. Jack felt an unexpected laugh bubble up, rough and tired, but real. Maybe this wasn't the legacy he imagined—models, research papers, citations in scientific journals. Maybe part of his legacy was right here, in the way his work had touched lives he would never meet, in forms he never anticipated.

The storm began to calm. The wind slowed down, the floor stopped shaking. The funnel disappeared in a wisp of smoke, leaving behind only a trace of ozone smell in the air. The audience broke into applause. Children were bouncing in excitement, adults were shaking their heads in bemusement, and the pre-recorded narrator's voice was thanking everyone for surviving the storm.

When the lights returned to normal, Jack stood in stillness for a bit, taking it all in. His granddaughter pulled on his arm, her eyes glittering. "Grandpa, can we do it again?"

He went down to her level, gently moving her hair away from her face. "Maybe," he said softly. "But don't forget- this is the safe storm. The real storm, there is nothing safe about it, and it's not a ride. It is dangerous."

She nodded solemnly, though the excitement in her expression lingered. For her, the danger only added to the thrill. But Jack could see the seed planted—the awareness that behind the fun was something real, something to be respected.

Darlie slipped her arm through his as they exited the ride, guiding him toward the sunlight outside. "Well," she murmured, "what do you think?"

Jack looked back one last time at the attraction's entrance, where bright letters spelled out Twister.

The crowd lining up was buzzing with anticipation, unaware of the deeper truths behind the spectacle.

He exhaled slowly. "I think… they got the feeling right," he admitted. "Even if the meaning got lost somewhere along the way."

Darlie smiled faintly, pressing her cheek briefly to his shoulder. "Maybe meaning isn't always the point. Maybe feeling is enough."

Jack said no more, and they walked back to the noise of the park. But inside, his mind was tumultuous as a storm, swirling with thoughts of legacy, of loss, of wonder. Seeing his granddaughter, holding tight to the railing, laughing as the storm raged around them — even as fake as it was — left Jack both humbled and haunted.

And while he couldn't predict how history will judge his work, he was certain of one thing: One way or another his storms would outlive him.

***

The crowd rushed away from the Twister attraction, giddy with excitement, but Jack was still standing there letting the patrons stream by, giggling and shouting, arms full of reflections of their experience in the form of souvenirs. His granddaughter held his hand tightly and was still recounting every detail of the experience: the flashing sparks, the rolling truck, the screaming wind. For her, this experience was not a terribly crafted piece of theme park entertainment. It was an adventure; for a couple minutes, they had conjured up a storm.

Jack, though, still felt the storm inside himself.

They walked together into the open air of the park, where the sun was setting in orange streaks across the Florida sky. A warm breeze carried the smell of popcorn and cotton candy, and roller coasters rattled in the distance. But Jack's mind was still in that dark room, still watching the funnel descend from the rafters, still hearing his granddaughter's laughter mixed with the simulated roar of wind.

She skipped ahead a few steps, her energy boundless. Then she stopped suddenly, turned, and ran back to him. Tugging on his sleeve, she looked up at him with wide, eager eyes.

"Grandpa," she said breathlessly, "was that really your tornado?"

Jack froze. The question seemed simple, innocent—but to him, it carried the weight of decades. He had spent his life chasing storms, building models, sketching theories in notebooks stained with rain and dirt. He had testified in courtrooms, fought for recognition, lost sleep, lost time, nearly lost his family—all to protect the integrity of what he had created. And now, here was his granddaughter, looking up at him, asking him to claim a storm that had been turned into a ride.

His first instinct was cynicism. *No, it wasn't mine. Mine were real. Mine were deadly. Mine weren't built to sell tickets.*

But then he saw her face—flushed with excitement, glowing with pride. She wasn't asking for a legal explanation. She wasn't questioning the dilution of science into spectacle. She just wanted to connect—to believe that the wonder she had just experienced was linked, somehow, to the grandfather she adored.

Jack leaned down until he was eye level with her. A small smile tugged at the corner of his mouth.

"That's my tornado," he whispered.

Her gasp was instantaneous. Her eyes widened, and her mouth dropped open as though he had just told her a secret no one else in the world knew. Then, just as quickly, she broke into a grin so wide it nearly split her face. She flung her arms around his neck, hugging him tight.

"I knew it!" she exclaimed. "I knew it was yours!"

Jack closed his eyes, the warmth of her embrace dissolving something hard and bitter that had lived inside him for years.

***

As Jack and his granddaughter pressed onward, he realized it was the lightest he had felt in a long time. The bitterness that had burdened him — the anger of watching his life's work become commodified, the impotent rage of standing in front of corporations who stripped his tempests of their storms and made them into an attraction — slowly started to wash away. He had always thought of legacy as a fight; a victory that would be solidified in the court documents years after the case; only to be bewildered by those who ridiculed his vision of legacy as a quiet and simple realization.

He looked at his granddaughter, skipping and humming to herself, re-running the ride in her mind. She had believed. She was amazed. She had asked him to believe.

Maybe that was enough.

The reality was that the ride had done something that none of his models could ever do before; it had allowed ordinary people to touch the storm, something they felt in their bones, if only for a moment, even if it was only an illusion. He wanted his research to save lives, create awareness, create curiosity, and in that moment, it was alive in her wide eyes and laughing out loud.

For years, Jack had thought commercialization cheapened science, that it sent it into the gutter, that taking science into a popular-controlled direction made it lose its color and its quirk. But, what if — that's a what if — commercialization also sent it deeper? What if the thousands of people that went through that ride every day walked away with a tiny thin sliver of respect for the awesome power of storms? What if it opened a question in some child that had opened the very same question in him as a kid running after clouds on the Kansas plains?

Maybe it wasn't so far removed from his original mission after all.

***

The family wandered deeper into the park, but Jack hardly noticed the other attractions. His attention kept circling back to his granddaughter, her voice tumbling out in bursts as she replayed every detail for her brother, for Darlie, for anyone who would listen.

"And then the truck fell, and the fire went *whoosh*—did you see it, Grandpa? Did you see how it felt like the floor was shaking?"

Jack chuckled softly. "I saw it all."

"Was it scary when you made it?" she asked innocently.

He hesitated, then smiled. "It was scary when the real ones came. But that—" he nodded toward the Twister marquee fading in the distance—"that was the safe kind. That was for fun."

"But you made the real kind," she said proudly, almost defensively, as if daring anyone to doubt it.

Jack nodded, his throat tight. "Yes. I studied the real kind."

She grinned again, satisfied, and skipped ahead to join her brother.

Darlie slid her arm through Jack's, walking close beside him. She didn't say anything at first, but he could feel the quiet understanding radiating from her. Finally, she whispered, "That meant something to her. To hear it from you."

Jack swallowed hard. "It meant something to me, too."

***

That night, back at the hotel, while the children slept and the hum of the air conditioner filled the silence, Jack sat on the edge of the bed. Darlie sat beside him, brushing her hair out slowly. He spoke softly, almost to himself.

"I think I've been looking at this all wrong," he said.

Darlie tilted her head, waiting.

"I spent so much time angry," Jack continued, "because they turned my storms into entertainment. Because they made it flashy and loud and… easy. But tonight, when she looked at me like that—like I'd given her something magical—I realized maybe that's the point. Maybe science doesn't always have to stay in a lab. Maybe sometimes it belongs in the world, even if it's messy, even if it's commercial."

Darlie reached over and took his hand. "You wanted people to understand storms, Jack. And now they do—even if it's in their own way. Isn't that worth something?"

Jack nodded slowly. "It is."

He exhaled, long and heavy, as if laying down a burden he had carried for too long.

***

The next morning, they returned to the park. This time, Jack let himself enjoy it. He watched his grandchildren ride the carousel, scream on the roller coasters, eat sticky cotton candy until their faces were covered in sugar. But when they returned once more to the Twister attraction, something had shifted inside him.

As the storm built again, he leaned down to his granddaughter and whispered, "That's my tornado."

She giggled, clutching his arm. This time, instead of bitterness, Jack felt pride.

He realized his legacy wasn't just in the models gathering dust on his desk, or the court rulings, or the recognition of scientists in journals he'd spent years trying to impress. His legacy was here — in the joy on her face, in the spark of curiosity that might lead her, or someone like her, to look up at the sky one day and wonder how storms worked.

That was the reconciliation he hadn't expected: to find peace not in a judge's gavel, but in a child's laughter.

***

As they left the park for the last time, Jack turned once more to see the bold letters of *Twister* shining against the evening sky. The crowd was as long as ever, parents and children lining up for their turn to feel the storm.

Jack smiled faintly. For the first time, he didn't feel like something had been stolen from him. Instead, he felt like he had given something away — something larger than himself.

And maybe that was the truest legacy of all.

The family stepped out of the dim corridors of the attraction and into the open air. The doors swung wide, spilling them back into sunlight. After the roaring wind machines, flashing lights, and manufactured chaos of the ride, the stillness of the Florida afternoon felt almost unreal.

The air was warm, heavy with humidity, and the scent of popcorn drifted faintly from a nearby stand. A soft breeze carried laughter from a roller coaster in the distance. The storm they had just left behind was artificial, but now, standing beneath the vast open sky, Jack couldn't help but feel its echoes inside himself.

For a moment, he didn't follow his family. He lingered just outside the attraction, lifting his face to the sun. The brightness made him squint, but he didn't look away. He let the light soak into him, warming the creases of his face, illuminating the lines carved by years of stress, trial, and weather-chasing.

Above, the Florida sky stretched wide and boundless, a brilliant blue scattered with drifting white clouds. Not storm clouds, not the towering anvils he had studied for decades. Just soft, unthreatening clouds, wandering across the horizon like idle travelers.

Jack exhaled, long and slow. For the first time in years, maybe decades, it felt like he was breathing *with* the world instead of against it.

He thought of the courtroom battles, the sleepless nights, the bitter arguments at home. He thought of the frustration, the gnawing hunger for validation, the sense that his life's work might vanish into someone else's pocket. And then he thought of his granddaughter's face—her wide eyes, her joyous laugh, the way she had hugged him when he whispered, "That's my tornado."

That was the moment he realized the truth: he didn't need a judge's gavel to confirm his worth. He didn't need corporations to stamp his name on their attractions. His legacy wasn't in contracts, or even in the models themselves. It was in the people who carried his wonder forward—his family, his students, anyone who felt awe when they looked at the sky.

The battle had been worth fighting, yes. But standing here now, with the Florida sun breaking through the clouds, he understood that peace came not from winning, but from letting go.

***

Darlie noticed he had fallen behind and turned, shading her eyes with her hand. She called out gently, "Jack? You coming?"

He nodded, smiling faintly, and walked toward her. She reached out and took his hand when he drew close. For the first time in a long time, there was no tension in her touch—only warmth, only the quiet reassurance of two people who had weathered their own storms and were still standing.

Ahead, the children were already darting toward another ride, their voices high with excitement. His granddaughter stopped to wave at him, urging him to hurry. Jack chuckled, shaking his head, then picked up his pace.

As he walked, he thought of how storms always moved on. Even the fiercest tornado left behind clear skies eventually. That was the rhythm of nature, and perhaps the rhythm of life, too.

Jack paused again, this time deliberately, and tilted his head back. The sky above seemed impossibly wide. A hawk circled lazily on a thermal, its wings catching the sunlight. He traced the outlines of the clouds, seeing in them the patterns he had studied so long ago—shear, lift, vorticity—but instead of equations and models, he simply saw beauty.

Once, he had only looked at the sky with questions: *What makes the storm? How can it be predicted? What secrets lie in the patterns of air?*

Now, he looked at it with gratitude.

It didn't matter that his storms had been turned into a ride. It didn't matter that his models had been simplified, packaged, and sold. What mattered was that the sky was still there—vast, humbling, eternal. And that he, after so many years of struggle, could finally stand beneath it and feel at peace.

Jack thought about legacy, that word that had haunted him through the trial, through his sleepless nights, through his fights with Darlie. Legacy wasn't something you won. It wasn't something you secured in court or cemented in contracts. Legacy was what you left in people—the awe, the curiosity, the courage to ask questions.

He had spent his life chasing storms. But maybe the real achievement was teaching others, even his granddaughter, to chase wonder.

That realization softened him in a way he hadn't thought possible. He smiled up at the sky, a smile not of triumph, but of acceptance.

***

Darlie squeezed his hand again. "You look lighter," she said softly.

Jack turned to her. "I feel lighter."

Together, they walked toward their family, into the golden stretch of the afternoon. The laughter of children mixed with the cheerful chaos of the park. And above it all, the sky arched wide and blue, scattered with clouds that would drift on, forever moving, forever changing.

For the first time in his long, storm-chasing life, Jack didn't feel the need to chase. He simply stood beneath the sky and let it be.

And in that sunlight, he finally found peace.

23

REFLECTION

The coffee had long gone cold, leaving a thin skin across the top of the cup. Jack barely noticed. It sat forgotten at the edge of his desk, surrounded by towers of notebooks, papers curling at the corners, and diagrams covered in looping arrows and numbers. His study smelled faintly of ink, dust, and the faint bitterness of old caffeine, the scent of years spent chasing storms on paper.

The desk lamp hummed softly, its pale light bending the shadows into long, reaching fingers across the room. Beyond the narrow window, the Kansas sky was ablaze. Streaks of orange, gold, and deep red bled together as the sun sank, painting the horizon in fire. Jack leaned back in his chair and watched; his weathered hands folded loosely in his lap.

It struck him, not for the first time, how storms had been his life's compass. He had followed them across open prairies, into classrooms, into labs where he dared to bottle them in glass. They had tested him, humbled him, and sometimes when the work broke through, they had lifted him higher than he ever thought he could stand.

But tonight wasn't about the chase. Tonight was about the quiet after. The silence that came when the questions ran dry and the papers lay still. He thought of his brother Vern, of his mother Elsie, of those first arrowheads tucked in a wooden box under a boy's bed. A life mapped not just in storms, but in the spaces between them.

Outside, the fiery dusk gave way to violet shadows. The world was winding down. Jack's pen, resting beside an open notebook, waited. He wasn't sure if he would write tonight. Perhaps reflection didn't always belong on paper. Sometimes it lived only in the heart, carried like weather that refused to pass.

***

Jack reached for a worn envelope tucked beneath a stack of journals. Its edges were yellowed, the flap no longer sealing shut. Inside were photographs he hadn't touched in years. One by one, he laid them across the desk, their corners catching the lamplight.

The first was grainy, black-and-white. A snapshot of his first successful vortex in the lab. The tiny funnel spun inside his lab, traced by smoke. He remembered the exhilaration, the disbelief that he had coaxed chaos into order. That moment had felt like lightning in a bottle, proof that storms could be studied and not merely feared.

Another photograph slid free, and his eyes tightened. The courtroom. The sharp suits, the skeptical stares. He had gone from a farm boy scribbling in notebooks to a man standing in front of judges and lawyers, defending not just his research but his very right to challenge the "gospel." The memory carried the sting of ridicule, but also the pride of standing his ground when the whole establishment rose against him.

The last photo made him pause longer. Hollywood. A glossy publicity shot from the film premiere where his work had been borrowed or maybe stolen, maybe celebrated, maybe both for entertainment. Actors smiled for cameras while his artificial tornado spun in the background like a circus trick. He remembered the applause, the flashing bulbs, the absurdity of tornadoes turned into spectacle.

Jack leaned back in his chair, the three photos aligned like a timeline: the lab, the courtroom, the red carpet. Three faces of a life spent chasing storms.

He rubbed the bridge of his nose, sighing. "What have I done?" he murmured under his breath, not as regret but as acknowledgment. He had advanced the science—no doubt. People were safer because of the work. Yet he had also fed the spectacle, let the mystery of storms drift into entertainment.

The contradictions sat before him like twin storms colliding. Genius and showmanship. Rigorous science and reckless spectacle. He wasn't sure if they balanced each other, or if they simply tore at him in different directions.

Still, as he stared at the fading photographs, he knew one truth: he wouldn't have done it any other way. Storms, whether in the sky or in the heart, never came without contradictions.

The photographs lay scattered on the desk, islands of memory in the lamplight. Jack sat still for a long while, hands folded, eyes unfocused, as though the past decades had rearranged themselves into a storm system, drifting across his mind in bands of color and sound. He felt the way he had as a boy lying on his back in the Kansas fields watching the sky churn above him, trying to decipher patterns that seemed too vast, too intricate, to ever make sense.

A shiver of recognition passed through him. This was no different. His life was its own storm. There had been whirlwinds of discovery, downbursts of failure, lightning bolts of triumph, and thunderclaps of criticism. And like any storm, its shape could only be seen from a distance, when you pulled back far enough to see the whole arc.

For years, he had measured his worth by the settings that defined him: the lab with its tornado chamber and humming fans, the courtroom where his credibility was dragged into question, the glittering theaters where Hollywood had turned his science into spectacle. Each place had carved an impression on him, left him feeling either validated or betrayed, respected or exploited. But as he sat there now, the truth drifted into focus like a clearing sky after rain.

It wasn't the places. It wasn't the stages or the settings.

It was the impact.

He leaned forward, elbows on the desk, and spoke aloud, as if the walls needed to hear it too. "The work lived beyond me."

The realization landed with weight. Whether the storm chamber sat in a university basement or in a theme park attraction, whether his theories were debated in journals or dramatized on a movie screen, the essence of what he had done was never confined to a single room. The ripples moved outward farther than he had ever imagined.

He thought of the warnings. The sirens that blared across small towns, the radio alerts that cut through baseball games and church picnics. Families who had seconds more to reach their basements. Children clutching blankets in the dark, mothers holding babies close, fathers bracing against rattling doors. They would never know his name. They would never see the data charts or the furious debates behind those sirens. But they were alive, breathing, because of the work. That mattered more than his pride, more than his bruised ego from academic fights.

Jack exhaled, eyes damp. Saving lives that was the truest measure of science. Not the prestige. Not the applause. The impact.

And then another memory rose, gentler but no less important. A letter he once received, decades ago, from a boy in Nebraska. The handwriting was shaky, barely readable. The boy had written after seeing Jack's miniature tornado on television. "I want to study storms too. I want to build machines like you." That boy, no longer a boy by now could be a professor, a researcher, or even an unsung meteorologist in a weather station, guiding people to safety. Jack would never know. The boy might not even remember sending the letter. But that spark that little ignition of curiosity was part of his legacy too.

He realized then that legacy wasn't just measured in sirens and survival. It lived in inspiration. In the countless unseen moments when a child looked up at the sky differently, saw order in the chaos, and thought, I want to understand this. Maybe that was the greatest gift he had left behind.

He took another sip of the coffee, frowning at its cold bitterness. The taste grounded him, reminded him of the long nights, the tireless research, the relentless persistence that had carried him here. He had doubted, many times, that the fight was worth it. The National Weather Service had mocked him, colleagues had called him reckless, and even friends had suggested he quiet down, let things be. But he hadn't. Because somewhere deep in him, he had always known: storms didn't listen to authority. They followed laws of their own, and it was his duty to uncover them, no matter who stood in the way.

The desk lamp hummed faintly, its glow steady. Jack traced a finger along the photograph of the laboratory tornado. That image, once controversial, had been shown in textbooks, classrooms, and museums. Children had pressed their fingers into the vortex, watching the smoky funnel spin. They didn't care if it was in a prestigious lab or a theme park; they only saw the wonder. Wonder — that was the seed of science. And he had planted it in more places than he could count.

A quiet chuckle escaped him. How strange, that the very thing he had once resented, the spectacle of his work might have carried the science farther than he ever could alone. If a Hollywood blockbuster made one person take tornado warnings seriously, if an artificial tornado behind velvet ropes nudged a child toward meteorology, then wasn't that impact too? Wasn't that part of the legacy?

He leaned back, letting the chair creak beneath him. His shoulders eased, a burden lifted. For the first time, he no longer felt the need to separate his life into categories of "serious science" and "showmanship." Both had mattered. Both had rippled outward. Both had saved lives in ways he would never fully trace.

The thought grew warmer the longer he sat with it. Legacy wasn't something you controlled. It wasn't a map you drew, with arrows pointing where you wanted influence to go. It was a storm itself, unpredictable, sprawling, sometimes destructive, sometimes beautiful. You released your work into the world, and it went where it needed to go. Sometimes it touched policy makers, sometimes it reached classrooms, sometimes it hid in the heart of a single child who would one day pick up where you left off.

Jack reached for his pen, opened his notebook, and scrawled a line across the page:

"Impact is not the place, but the ripple."

He stared at the words, nodded slowly. Yes. That was it. That was what he had been circling around all evening, what the photographs had been trying to tell him. Not lab, not courtroom, not theater. Ripple

His thoughts drifted again, this time to Vern. His brother's steady voice came back to him, faint but certain: "Storms come and go. What matters is how you stand through them." Jack realized now that legacy was the same. It wasn't about stopping the storm. It was about how you stood and how others stood because of you.

He felt the room soften around him, shadows lengthening as the last streaks of sun bled out of the horizon. The storm of contradictions within him had quieted. For once, he didn't feel the need to justify, to defend, to argue. The realization was simple, almost humbling: his work had gone farther than he ever could.

Jack placed the photographs back into the envelope, but more gently this time, like handling fragile artifacts. He didn't need them to prove anything anymore. The proof was out there in sirens, in textbooks, in children's wide eyes, in families alive after storms.

As he folded the envelope shut, he whispered into the silence, "It was never about me."

And the truth of it filled him with peace.

The lamp's glow dimmed as Jack pressed the photo album shut. Its cover, worn soft by years of handling, felt heavier now as though every page carried not just images, but the weight of an entire life. He rested his hand on it for a moment, then slid it aside, letting the desk return to stillness.

With a quiet click, he switched off the lamp. The shadows swallowed the room, leaving only the faint outline of the window, where the last streaks of dusk had bled into indigo. For a heartbeat, he remained in the darkness, listening to the silence, broken only by the tick of the old wall clock and the faint hum of cicadas outside.

He rose slowly, stretching the stiffness from his legs, and walked to the door. The air outside met him like a bomb, cooler than the heat of the day, carrying with it the scent of grass and distant rain. He stepped onto the porch, feeling the boards creak beneath his weight, and looked out over the horizon.

The prairie stretched wide and endless, just as it had when he was a boy lying in the fields. But now, it was no longer the vast unknown. It was familiar like an old friend whose moods and tempers he had spent a lifetime trying to understand.

In the distance, the sky pulsed. Heat lightning flickered, illuminating the edges of clouds in silent bursts. No thunder followed just flashes, here and gone, as if the heavens were practicing storms without unleashing them.

Jack watched, his lips curving into a faint smile. How many storms had he chased, measured, battled, feared, and admired? And now here was another—quiet, harmless, offering light without fury. A reminder that not all storms tore things apart. Some simply lit the sky for those who bothered to look up.

He folded his arms, leaning against the porch rail, and let the moment wash over him. The storms would go on, long after him rising, breaking, vanishing into memory. And maybe that was right. Maybe that was enough.

For the first time in a long time, Jack felt no urge to measure, to record, to analyze. He simply stood there, watching the horizon flash in silence, and smiled knowingly as if sharing a secret with the sky.

24

A STORMY LEGACY

The sky had turned a sickly green. Even decades later, Jack could still remember that color, the hue of dread that only tornado skies seemed to carry. He was young then, lean with restless energy, standing ankle-deep in a splintered street in Topeka, Kansas. Around him, the world looked as though some enormous, careless hand had swept across the land, toppling homes, uprooting trees, and leaving lives scattered in pieces like broken toys.

The pungent smell of splintered wood and damp earth hung heavy in the air. Mixed with it was the copper tang of dust and something else, something raw and human that he didn't want to name. Sirens wailed faintly in the distance, weaving in and out of the cries of families searching for one another.

The wind that followed the storm was still restless, as if the atmosphere hadn't decided yet whether to calm or strike again.

Jack walked forward slowly, boots crunching against glass and plaster. He didn't yet know that this moment would cement his life's path. All he knew was the weight in his chest, a mixture of horror and awe, as if he had stepped into the pages of a story too big for him to understand.

To his left, a roof had collapsed inward on itself, crushing the front of a small house. A man staggered in the yard, holding a child whose face was streaked with mud and tears. Jack could hear the man's voice, broken, calling for his wife. He wanted to help, but he was just one young man, with no training and no tools, only a notebook in his pocket and an ache in his gut that this devastation could not be left to chance.

He moved on, his eyes scanning everything the way they always did. He noticed how one house was flattened completely, while the one next to it still stood, windows shattered but walls intact. Why? The question burned inside him. Why had one family lost everything while another still had shelter? Why did the storm choose one path of ruin and spare another?

He crouched near the ruins of a basement, peering into the jagged pit where cinder blocks and furniture lay tumbled. His mind, even in the chaos, started sketching invisible diagrams: wind direction, angles, the way debris had been flung. A woman's voice behind him jolted him from thought, "Sir! Sir, can you help?" and he turned to see her trying to lift part of a wall off a boy no older than ten. Jack scrambled over, his hands slipping on wet wood, straining with her until the boy wriggled free, coughing but alive.

The woman wept with gratitude, clutching her son. Jack stood there, his hands scraped and bleeding, his shirt torn, and thought: This can't just be chaos. There has to be a pattern. If I can see it, maybe I can prevent this.

That night, he couldn't sleep. The images replayed again and again, families torn apart, houses collapsed, the silent gaps where people used to live. He sat on the porch of a borrowed cot at the edge of town, notebook open on his knee, scribbling by the light of a weak lantern.

He drew crude maps of neighborhoods, marking where houses had been destroyed and where some had survived. He sketched arrows showing the storm's path, lines crisscrossing like veins on a leaf. And as he wrote, one thought kept pulsing in his mind: The experts say southwest corner. But I saw families crushed in that corner tonight.

The official "gospel" of tornado safety taught by the National Weather Service was firm: if a tornado struck, hide in the southwest corner of your basement. It was advice repeated like scripture, accepted without question. But what Jack had witnessed told a different story. In house after house, the southwest corners had collapsed under the force of debris. Survivors, the lucky ones, often crowd together in the northeast.

He gripped his pencil tighter, the words scrawling across the page as though they were bigger than him: If the gospel is wrong, people will die.

The memory of that night was burned into all his senses. He remembered the dampness of his shirt, soaked through with rain and sweat. He remembered the grit of sawdust in his teeth, the sting of smoke in his eyes from gas fires flickering in the ruins. He remembered the silence that came after the sirens, when darkness swallowed the town and only the distant voices of searchers carried across the fields.

Most of all, he remembered the smell, the acrid, living smell of a storm's aftermath. Splintered pine mixed with wet earth, the faint bite of ozone still lingering from the lightning. For years afterward, whenever that smell hit him, he felt his stomach twist with the same urgency he had felt that night. It wasn't fear anymore, it was responsibility.

At dawn, he stood on a rise outside the city, looking back at the scarred landscape. The storm had carved its mark straight through the heart of Topeka, leaving behind a sharp wound that would take years to heal. He stared until the first light gilded the wreckage, and in that fragile light, he made a vow.

He would not rest until he understood storms. He would measure them, dissect them, challenge every old belief about them. He would fight the institutions if he had to. Because behind every collapsed wall and every shattered window were lives. Ordinary people who trusted experts to tell them the truth. If the experts didn't know, then he would find out.

That promise, whispered into the dawn, was the true beginning of his legacy. Long before television cameras or courtroom battles, before the fame and the ridicule, before Hollywood ever turned his science into spectacle, there was only this: a young man in muddy boots, standing in the ruins of Topeka, vowing to seize order from chaos.

Now, decades later, as Jack sat at his desk in the twilight of his career, the memory came back with aching clarity. The photo album at his side held the images of his life laboratories, experiments, movie premieres but none of those mattered as much as the storm that had first broken him open and remade him.

He leaned back in his chair, closing his eyes, letting the sounds of that night echo through his mind. The wailing sirens. The sobbing families. The steady, determined scrape of his pencil against paper. It was there, in the rubble, that he had begun to build his true life's work — not in a classroom, not in a laboratory, but in the wreckage of human loss.

That storm had not just destroyed Topeka. It had shaped him, hardened him, sharpened him into the man who would spend his life chasing, studying, and sometimes defying storms.

Jack opened his eyes, the present and the past blurring together. The dusk outside his window glowed with the same fiery red he had seen over Topeka so long ago, as if the sky itself remembered. He touched the edge of the photo album, then pulled his notebook closer. Even now, after all the years, he was still writing, still trying to understand.

Because storms, whether they tore through cities or haunted families, never really ended. They lived on in memory, in data, in the determination of those who survived.

And Jack Engle had made it his life's work to make sure those storms never claimed more than they had to.

***

The study was quiet except for the faint hum of the desk lamp and the ticking of an old clock that had been with him for decades. Jack sat slouched in his chair, fingers tracing the worn edges of a photograph that had slipped from the album. It was a black-and-white print, grainy with age, showing a street in Topeka the morning after the tornado of 1966. He stared at it for a long while, as though the picture itself might still carry the smell of damp wood and the echo of distant sirens.

So much of his life had grown from that one day. Sitting here now, his study lined with shelves of journals, research papers, and dusty instruments that once seemed revolutionary, he could see the thread that tied it all together. A chain reaction, ignited by that single storm.

The photograph shook slightly in his hand. Not from weakness though age had crept in steadily but from the weight of what it represented. That day made me who I am, he thought. That day planted every question I ever tried to answer.

Jack leaned back, letting his eyes drift to the window. Outside, dusk was settling into night, the horizon glowing faintly orange before surrendering to gray. He thought of how the world outside had changed since that summer in Topeka. Towns had grown into cities, the science of weather had leapt forward, and communication had become instantaneous. Yet storms, those swirling, violent tempests remained just as indifferent, just as merciless.

It was strange to think how his own journey mirrored that. He had grown, aged, weathered successes and failures, but the questions remained. The tornado did not evolve to suit man. Man had to adapt, to understand, to survive.

And for decades, he had poured himself into that very task. The modeling systems that tracked storm behavior in real time, the warning networks that stretched across states, the simulations that allowed entire generations of students to see how chaos could be studied all of it had roots in that splintered Kansas street.

Sometimes, in quiet moments like this, Jack wondered: What if I hadn't been there? What if I had looked away? Would someone else have carried the fight? Would families have had those precious extra minutes of warning? Would families still seek shelter in the southwest corner?

It was a dangerous line of thought, tempting but endless. He pushed it aside gently. It wasn't about being irreplaceable. It was about being placed in the right moment, with the right stubbornness, to ask questions no one else dared ask.

His gaze moved from the photograph to the shelves around him. He could see the worn spines of academic journals where his most controversial articles had first appeared, the ones that drew both admiration and anger. He remembered the sting of rejection letters, the lectures where colleagues dismissed him as reckless, the quiet satisfaction of watching data prove him right.

But more than that, he thought of the letters in a box near his desk, letters from strangers. Mothers who wrote to thank him for safety drills their children now practiced at school. A farmer who wrote to say he moved his family out of the southwest corner of their cellar, and when the storm came, they survived in the northeast. Students who had read his work and gone on to become meteorologists themselves.

These were the real measures of his life's work. Not the awards on the wall, not the interviews on television, but the lives shaped in ways he would never fully know.

The ripple effects stretched wider than he could trace. A boy in Oklahoma who decided to study weather after seeing a television segment on Jack's experiments. A girl in Illinois who survived because her teacher drilled a new safety routine inspired by his research. Policymakers who fought to fund radar networks after his relentless testimony.

Jack knew that storms were bigger than any one man, but he also knew the ripples mattered. Even the smallest stone, thrown into the current, reshaped the flow.

He picked up his mug of coffee, cold now, and took a sip anyway. The bitterness sat heavy on his tongue. Contradictions — that was another legacy of his life. He had always wrestled with them.

On one hand, he had advanced tornado science, saved lives, and stood firm against authorities who preferred tradition over truth. On the other, he had lent his work to entertainment. Theme parks, Hollywood productions, exhibitions that made storms into spectacle. Some of his peers had sneered at that. They claimed he cheapened science, turned fear into amusement.

He understood their criticism, but he had his own defense. For every child who screamed in mock terror as a simulated vortex spun overhead, there might be one who left inspired. One who realized storms were not just monsters but mysteries. If even a handful of those children grew into scientists, wasn't that worth it?

Jack admitted to himself that part of him enjoyed the showmanship. He liked bottling the impossible, showing the public what nature could do in controlled miniature. He liked proving that storms could be understood, not just endured. And perhaps, deep down, he had needed the applause too—a way of silencing the years of being told he didn't belong.

He sighed, rubbing his temple. Contradictions, always. He was proud and ashamed, certain and doubtful, stubborn and weary. But he had lived, fully and without retreat. And that, he thought, was no small thing.

The photograph slid back into the album, his hand lingering on the page before closing it. He let his thoughts drift, not to moments of fame, but to the chain of cause and effect that began with Topeka.

The storm had led to questions. The questions had led to studies. The studies had led to conflict. The conflict had led to breakthroughs. Each link forged under strain, each one necessary.

Had he known, standing among the ruins that day, how long and lonely the road would be, would he have chosen it? He believed so. Because when he thought of the alternative — silence, ignorance, families dying under false assurances — he knew he couldn't have walked away.

The storms demanded an answer. He had simply been the one stubborn enough to answer back.

Jack leaned forward, elbows on the desk, staring at the glow of the lamp. His hair was thinner now, his shoulders less square, his breath heavier than he would admit. He knew time was running short. Legacy was no longer an abstract concept — it was the air he breathed each day, wondering what would remain when he no longer did.

And yet, strangely, he felt lighter now than he had in youth. Back then, the fight had consumed him. Every criticism had stung; every setback had felt like failure. Now he saw the larger pattern, as he always had with storms: turbulence first, clarity later.

He thought of Vern, his quiet brother, whose patience had been his earliest teacher. Vern had told him once, "Everything has its season. Fish, storms, even us." Jack smiled faintly at the memory. Vern had been right. His own season was ending, but not without fruit.

He wondered, briefly, about the students carrying his torch now. Some had built careers in research and as college professors, others in policy, others in public outreach. Some he had watched giving weather forecasts on TV. They might not all remember him directly, but they carried pieces of him in their work. That was enough.

He imagined a child decades from now. Maybe one not yet born—sitting in a classroom, learning tornado safety. The teacher would say, "Don't go to the southwest corner. That's outdated." The child would nod, never knowing that advice had been fought for, tested, and earned through years of resistance. Never knowing the name behind it.

And that was how it should be. Legacy wasn't about being remembered. It was about being useful long after memory faded.

The clock ticked on. Outside, the horizon deepened to purple, and a soft rumble rolled across the plains, heat lightning flickering in the distance. Jack didn't move for a long while, his thoughts circling, settling, rising again like the air before a storm.

He thought of that young man he once was, standing in Topeka's ruins with mud on his boots and eagerness in his chest. If that person could see him now—older, grayer, worn but unbowed— what would he say?

Jack smiled faintly. He'd say, "You kept the promise."

And that was enough.

***

Jack sat in his study, the photograph album still open, though he was no longer looking at it. His gaze had drifted to the horizon outside his window, where dusk had settled into full night. Beyond the darkened glass, lightning flickered silently in the distance, illuminating the edge of the plains. Each flash reminded him of how the world once trembled before storms, helpless and uninformed.

But things were different now. Not because storms had changed—they never would—but because people had.

He leaned back in his chair and let his thoughts expand outward, away from the narrow confines of his own life and toward the wide sweep of history. What he had done, what he had fought for, was no longer just his story. It had become part of the fabric of society, woven into how people thought, prepared, and survived.

Jack remembered stories his mother used to tell about the old days, before radio broadcasts and radar, when storms came like thieves in the night. Families would huddle in cellars, not because they had been warned but because instinct told them danger was near. Lives were left to chance. Survival was often luck rather than preparation.

Back then, storms were spoken about in whispers, as though naming them too loudly might summon them. Whole communities could be flattened in minutes, leaving nothing but questions. Why here? Why us? The answers, if there were any, belonged to preachers in pulpits, not scientists in labs.

That was the world Jack had been born into—a world where storms were gods and people their trembling subjects.

Now, decades later, he could see the gulf between then and now. Tornadoes were no longer mysterious terrors whispered about after church. They were measured, tracked, studied, broadcast. Sirens wailed in towns long before the funnel touched down. Schools practiced drills. Families kept weather radios on their kitchen counters. Meteorologists spoke with authority about probabilities, trajectories, and safe havens.

This shift, the transformation from helplessness to readiness was not born overnight. It had taken stubbornness, mistakes, and sometimes ridicule. And yet, as Jack reflected, it was undeniable: the way people thought about tornadoes had changed.

Society itself had changed. And his fingerprints were all over that change.

The chaos of Topeka still lived vividly in his memory—the splintered wood, the choking smell of destruction, the sight of families standing barefoot in the rubble of their lives. That day had been a wound. But it was also a seed. From it had grown new ways of thinking, new approaches to safety, new standards for survival.

His models, born from sketches and calculations scrawled in frustration and defiance, had been mocked at first. Yet here they were now, folded into government protocols, taught in classrooms, reinforced in emergency drills. Town by town, school by school, family by family—his work had rippled outward until it was no longer "Jack's idea." It was history's idea. It was common sense.

The southwest corner myth—once gospel—was gone. His damage statistics and persistence had buried it. The irony made him smile faintly. At one time, that fight had felt like the end of the world. Professors had dismissed him; officials had told him to stop stirring trouble. Now, children who had never heard his name still learned to take cover in the central or northeast corner. The myth was gone, but the truth remained.

Jack thought about the communities he had visited over the years—Oklahoma, Texas, Kansas,

Missouri, Illinois—places where tornadoes were not possibilities but inevitabilities. He remembered standing in gymnasiums where children practiced crouching low against walls. He remembered speaking to town councils about funding sirens, and hearing the quiet thank-yous from parents afterward. He remembered the look in survivors' eyes when they spoke about the warnings that had given them minutes—precious, life-saving minutes—to run, to hide, to live.

He realized now that society no longer braced for storms blindly. It prepared with knowledge, with systems, with trust in data. That trust hadn't always been easy to win, but once it took root, it grew like prairie grass—stubborn, resilient, unshakable.

And while Jack knew his own name might fade into the background, he also knew his work lived on in the very fabric of that trust. When a siren blared in the middle of the night and a family rushed to shelter, his fingerprints were there. When a teacher lined her students against the safest wall, his fingerprints were there. When meteorologists used data to give communities ten, fifteen, even twenty minutes of warning, his fingerprints were there too.

That was legacy—not the memory of a man, but the survival of many.

Jack set the coffee mug down gently, almost ceremonially. A simple truth lay before him: storms would always come. Nothing could stop them. They were as old as the earth itself, and they would outlast humanity. He had long since accepted that.

But he had also accepted another truth: people would always fight to survive. And because of his work, they fought smarter. They fought with tools, knowledge, and a sense of agency. They didn't simply cower anymore — they prepared, they acted, they endured.

That permanence mattered. His life's work, forged in arguments and written in sweat, had become part of that fight. Tornadoes would outlive him, yes, but so would the systems he helped create. And in that way, he had carved something permanent out of impermanence.

It was a humbling thought. He was not bigger than the storms. But he had shaped how humanity met them. That was enough.

Jack's mind stretched outward again, beyond his own small office, beyond Kansas, beyond the Midwest. He thought of how other nations had begun adapting tornado protocols, how his work had influenced not just the United States but the global conversation on severe weather. Storms were not confined to American plains. They struck in Asia, in Europe, in South America. And everywhere, the questions were the same: How do we prepare? How do we survive?

Pieces of his research had traveled further than he ever could. Citations in journals in languages he couldn't read. Students he had once mentored now presenting at international conferences. Government officials across oceans debating safety measures born from his ideas.

History was not a neat story, Jack realized. It was a scattering of seeds, some growing in places you'd never expect. His seeds had taken root in soil far from Topeka. And that realization filled him with a quiet awe.

He thought, briefly, about his own name. Would people remember it fifty years from now? Would textbooks mention him, or would his work simply become anonymous safety protocol?

The question no longer troubled him. In youth, he had craved recognition. He had wanted his name in print, his theories respected, his place secure. But with age had come perspective. Legacy wasn't about being remembered — it was about being useful.

If his work lived on without his name, so be it. If children grew up safe without ever hearing of Jack Engle, that was a victory. He had fought not for fame but for survival. The storms did not care about names. Neither did he, not anymore.

Jack rose from his chair slowly, his knees stiff, his shoulders sore. He walked to the window, resting a hand against the cool glass. Outside, the heat lightning flickered again, illuminating the plains in fleeting bursts. He watched it with the same mixture of awe and respect he had carried all his life.

Storms would always come. That truth had never changed.

But now, thanks to his work and the work of others who followed, people would always be ready.

And that truth would never leave.

***

The study felt too small for his thoughts. The lamp on his desk still glowed faintly, but Jack no longer needed its light. He had been staring at the window for too long, waiting for something beyond glass and wood and paper. Finally, with a quiet exhale, he pushed his chair back, the wooden legs creaking against the floor, and stood.

The house was still. The kind of stillness that only Kansas nights carried, a stillness stitched with patience. Outside, the horizon pulsed faintly with lightning, as though the sky itself were breathing. He reached for the doorknob, hesitated for a heartbeat, then stepped out into the night.

The first thing that met him was the wind. Not violent, not roaring, but steady—a breath of the prairie moving past his skin. It was a wind he had known since boyhood, the same current that had filled his lungs when he chased storms barefoot across fields, when he stood trembling beside Vern at the lake, when he first looked up at towering thunderheads and whispered questions no book could answer.

It was the Kansas wind. His oldest companion.

Jack closed his eyes for a moment and let it move across his face, through his thinning hair, tugging gently at the collar of his shirt. It smelled faintly of earth and grass, damp from the distant storm.

He thought: I was born in this wind, I grew in it, and someday I'll return to it.

Far away, a low rumble rolled across the night. Not sharp thunder, not yet. Just the voice of a storm too far to see but close enough to remind him that the world was always moving, always shifting.

How many nights had he stood like this? Listening, waiting, measuring distance by the seconds between lightning and sound. As a boy, it had been a game. As a scientist, it became method. As an old man, it was simply habit, an instinct etched so deeply it would never leave him.

The storm out there was not his to chase anymore. His body could not keep up with the roads, the instruments, the hours of watching. But he still listened. He still learned.

Jack tilted his head back, his eyes finding the restless ceiling of the sky. Above him stretched the canvas of night—clouds illuminated in fleeting bursts by heat lightning, stars blinking between their edges. He had spent a lifetime looking up, and even now, in this quiet moment, the sight stole his breath.

Storms had never frightened him, not even as a child. They humbled him, yes, but they also invited him. They asked him to pay attention, to search for the rules within chaos. Looking up had always meant possibility.

Now, it meant gratitude.

As the thunder rolled again, Jack thought of all the storms that had shaped him, not just the ones that tore across Kansas soil, but the storms inside his own life. The ridicule from colleagues, the fights for recognition, the loss of Vern, the long nights when experiments failed, the moments when he questioned whether it was all worth it.

Every storm had left its mark. Every storm had carved him into the man standing here tonight.

And just as real storms cleared the air after rage and rain, so too had his storms left behind clarity. They had given him a purpose larger than himself.

He wondered, as the wind pressed against his chest, if somewhere maybe in another state, maybe in another country, a child was crouched beside a window, watching clouds gather with the same curiosity he had once carried. Maybe that child would grow up with safer warnings, with stronger buildings, with parents who knew where to shelter. Maybe that child would one day take his work further, asking questions he himself had never dreamed.

That thought comforted him more than any award or title ever could. His life had rippled outward. The storm of his work had reached places he would never see.

The wind picked up slightly, carrying with it the faint creak of the barn door down the road, the rustle of leaves in the trees. Jack breathed deeply, feeling not just the air, but the memory of all who had walked these fields before him farmers, dreamers, storm-watchers, survivors.

He thought of his mother's steady voice, his father's stern grip, Wanda's teasing laughter, Vern's quiet encouragement. He thought of his mother scolding him for muddy boots, of classmates who called him daydreamer, of professors who doubted him, of survivors who thanked him with tears in their eyes.

They were all part of the storm inside him, part of the legacy he carried.

The thunder came again, closer now, its edges sharp. Jack smiled faintly, the corners of his mouth pulling upward in a line worn by both struggle and joy. He was older now, slower, no longer chasing funnels across highways with a notebook in hand. But in his heart, he was still that boy in the Kansas fields, ears tuned to the sky, eyes searching for patterns.

He whispered to the night, not as a challenge, but as a vow:

"I'm still listening. I'm still learning."

The words disappeared into the wind, carried outward into the vastness where storms lived.

Jack lowered his gaze from the sky to the fields stretching outward, silvered by moonlight. Life had always been this—storms and silences, destruction and renewal. He was only a man, but he had given his years to decoding the rhythm of it all. And in that rhythm, he found peace.

Storms would come again tomorrow, next year, long after he was gone. They would tear roofs from houses, uproot trees, scatter lives. But alongside them would come warnings, shelters, drills, hope. And in that hope, his work would live.

A gust of wind swept past, ruffling his shirt and whispering through the grass. Jack drew in a long breath and exhaled slowly, as though releasing the weight of years. He closed his eyes, tilted his head once more toward the heavens, and let the night wash over him.

Somewhere far off, lightning split the clouds, brilliant and fleeting. For just a second, the sky burned alive, and Jack's face glowed with it.

He smiled knowingly not with pride, not with regret, but with the quiet satisfaction of a man who had walked through storms and left behind more than he ever took.

The thunder murmured again, softer this time, like a lullaby across the plains. Jack stood in the wind, head lifted, eyes open. Still listening. Still learning. Always.

25

THE SCIENTIST'S FINAL CHAPTER

The porch creaked beneath Jack's boots as he eased himself into the chair he had claimed as his own for decades. Dawn stretched slowly across the Kansas prairie, the horizon glowing lavender, then soft rose, then edged with gold. The air carried the chill of dew, sharp against his lungs. He wrapped his hands around a mug of black coffee, letting the heat bleed into his palms.

Inside, the house was still asleep. Darlie's steady breathing was faint through the screen door, a comfort that had become the background rhythm of his life. The silence was fragile, almost reverent. For the first time in weeks, he didn't feel pressed by meetings, data, or students. Retirement loomed on the edge of his thoughts, demanding his attention like thunder muttering far off.

He had been circling the idea for months, sometimes prompted by well-meaning colleagues who told him he had earned a rest, sometimes by Darlie herself, who would watch him rub his temples after a long day in the lab and gently suggest it was time to slow down. Even his own body whispered it — the stiff joints, the shallow breath, the cough that came too often.

But what did it mean to stop chasing storms when storms had been his life?

He set the mug on the rail and pulled a leather-bound notebook from his lap. It was cracked and worn, stuffed with scraps of yellowed paper and faded notes scrawled in pencil. The book had traveled with him everywhere: across prairie fields, into courtrooms, into laboratories where tornadoes spun from the ceiling. Its pages smelled faintly of dust, graphite, and time.

This morning, though, no equations or storm tracks came to mind. His pen hovered, but the familiar flow of numbers refused him. Instead, he wrote a single word, pressing hard enough to etch the paper:

Legacy.

He stared at the word, its finality sinking into him. Legacy was not data. Legacy was not peer review. Legacy was not something he could graph or chart. It was what lingered after storms passed — the imprint left behind, visible only when the wind had gone still.

The prairie was quiet except for the birds. His coffee cooled, untouched. Still, he sat there, staring at the word until it felt heavy in his chest.

***

His gaze drifted to the horizon, where faint thunderheads were gathering. Not threatening, not yet — just a reminder that storms never stopped building. As always, Jack saw himself reflected in them.

Storms. Always storms.

He remembered the calm build-up of his boyhood. Jack, then, not Jack yet. Barefoot at the creek, catching crawdads, sketching their movements in a scrap notebook. Whittling a slingshot, learning angles and arcs without knowing the word "trajectory." Standing on the farm fields, watching towering clouds roll in, not with fear but with awe. That was the air before the storm: curiosity swelling quietly, gathering unseen force.

Then came the Topeka tornado. He was no longer just the boy staring at clouds; he was the young man standing in wreckage, the acrid scent of splintered wood and damp earth burning his lungs. Sirens wailed faintly in the distance, the world split open in chaos. That was the storm's first surge — violent, defining. He hadn't known it then, but Topeka had set the course of his life. It was the spark that told him storms were not just wonders but questions demanding answers.

The violent peak of his life's storm came later. The battles. The backlash. His warnings against the gospel of tornado safety drew ire from the establishment. Professors who once nodded politely began to dismiss him as reckless. The National Weather Service branded his work dangerous. He remembered letters filled with sharp words: "Irresponsible." "Unscientific." "Reckless." He remembered Darlie at the kitchen table, worry etched into her face as he poured over charts, shouting that lives depended on proving them wrong.

Those were the winds at their fiercest. His storm had torn through his peace of mind, strained his marriage, shaken his health. And yet, he kept chasing it. Because storms, he knew, didn't care for politics. They only cared for truth.

But even the fiercest systems weaken. His storm began to dissipate in later years. The models he had fought for became standard. Communities drilled for tornadoes using the very diagrams once called dangerous. His courtroom battles turned into citations in textbooks. He walked through labs and saw young students running simulations built on his work as if they had always existed. He visited amusement parks and watched children, gasp at the sight of artificial tornadoes spinning in front of them, never knowing their wonder was partly his doing.

And his granddaughter, he thought of her often. The way her eyes lit with the same curiosity he once carried, her notebook filled with weather sketches and questions. She was the calm eye of his storm: proof that the cycle didn't end with him.

Storms built. Storms raged. Storms faded. And yet, every storm left something behind. Scars, yes, but also renewal.

So had he.

The realization came with surprising gentleness. Legacy wasn't permanence. Legacy was impact — the way land changed after the rain, the way people rebuilt after the winds. Maybe his life's storm had torn through him, but it had also left fertile ground behind.

He leaned back in the chair, exhaling. For the first time, he could look at the word Legacy in his notebook without flinching.

***

The prairie wind shifted, carrying scents of wheat and dew. As he sipped the last of his cooled coffee, Jack let his thoughts wander through the wreckage and triumphs of his past.

He saw Vern, pale and coughing by the lake, telling him, "Everything has its season, Jack. Fish, storms, even us." At the time, he hadn't understood. Now, decades later, he did. Vern's season had ended too soon. Jacks was finally tapering.

He saw Elsie, her voice strong in defense of her children during a stormy dinner, lightning cracking outside as Edger sat at the table. The metaphor had branded itself into him: storms didn't just live in the skies. They lived inside people, too. That lesson had guided not just his research, but his empathy.

He saw the courtroom, crowded with skeptics, when he had stood at the witness box insisting the gospel of tornado safety was wrong. His voice had shaken, but his conviction had not. "If the gospel is wrong, people die," he had said. And though they mocked him then, he knew it had been the right fight.

He saw the Hollywood premiere — lights, cameras, a crowd gasping at a movie tornado bigger than any real one. He had felt torn that night.

Pride, yes, but also unease. Was this science, or spectacle? Did it matter, if it made people pay attention? His life had always balanced on that fault line — between wonder and rigor, chaos and control.

And finally, he saw his granddaughter, wide-eyed at the laboratory tornado, pencil scratching furiously in her notebook. She didn't see him as the tired, gray-haired man. She saw the storms reflected in his eyes; the same way he once saw them in Vern's.

The images swirled, but instead of chaos, they settled into pattern. He had lived enough storms to know that even the wildest system carried order, if you looked closely enough. His own life was no different.

***

The sun had climbed fully now, golden light spilling across the prairie. Jack closed the notebook, resting his palm on the cover, as if sealing the word inside it.

Retirement was no longer a question of if, but of when. And when it came, it would not mean stopping. It would mean handing the chase to others. It would mean becoming a witness instead of a participant, a mentor instead of a fighter.

The storms of his life had shaped him, scarred him, given him purpose. And like every storm, they had left something behind — students, models, warnings, a granddaughter's dreams.

He lifted his mug, cold coffee bitter on his tongue, and let the prairie wind wash over him. Somewhere far off, thunder murmured, low and steady. Instinctively, he tilted his head, listening. Measuring.

And then he smiled.

The storms were not finished, and neither was he. But he no longer needed to chase them. He had already left his mark in their paths.

The scientist's final chapter wasn't about the storm itself. It was about the calm after — the place where you finally see what the storm has changed, and accept that it's enough.

26

PASSING THE TORCH

The corridors of the University of Kansas Atmospheric Sciences building were unusually quiet. Classes had ended hours ago, and only the faint echo of a janitor's rolling cart drifted from the far end of the hall. The air inside smelled faintly of dust and ozone, as though the walls themselves remembered the countless storms that had once been simulated within.

Jack Engle—his shoulders stooped with age, but his stride still carrying that stubborn prairie steadiness pushed open the heavy double doors to the lab. The hinges groaned, a sound he had heard for decades, as familiar to him as the groan of wind through barn rafters from his boyhood.

Inside, the room was illuminated by the dwindling day. Orange light streaked through the half-closing blinds, casting long shadows across the concrete floor. The vortex chamber remained, waiting for action Jack's hand unconsciously reached out to the cool space of the vortex chamber.

The hum of the machine still echoed faintly, as if the giant still breathed, but was presently at rest. To an untrained observer, the vortex chamber might appear to be just a collection of fans, ducts and polished steel. To Jack, this was a cathedral. This was the place where he had bottled the sky. This was where the impossible turned into the tangible. This was where chaos was tamed into structured existence.

He lingered, his fingertips trailing along the rim of the control panel. The worn buttons bore the faint polish of decades of use, smoothed by countless presses of his hands and those of eager students. He could almost hear the excited voices of grad students that once filled this space, the gasps of visitors as the swirling funnel rose from the chamber floor, the clicking cameras of journalists who came to marvel at the man who made tornadoes in a room.

But now, the lab was silent. The desks were empty. The chalkboards along the side wall still bore ghostly white traces of equations rubbed half-clean. A calendar on the far wall, months out of date. Jack allowed the silence to settle over him, not as loneliness but as recognition. Everything has its season.

He walked slowly to the control console and rested both hands on its edge, leaning forward slightly. His reflection stared back at him from the glossy black surface — lined face, thinning hair, eyes that still held a glint of curiosity. How many times had those same eyes squinted against Kansas winds, scanning the horizon for a funnel cloud? How many nights had they stayed open under the dim glow of lab lamps, waiting for equations to finally align?

The hum of the chamber deepened slightly as the standby motor kicked in, a mechanical heartbeat still pulsing within the machine. Jack smiled faintly. Still ready. Still waiting for someone to ask the right question.

He thought of his first days here — an outsider, a farm boy with mud still on his boots, mocked for his accent and his lack of polish. He had walked into this university not knowing if he belonged. And yet, this room had been his redemption. Here he had proven that curiosity was not childish, that persistence was not weakness, that even the fiercest storm could be coaxed into revealing its secrets if you listened carefully enough.

His hand lingered on the start switch, but he did not press it. For the first time in his life, he did not feel the urge to summon a storm inside this laboratory. He didn't need to see another funnel form in the artificial air. He had seen enough. What mattered now was that the machine stood ready not for him, but for those who would follow.

He took a deep breath, filling his lungs with the familiar dry, metallic air of the lab. The scent carried with it decades of memory: the sharp tang of solder from late-night fixes, the smell of chalk dust settling on fresh equations, even the faint whiff of burned wiring from experiments gone wrong. Each smell was a fragment of his life, stitched together into the fabric of a career that had outlasted storms and critics alike.

Jack stepped back, surveying the chamber one final time. He whispered softly, almost reverently, "You're theirs now."

The words hung in the air, absorbed by the silence of the room. It was no longer his cathedral alone. It was an inheritance, a torch waiting to be lifted.

***

The sound of the lab door opening broke the quiet. Jack turned his head, and for a moment, the golden light spilling in from the hallway blinded him. Then she stepped inside, his granddaughter, Leda.

She carried the energy of youth, her steps brisk, her notebook clutched tightly against her chest. Her hair was pulled back in a hurried ponytail, her cheeks flushed not from exertion but from anticipation. She had that spark, the same restless curiosity Jack had carried into this very lab decades earlier.

"Grandpa," she said softly, almost reverently, as though she knew this moment mattered more than an ordinary visit.

Jack's lips curled into a tired smile. "You found your way back here."

Leda nodded, her eyes darting around the room, taking in the equipment, the chalkboard still dusted with equations, the looming vortex chamber. She had heard stories all her life — at family gatherings, in news clippings, in textbooks that mentioned his name in passing. But standing here, in the temple of his storms, it felt different. Real. Sacred.

He gestured for her to come closer. She moved to his side, notebook already open, pen ready, though her hands trembled just slightly. Jack noticed and smiled. "Don't worry. Every good storm chaser shakes a little before the first storm."

Her laugh was nervous, but it loosened the air.

Jack turned to the vortex chamber, resting his palm against the cool metal once again. "This machine… people think it's about power. About control. They look at it and see a man making an artificial tornado. But that's never what it was for."

Leda leaned in, her pen hovering. "Then what was it for?"

"Respect," Jack said simply. His voice was gravelly, but steady. "Respecting the storm. Learning that it isn't a monster to defeat or a spectacle to sell tickets for. It's a force, ancient, mathematical, humbling. If you listen, if you measure, if you study long enough… the storm will teach you."

He moved slowly to a cabinet tucked along the wall. The hinges squeaked as he opened it. Inside were rows of binders, worn at the edges, their spines faded from years of handling. He reached for one in particular, thicker than the rest, its cover patched with tape and scrawled with notes in his uneven handwriting. He pulled it out carefully, as though it were something fragile.

Leda's eyes widened. "Is that—"

He nodded. "My life's storms."

The binder was heavy in his hands, not just with paper but with decades of effort: annotated research, raw data, trial runs, hand-drawn diagrams of wind funnels, notes scribbled in margins at 3 a.m. Entire seasons of his life pressed flat between those covers.

He turned and held it out to her. She hesitated. Her breath caught. This was no ordinary book, it was the weight of history, the passing of a legacy.

Her fingers brushed the worn cover as she accepted it, and for the briefest second, Jack thought of himself as a boy on the farm, clutching arrowheads he'd dug up from the Indian mound, feeling the pulse of history in his palms. Now, the roles were reversed. He was the one entrusting artifacts, knowledge, a piece of himself to the next seeker.

Leda swallowed hard. "Grandpa, I— I don't know if I'm ready for this."

Jack chuckled, a deep, warm sound. "Neither was I, when I started. I was just a farm boy who thought storms were puzzles. Truth is, no one is ever really ready. But storms don't wait until you are. They come when they come. The best you can do is meet them with open eyes."

She clutched the binder to her chest, the way a believer might hold a holy book. Her hands trembled slightly under its weight, and Jack saw in her expression the exact blend of awe and fear he'd once felt when faced with his first real tornado on the Kansas plains.

He placed a hand on her shoulder, steady and reassuring. "Leda, this isn't just about predicting storms. It's about understanding them, respecting them. Some people look at weather and see chaos. But you—" he tapped the binder gently, "—you'll see the patterns. You'll listen."

Tears pricked at the corners of Leda's eyes, but she blinked them back, nodding firmly. "I'll try. I promise."

Jack studied her face in the fading light, the set of her jaw, the fire in her eyes. She reminded him so much of himself at her age, restless, searching, unwilling to accept easy answers. For the first time in years, he felt certain that the work would continue, not as a monument to him, but as a living flame carried forward.

The room grew quiet again. Dust particles floated lazily in the slanting sunlight, and the vortex chamber hummed softly in standby, like a storm waiting in the wings. Jack felt the weight of the moment settle; this was not just a handoff of data or research. It was the passing of trust, of responsibility, of reverence for the very forces that had shaped his life.

Leda held the binder close and whispered, almost to herself, "It feels alive."

Jack's smile deepened. "That's because it is. Every page in there is a storm still speaking. And now... they'll speak to you."

They stood together in silence, side by side, the old scientist and the young seeker bathed in the last golden light of day. The machine, the notes, the room itself all seemed to breathe with quiet continuity.

Jack exhaled slowly, as if releasing a burden, he had carried too long. The storms were no longer his alone.

***

The lab was quiet again after Leda left for the evening, the heavy binder pressed tightly to her chest as she stepped out into the darkening corridor. Jack remained behind, standing in the fading light of the setting sun, his hand still resting on the edge of the vortex chamber.

For the first time in years, he didn't feel like a man clinging to something fragile and finite. He felt lighter as though the storms, the data, the endless chase that had once consumed him had finally found a new home, a future beyond him.

Jack sank into the worn leather chair beside his desk. The room smelled faintly of chalk dust, machine oil, and the sharp metallic tang of the vortex generator. He poured himself the last of the cold coffee from his mug, took a sip, and grimaced at its bitterness. It didn't matter. Tonight wasn't about comfort. Tonight was about release.

He closed his eyes, leaning back, and let the memories play.

There had been so many storms. Too many to name, but each one carried an imprint: the Topeka tornado that had set his path, the long nights of data scribbled on notepads by lantern light, the courtroom battles where his voice shook but his conviction held steady, the exhilarating day the first lab-built tornado spun perfectly, defying all the skeptics. And later, the compromises — Hollywood sets, tourists gasping at artificial storms, the fine line between science and spectacle.

He had carried them all, like weights on his shoulders, believing it was his job to protect, to preserve, to prove. He had feared, deep down, that if he stopped holding on, the storms would swallow the truth, and people would return to myths and misplaced "gospels" that cost lives.

But tonight, for the first time, he felt something new. Relief.

The binder was no longer his to guard. It was in Leda's hands now, in her bright young mind, in her fierce determination. His storms would live on, grow, and adapt. The science would keep breathing.

Jack opened his eyes and looked toward the window. Outside, twilight deepened, and clouds gathered low on the horizon. Not threatening ones, just the kind that caught the last light of the sun, glowing pink and purple like bruises fading on the sky.

He whispered to the quiet room, "A storm doesn't belong to the one who tracks it. It belongs to everyone it touches."

The words surprised him. They had been simmering in his mind for years, but he had never said them aloud. Now, spoken, they felt final — not an admission of defeat, but of truth.

All along, he had tried to claim storms in some way. To capture them in jars of equations, to bottle their chaos in chambers of glass and steel, to pin them down with theories and warnings. But storms were never his. They were never any one persons. They were wild, democratic forces — touching farms, cities, children, scientists, skeptics alike.

And so too was his legacy. It wasn't in his name imprinted in textbooks, or in the articles that carried citations of his work. It was in the thousands of people who ducked into basements because of improved warnings, in the children who looked at thunderheads with curiosity instead of fear, in the young scientists who dared to question authority because they saw that even "gospel" could be wrong.

Jack leaned forward, elbows on his knees, and let the realization wash over him: It was never about me.

That thought, instead of stinging, soothed him. He laughed under his breath, shaking his head. How many sleepless nights had he spent agonizing over his reputation, his credibility, his battles with the National Weather Service, his mistakes? Yet none of it mattered as much as the ripple effects that moved outward, unseen.

Leda or whichever young scientist picked up where he left off would not carry forward his storms exactly as he had. They would make new mistakes, forge new paths, chase new questions. And that was right. That was how it was supposed to be.

Jack reached for one of the remaining binders in the cabinet, flipping it open. Inside were weather maps from the 1970s, annotated with his looping handwriting. He smiled at the messiness of it, at the half-finished thoughts scribbled in margins, at the equations he now knew were clumsy first drafts.

Once, he would have hidden this away, embarrassed that it wasn't polished or perfect. But now he saw it differently — not as weakness, but as a record of human effort. The real legacy wasn't a flawless theory. It was persistence. It was the willingness to wrestle with chaos and not give up.

He thought of Vern then, his older brother by the lake, teaching him that patience was as important as the catch. He thought of Elsie, whose kitchen storm all those years ago had taught him that tempests lived in human hearts too. He thought of Edger, gruff and unyielding, but a man who had given him the gift of discipline. They were all gone, but they had shaped him, and through him, they would shape others.

Legacy was not linear, he realized. It was a web — a storm front spreading, touching lives he would never see.

A breeze drifted through the slightly cracked window, stirring the papers on his desk. Jack smiled faintly. It felt as if the wind itself was agreeing, affirming what he had just accepted: the storms would go on, with or without him.

And so would the learning.

He rose from his chair, joints stiff but heart lighter than it had been in years. He walked slowly around the lab one last time, running his fingers across the vortex chamber, the chalkboard, the shelves of instruments. They no longer felt like burdens to guard, but old friends he could finally release.

At the door, he paused and looked back. The room glowed in the soft amber of the desk lamp, humming with quiet energy, as though it too understood the transition. For decades, this had been the center of his world. Now, it was ready for another's hands.

Jack whispered again, not to the room, not even to himself, but to the storms he had chased all his life:

"Thank you. For humbling me. For teaching me. For letting me listen."

With that, he turned out the light and stepped into the hallway, the echo of his footsteps fading. Behind him, the lab stood ready — alive, waiting for the next storm, the next seeker.

And ahead of him, for the first time, stretched a horizon without the weight of unfinished business.

Jack felt peace.

The heavy laboratory door swung open with a creak, spilling them both into the late evening air. Jack squinted at the sudden brightness, the sun had nearly set, and the Kansas sky was painted in deep layers of orange, lavender, and gold. The world felt stretched wide, as if the prairie itself was exhaling after a long day.

Leda walked a half step ahead; the thick binder cradled against her chest like a treasure she wasn't sure she deserved. Her notebook, still filled with fresh scribbles from Jack's explanations, peeked out from under her arm. She moved with the eager bounce of someone standing at the edge of a new world.

Jack followed more slowly. His legs weren't what they used to be, but he didn't mind. Tonight wasn't about keeping pace. It was about letting go.

They stepped into the open air, the faint hum of cicadas rising in the fields beyond. A warm breeze curled past them, carrying the earthy scent of wheat and the distant sweetness of wild clover. Jack tilted his head back, breathing it in. For decades, storms had defined his life — the rush of chasing them, the weight of warning against them, the endless effort of trying to capture them in models and theories. But tonight, the sky was still. Balanced.

Balanced, but not empty.

On the horizon, he saw them: towering cumulonimbus clouds, rising like cathedrals of vapor into the darkening sky. Their tops blushed with the last light of the sun, while their bases were already sinking into shadow. The promise of a storm. A reminder that nature was always writing new chapters, whether or not he was the one to read them.

Leda followed his gaze. Her eyes widened, reflecting the glow of the horizon. "Looks like something's building out there," she murmured, almost reverently.

Jack smiled. He had said those exact words, decades ago, to Vern by the lake, to colleagues in the field, to television cameras during interviews. And now his granddaughter or maybe simply the next in line was saying them with the same spark, the same awe.

"That's right," Jack said softly. "Something's always building."

They stood side by side in silence for a long moment, watching the storm tower rise. Leda's posture leaned forward, her entire being tilted toward the horizon, as though she could walk straight into the sky and ask it questions. Jack recognized that hunger, that restlessness. It was the same thing that had driven him to argue with professors, to spend long nights in cramped labs, to face ridicule from institutions more comfortable with tradition than truth.

And in her eyes, he saw something more, not just curiosity, but determination. She wasn't going to be satisfied with easy answers. She would test, challenge, and refine. She would take storms apart piece by piece, as he had done, and maybe put them back together in ways he couldn't yet imagine.

Jack didn't need to say anything. He didn't need to tell her she was ready. The sky was telling her, louder than he ever could.

The binder shifted in her arms. She adjusted it carefully, almost ceremonially, as if sensing the weight of responsibility it carried. She turned her head slightly toward him. "I'll take care of this, Grandpa. I promise."

Jack's chest tightened. For a second, he wanted to reach for the binder again, to hold onto it one last time, to make sure the notes were safe. But then the impulse passed. He had already done his part. Now it was her turn.

"You won't just take care of it," he said. "You'll make it better."

Leda's lips curved into a small, confident smile. She looked back to the horizon, eyes catching the first flicker of lightning in the distant clouds.

The soundless flash lit her face for a heartbeat. Jack felt his breath hitch — because in that instant, he saw himself. Not the tired, aging man he had become, but the boy standing barefoot at the creek, lifting crawdads out of the water, scribbling rules into a notebook, wondering if chaos had patterns. He saw the young man walking into his first lecture hall with scuffed farm boots and too much self-doubt. He saw the scientist in the lab, trembling with pride as the first vortex swirled to life.

Now, that same hunger, that same fire, burned in her.

Without a word, Jack knew: the work would continue.

He felt the wind brush across his face, ruffling his thinning hair, nudging the binder in Leda's arms. It was as if the sky itself was acknowledging the hand-off, whispering that storms belonged to no one — they were carried from one generation to the next, just like stories, just like responsibilities.

Leda broke the silence first. "Do you think… storms will ever give up all their secrets?"

Jack chuckled softly, the sound low and warm. "No. And that's the point. If they did, there'd be nothing left to chase."

She nodded, her eyes still fixed on the glowing horizon, as though storing his words in the same place she had tucked away his binders of data.

The light continued to fade, and the first true stars of evening blinked awake above them. Jack's body felt heavy, but his spirit felt lighter than it had in years. Watching her, he realized this was the moment he had been working toward all along — not the papers, not the conferences, not even the warnings that saved lives. This. The torch passing into hands ready to carry it forward.

Another flicker of lightning illuminated the sky, brighter this time, followed by a faint murmur of thunder. Leda's face lit up, her eyes wide with the thrill of it.

Jack didn't move. He didn't need to.

The storm on the horizon belonged to her now.

He glanced at her once more, then at the clouds. And with a faint, knowing smile, he let the silence carry the truth neither of them needed to speak: the legacy was safe. The work would live on.

The torch had been passed.

ABOUT THE AUTHOR

Joe R. Eagleman (1936-) was born on a farm near West Plains Missouri. He received the PhD from the University of Missouri in 1963 and was a professor at the University of Kansas for 39 years. He taught thousands of students about Atmospheric Science through his courses there and many thousands more  through four different textbooks used by over a hundred universities over a span of several decades. He directed a successful experiment on Skylab, funded by NASA, and invented a tornado in his laboratory that was used by Universal Studios for a 50 ft. tornado attraction in the Twister Building in Orlando Florida for several decades. It can still be seen at the Exploratorium in San Francisco.

He is the author of a technical book on severe thunderstorms that includes his tornado safety research which resulted in changes that were adopted nationally. His autobiography, *Name Your Price*, tells of his early life on a farm where he was the 11th of 12 children. It includes his work as a scientist as well as a number of unusual hobbies including those as an artist, musician, luthier, marksman, taxidermist, world traveler and other endeavors.

He has also published his second autobiography, *Monumental Moments*, that captures the most significant times of his life and *Eagleman Stories* that contains stories from his life as well as his 11 siblings and his parents.

Since his retirement he has published numerous books and recorded four albums of original music. For more information see http://www.JoeEagleman.com.